Soul Symbol

JEREMY B. KENT

Gorilla Spirit Publishing, Charlottesville, VA

ISBN: 0989248801
ISBN-13: 978-0989248808

Cover Design by Evpoe

DEDICATION

To my family.

PREFACE

L EONARDO DA VINCI once said, "The noblest pleasure is the joy of understanding." The quest for greater understanding is never more evident than in medicine. Medical knowledge is relentlessly evolving. On a near daily basis, newly published medical studies detail improved methods to diagnose and treat illness, leading to better medical care. Accordingly, the latest scientific studies and tested theories on symbolism, evolution, dreams and spirituality have uncovered innovative concepts of our relationship to self and others. Our quest for knowledge has pushed humankind's understanding of itself and its place in this world to new heights. By using these studies, not only can we improve our health, but we can enlighten our soul. This new and exciting scientific research is the basis for this novel.

ONE

I PRESSED MY HAND to my chest—no help. I took out my stethoscope and listened.

Lub-dub, lub-dub.

Normal, yet my heart still pounded. The stress was prevailing against me. Only a few days had passed, but I was already having difficulty coping. And I still needed to tell Sara and the girls. My office door opened. Ms. Kelly, my medical assistant, poked her head in.

"Your first patient is in the room, Dr. Handling."

"Thanks, Ms. Kelly. I'll be right in."

This was a day like every other in my career as a family medicine doctor, but its end was almost insurmountable at this point. I pushed myself up from my desk chair and slowly made my way to my office mirror. I bent down. The previous occupant of this office must have been much shorter. In spite of spending ten years in this office, I hadn't found time to do move it. And that wasn't going to happen anytime soon.

Just like the mirror, my life hadn't changed much since I started my practice. I grew up and attended school in Maryland. After serving as a physician in the Army, I found a good position in a suburban practice outside of Baltimore and settled down with my family. My

flabbier torso and growing girls were all I had to show for my time
since. Life had so many more opportunities back then. Long gone
was the freedom to pick up and go with little responsibilities tying
me down. Backpacking to another country or rucking around in the
desert playing Army was no longer in the cards. Unfortunately, my
ambitions had slipped away and my expectations had dulled over
time. One thing was for sure, there was never a time I didn't want to
be a doctor. For good or bad, I chose this life.

I faced myself in the mirror. My tie was in order and my graying
hair in place. By all normal measures, I was ready for the day. But it
stuck in my mind like a bad smell. My recent test results had sucked
the life out of me and created an anxious shell. Visits to my primary
care doctor and urologist had left me with the same question; was it
malignant? All they could say was that my PSA was elevated.

PSA was an acronym for prostate specific antigen, which was a
protein made by the prostate and found in all men. Elevated levels
could suggest a number of illnesses, but cancer was the most concerning. My surgical appointment would give more answers.

Regardless of my mood, it was time to get to work. I looked myself in the mirror again—no change. I grabbed my stethoscope and
pen and opened the door to another day.

The first few patients were follow-ups. Nothing new or interesting,
but I enjoyed talking and treating them nonetheless. In spite of a
tedium that had been setting in over the last several months, I had
always felt a certain idealistic satisfaction for my work; chatting with
my regulars, diagnosing illnesses and educating.

My next patient was new to the practice. Her concern was a *personal problem.* This was a loaded statement and could mean anything
from a rash on the genitals, to a headache, or even suicide. She could
end up taking five minutes or as long as one hour. I met her in my
first exam room.

"How are you? I'm Dr. Handling."

"It took you long enough. I've been waiting here all day." She looked at her wrist, which was watchless. Her appointment time started five minutes before my entrance. "At least you could see me on short notice. I'm Kim Travers."

She was a short, plump woman with large blue eyes and blonde, frizzy hair that engulfed her head in a frenzied heap. She wore hiking boots half hidden under an ankle length, tie-dye dress. Her appearance was unconventional to say the least.

"Sorry for the wait. What brought you in?" At this point, I wasn't sure what she was going to say and nothing would have surprised me.

"A personal concern."

"Tell me about your concern."

"I'm concerned about you." She fixed her intense blue eyes squarely on mine. I looked away.

This woman was a stranger, but spoke as if she knew me. Sometimes I'll forget a name as I see a hundred patients a week, but I usually don't forget a face especially not this one.

"I'm sorry. I didn't hear you right. What did you say?" I asked.

"I have a concern about you."

"I don't understand what you mean."

"I had a dream last night and it told me to warn you," she said, "or things don't end up well for you."

"Is this a joke?"

"No, it isn't."

Her big, blue eyes expressed no amusement.

"You don't remember me, do you?" she asked.

"No, I don't. Have we met before?"

"Yes, about twenty-five years ago."

"Twenty-five years ago? That's a while back."

"In a previous life, I used to be a psychic artist. Now, I have a pet grooming and clothing business. Would you like a tie-dye sweater for your dog?" She smiled, causing her lips to curl up and her eyes to squint revealing wrinkle lines covered by make-up.

"Twenty-five years ago I would have been about fifteen. When I was younger, I had visited a psychic artist with my dad. We also attended a medium party and a tarot card reader. All three had interesting takes on my future"—and were a little odd. "Remind me again what a psychic artist does?"

"A psychic artist is one who receives inspiration intuitively and expresses it through art such as watercolor or oil. They can work from a general idea like nature. They can also work for a specific person who wants to know their future or help with a certain question."

"And I visited you back then?"

"You saw me with your father, and I created a painting for you about your future," she said.

The experience was a vague memory.

"I don't have a strong recollection of that day. I remember the psychic artist, but I don't remember her looking like you."

"Well, the years haven't been kind and my hair wasn't this beautiful shade of blonde back then. I was a sultry brunette." She ran her fingers through her hair as she flipped it up.

"I don't remember what happened to that painting. I may have given it away."

"Given it away? Why did you do that? That painting is important. It can change."

"What do you mean?"

"The image changes as you change."

"That doesn't make sense."

"I don't make the rules. That's just how it works, but you have to take a picture of it from the beginning or the change won't be noticeable to your eyes. As we grow with the painting, it looks the same," she said.

I studied her, unsure if this was a hoax or if she was malingering for an as yet unspecified medication. But she knew something few did about my earlier life. My visit to a psychic artist was not an event I advertised.

"I still don't understand why you're here."

"My dream is why I'm here. I already told you that," she said, shaking her head. My inability to read her mind frustrated her. "My dream showed me that you need to remember the painting."

"What about the painting?" I asked. "Like I said, I don't remember much about that day, much less the painting."

"That's a good piece of art."

"So good that now you're a tie-dye dealer?"

"That hurts."

"I don't mean to be unkind, but I have only a few memories of that day. And you must admit that if you were in my shoes you would be wondering what was going on right now. Most patients don't show up with cautionary remarks from their dreams."

"That is probably true, but I dream what I dream."

Taking the bait, I asked, "Can you go into specifics about the painting?"

She looked at me with a befuddled expression. "How should I know what answers that painting holds? That was twenty-five years ago. Do you think I can remember that long ago?" She shook her head as if my obvious question was preposterous.

"I guess not." Too much bleach I suppose.

"But my dream did show me bubbles floating above your head. In the past, bubbles in my art usually symbolized the person's ideas and life goals," she said.

That actually did jar a memory. I remembered a chalk painting with bright colors and bubbles floating over a face with my likeness. It looked a little ridiculous.

"I remember the bubbles."

"Well…?"

"My ideas back then are different then they are now. I was young. Things change."

"And your father? He was there. What about him?"

"They were his ideas, not mine. Not anymore. I was a dutiful son—impressionable. I wanted to spend time with my dad, but we have different opinions now."

"Maybe that's the problem."

"What problem?"

"The problem I saw in my dream was that you have to make a decision and you're stuck. One path leads to a discovery and the other leads to," she paused. "Let's just say, if you're stuck for too long, you sink."

"Sink? Where do I sink?"

"I don't know. My dream ended." She shrugged and then began to get her things together.

"What do you mean your dream ended?"

"Don't know. My dream just ended. Nothing else." She stood up and was about to leave. "Sorry, gotta go."

"There has to be something else."

She sighed. "Let me think." Her countenance changed. Her face softened and sympathy spread over her eyes. "You were alone and without your true self."

"What does that mean?"

As if a light switched back off, her expression reverted to her previous flippant indifference. "Don't know. Sometimes I say things that make no sense. Sorry, I really gotta go," she said. "I have an important date with my ink distributor. I'm getting new colors today. I can't wait." She giggled and then flittered out the door.

The rest of my day passed without incident, but the blue-eyed, frizzy haired women never left my mind. That was the strangest encounter I'd ever had with a patient.

TWO

MY PHONE RANG as I was finishing my work for the day. Sara.
"Hey, Honey, I'm almost done," I said.

"Are you going to be late?"

"No, not this time."

"Are you sure?"

"I'll be home for dinner, I promise."

"Okay. Good. Can you please drop off the movie rentals before coming home?" Sara said.

"Sure thing."

"Everything okay?"

"Yeah, everything's fine."

"Are you sure?"

"Yeah, I'll see you at home."

Sara always knew when something wasn't right. After nearly twenty years of marriage, my voice inflections were obvious. Regardless, I didn't want to discuss my results over the phone. It could wait until tonight. Hopefully, I'd be able to alleviate her fears better than I did mine.

I finally made it home after passing the video store once and getting another call from my wife for requests by our kids for a certain movie rental about some high school kid who was in love with an-other high school kid. I wasn't familiar with the title, but it sounded like my evening entertainment was going to be a book.

Our family home was nestled in a quiet cul-de-sac, pushed off the street and surrounded by large pine trees. When we bought it ten years ago, only forest marked our property line. Now a multitude of more modern, domestic edifices dwarfed our modest home. The house was large enough to give each of us our own space, but small enough to cause regular familial interactions. It usually offered a res-pite from my stressful workday, but since learning of my test results, nothing lifted my mood. I arrived home in one piece, but I felt bro-ken. The lab results had shattered my healthy self-image. My family usually rejuvenated me, but tonight I needed my space—something I was unlikely to get.

My wife and I made a good parental team. My daughters, Jamie and Anna, were good kids and luckily not difficult yet in spite of their teen and pre-teen age. I worked and Sara took care of the girls. Our relationship wasn't perfect. We had good months and bad months with more bad months than I would like to admit recently, but we loved each other and we knew how to make it work. Unfor-tunately, this month was not going as smoothly, which meant we weren't as patient with each other and we didn't always have the warm fuzzies. Hopefully, we'd be able to make it through dinner without any major clashes. I wanted to tell her about my test results from a positive place.

Anna was the first to greet me. Her straight, dark hair flapped behind her as she ran to meet me at the door. She wore a cooking apron, which was much too long for her thin, nine-year-old frame. She stopped abruptly in front of me.

"Hi, Dad."

"Are you helping Mom cook?" I asked.

"Yeah, I get first dibs," she said, grinning.

She continued to look at me as I hung my coat up.

"Are you okay, Dad?" she asked.

"Yes, I'm fine. Why do you ask?"

"You look like something is wrong."

"I'm fine. How was your day at school?"

"It was okay."

"Just okay? You're normally ecstatic about school."

"Tim, this boy I sit next to, got in trouble."

"How were you involved?"

"He ran out of the classroom and stepped on my lunch, smashing it."

"That's not nice."

"He didn't mean to do it."

"Why did he run out?"

"First, the teacher asked him to put his phone away, but he wouldn't and kept playing games. Then, she came over and told him she would take it away from him if he didn't stop."

"He didn't stop did he?"

"No, he didn't. Then it got real bad. He yelled at the teacher and she yelled back and said that he was going to get in trouble."

"It must have been pretty bad if he ran out."

"I tried to tell the teacher that he wasn't upset at her, but with someone else."

"Who?"

"His dad."

"How did you know that?"

"I just did. I saw Tim get out of his car this morning and I could tell something was wrong." I didn't question her. Anna had reported similar things in the past and had oftentimes been right. She had the uncanny ability to sense another's feelings.

"Did you tell the teacher?"

"Yeah, but she didn't believe me."

"Well, it sounds like you were a good friend and did all you could do."

She was only partially satisfied with my fatherly rationalization and was about to say more, but instead frowned.

"Dad, are you sure you're okay?" Her small fingers wrapped around my free hand. I looked into her perceptive, innocent eyes, unsure of exactly what she knew or how she knew it. I loved her more than life itself, which made my earlier news no less difficult to deal with.

"Where's your mom?" I asked.

My eldest daughter Jamie then walked past.

"Hey, Dad, did you get the movie?" she asked, marching through our family room without losing stride.

Jamie was tall and thin with wavy, brown hair, which she habitually kept in a ponytail. Her stride was purposeful and confident. At sixteen, she was already plotting her means to change the world.

"I did and it only took one U-turn this time and some daring driving to pick up this Oscar winner. How was your day at school?" I asked, trying to break her pace.

"Dad, you're not very funny, but I still love you. It was fine. Nothing exciting. Just six hours, six bells and one crazy lunch hall. The usual."

"How did you do on your biology test?"

"Aced it."

"Finish your homework before you start watching the movie."

"I already finished."

"When?"

"Before swim practice."

"Good. Where's your mom?"

"She's in the kitchen. Dinner is almost ready. Oh, and Dad, don't say anything about her hair. She had it cut today and is very upset about it."

"What do you mean, 'don't say anything'? If I don't, she'll know something is wrong."

"Maybe your right, but just don't say it like you did the last time." She disappeared in a flash before I could ask what I had previously done wrong. As I was trying to recall this piece of pertinent history, Sara walked in. Before I could say a word...

"I knew you wouldn't like it."

"What? I didn't say anything."

"I knew by the look in your eyes when I walked in."

"That was a look of surprise by your beauty."

"I know your looks and that's not how I would describe it."

Sara and I had met in college, in art history class. She was interested in the subject and I needed to fill a requirement. She was a pleasant distraction. I couldn't resist her dark, passionate eyes and her curvaceous, Hispanic heritage. Her wavy, black hair was a little longer then and always in a ponytail like Jamie's now. While she argued incessantly with the teacher about the importance of Brazilian art in our European centric curriculum, I plotted my pick up line. Needless to say, I didn't spend much time paying attention in class. She breezily aced her way through the course and I barely made a decent grade, but I did secure a date.

Tonight, like most nights, she wore jeans and a comfortable t-shirt that subtly accentuated her athletic form. In spite of being a busy mom of two, she took good care of herself, ate well, and exercised.

I moved in to give her a kiss on the forehead. "You're beautiful."

She looked at me with skeptical eyes and then smiled. "Thank you. Now wash up. Dinner is ready."

We took our seats at the table, each in our usual place. Anna sat on her knees at which Sara then patiently asked her to unfold them and so they dangled from the chair. My elbows rested on the table with fork and knife in hand making eating sounds like Cookie Monster as I prepared to consume my meal. Anna laughed and Jamie shook her head in amused disapproval. Sara sat straight and proper as she normally did with a napkin in her lap. Jamie with her ponytail and upright posture emulated her mother. Both girls had distinguishing characteristics from Sara and me. Jamie looked and moved like her mother. From me, she had that singular drive that I remembered feeling in school. Anna had her mother's coloring, but facial features and a lighthearted attitude that reminded me of my father. Our backgrounds couldn't have been more different, but our dissimilarity created two beautiful girls.

Sara grew up in Brazil. Her father worked with the U.S. State Department and her mother was Brazilian. She received her political science degree and with her fluency in Portuguese and her father's connections, she planned on following in his footsteps. That was until she met me. Her focus then switched to our growing family.

Dinner was civil with no major happenings except for a chiding look from Jamie for my blunder with the haircut. I looked at her in utter confabulation, but conceded my error and didn't try to dissuade her otherwise.

"I'm reading a new book. It's called *Spiritual Connections 1.0*," Sara said. "Your dad gave it to me last Christmas. I think you'd like it."

"Sounds like the type of book my dad would give," I said.

"It's about how individual spiritual awakenings will lead to a growth in the collective consciousness."

"I'll take a look at it if I get time." I already had a stack of unread medical journals on my desk a month old. "The problem I have with those books is that they all say the same thing."

"You don't sound convinced," Sara said.

"Spiritual awakenings and collective consciousness? I've heard it all before."

"It has some interesting insights."

"I think the publishing companies have a grand plan to release a new book promoting New Age spiritual answers just as our memory of the previous book wanes. They should write a book on how to keep from forgetting that stuff."

"Grand plan or not, I'll leave it on the bookshelf when I'm done," Sara said.

"What is New Age?" Anna asked.

"New Age is a set of beliefs," Sara said.

"Like the Bible?" Anna asked.

"Sort of, but a little broader than that."

"I thought Buddhism was part of it," Jamie said.

"There are a lot of different beliefs that make up New Age thought including Eastern religions. It's also called metaphysics, spiritualism, and Western Mysticism to name a few."

"Sort of like what Grandma Judith does. Meditation and stuff," Jamie said.

"Yes, meditation would be included. In its simplest form, New Age beliefs are a different way of expressing your spirituality that is not always in line with standard Western religions."

"I still don't understand what it is," Anna said.

"You're not the only one," I said. "Another side of New Age beliefs is alternative medicine."

"That's what Grandpa does," Jamie said.

"Yes, Grandpa would be part of it," I said. "But like New Age beliefs, alternative medicine entails many different and unproven medical treatments."

"That's not what Grandpa says," Jamie said.

"It also has different terms such as holistic medicine, mind, body, spirit, and complementary and alternative medicine. Grandpa likes to combine New Age beliefs and alternative medicine into what I call his spiritual medicine," I said.

"Grandpa says some of those treatments can help," Jamie said.

"I know what Grandpa says, but that's your grandfather and you have to take it with a grain of salt."

"You don't believe in it, Dad?" Anna asked.

"No, I don't."

"Why not?" Anna asked.

I looked at Sara.

"Okay, enough questions," Sara said. "We'll continue this discussion later."

I was a traditional doctor educated in Western medicine. When I diagnosed a patient with an illness like cancer, I referred them to the appropriate specialist for treatment. I was fully versed in complementary and alternative medicine, but unless a patient requested the alternative treatment, I didn't recommend it. Medical studies had demonstrated some alternative treatments to be effective. Traditional medicine had many answers, but not all.

Alternative medicine was not foreign to me. I grew up in a circle of family and friends who were open to health care beyond Western medicine. This group initially shaped my beliefs. At one time, I believed that alternative medicine offered further options for the patient. However, during my medical training, my viewpoint changed and I disregarded those treatments many years ago.

We had finished eating, except Anna, who as usual did most of the talking. She sat on her knees and gave a detailed account of an upcoming violin recital. I was only partially involved in the discussion, nodding my head when a question was directed at me.

"Do you remember what this Saturday is?" Sara asked me.

"No, what is this Saturday?" Jamie asked.

Sara's question pulled me back to the present for something I didn't want to discuss. It was a memory I forced myself to embrace each year.

"It's the anniversary of Gary's death," I said.

"Who's Gary?" Anna asked.

"You asked that last year," Jamie said. "Gary was Dad's friend who died."

"Why did he die?" Anna asked.

They all paused to look at me.

"It's complicated," I said, without looking up from my plate.

Anna was not satisfied with my answer and looked over to Sara.

"Mom?" Anna asked.

"Yes."

"Who's Gary?"

"He was your Dad's friend who died about fifteen years ago."

"Sixteen years," I said.

"He was a very good friend of your father's and me."

"Dad always said he was like a brother," Jamie said.

"How did he die?" Anna asked.

Everybody looked at me again. I sighed.

"He died from cancer," I said.

"Your dad doesn't like to talk about it. It was a difficult time."

"Okay," Anna said and the conversation shifted.

We finished dinner and were cleaning up.

"Dad, we're going to make the special cookies tonight. Do you want to help?" Anna asked.

"No, I have to do some work."

"You haven't made the cookies with us in a while," Anna said.

"Maybe next time."

"They taste much better when you help," Jamie said.

"Not tonight girls."

"Your dad has work to finish girls," Sara said, but not before giving me a disappointing look.

THREE

I COULDN'T FIND A chance to talk to Sara about the lab result until we were getting ready to go to sleep. As I delayed my news, she flipped through a magazine in bed, wearing sweat pants and a t-shirt, her dark, shiny hair lying on her shoulders.

"John, I wish you would make more time for the girls and me. You've been missing the small things, like making cookies, more and more. The girls get disappointed and wonder why, especially Anna. You know how sensitive she is."

I had no answer and no energy to delve into that black hole of a conversation. I was preoccupied with my lab test.

"You're right. I'll help out next time. Hey, Honey, we need to talk."

Sara looked up from her magazine with a frown across her face.

"One of my labs came back positive," I said.

"What do you mean, 'positive'?" She closed the magazine "I thought you said everything was okay."

"I did. And everything is probably okay." I tried to convince her and me. "My PSA is high. The urologist wants to do a biopsy."

"What is your PSA and why do you need a biopsy?"

In a long diatribe, I explained the significance of the PSA. I tried to delicately leave out the cancer part, but she could sniff me dancing around that issue from a mile away.

"Are you concerned about cancer? I need to know. You need to tell me if you're concerned about cancer. Please," Sara said.

"I'm a little concerned, but there are many more common things that can elevate a PSA other than cancer."

I tried to inform Sara as I would any patient or family member. After years of objective decision-making, I usually found it easy to distance myself emotionally to make the right decision. However, I still had the pit in my stomach. I still had few answers. And I still may have cancer, but I didn't want to tell her this. I wanted to convince myself that the odds were in my favor. They just didn't feel in my favor.

She could sense my unease, but didn't say anything. Instead, she stood up and gave me a hug.

"I love you," she said in my arms.

"I love you too."

"When will we know more?"

"My biopsy appointment is on Thursday. We'll have a better understanding of what we're dealing with after that."

"What are we dealing with, Jeff?"

"I'm not sure."

I lay awake unable to sleep. My mind raced. What would I do if I had cancer? What would my family do? I tried to push the anxiety from my thoughts, but it persisted.

"What would I do?" I said, almost waking Sara.

I slept, finally, but not well. My thoughts and dreams were a jumbled mess, twisting in my head. The next few days were a blur. I went to work and came home. Sara and I didn't discuss it. We didn't have any fights either. We delayed telling the girls until I had more answers. The days passed as if I had no impending doctor's visit. She did give me a few extra-long hugs, but otherwise it was a normal week. That changed at my urology appointment.

I felt as if I were in a dream that wasn't my own. I hadn't had surgery in years. As I entered the exam room, the bare impersonal walls greeted me. A small framed picture of a snake coiled around a rod, symbolic of medicine for hundreds of years, was the only adornment. I eased myself into a seat. I could feel the eyes of the snake glaring at me from across the room as if I had invaded its space. The fluorescent lights bore down as the chill of the air and the aseptic smell of cleaning products made my stomach queasy. Something didn't feel right. But then again, my anxiety was probably due to my impending procedure.

The urologist, Dr. Palmer, entered with a starched, glowing white lab coat under a pair of tailored, dark slacks and white shirt. He was an esteemed specialist in the area. He was also well liked beyond his surgical skills.

"Morning, Jeff. How are you?"

"I'm doing well, except for the little problem that I present to you today with."

"How's your family?" he asked.

"They're doing well." I wasn't interested in small talk. I wanted to get to the point of the visit. He picked up on my cues.

"You're here for the biopsy."

"Yes."

"I don't need to explain the procedure to you."

"No, I got it."

"Well, then let's get things moving. The nurse and the anesthesiologist will be in here in a moment. I'll see you in the surgery room."

I lay on the gurney, waiting to speak to the anesthesiologist. I was seven years old the last time I had undergone surgery. I was playing around on my dad's woodpile when I slipped and fell awkwardly on my arm. The break was severe and the surgeon had to manually reduce it while I was under general anesthesia. Both my parents were present. It was one of the last times I remember them showing affection even though they wouldn't divorce for another five years. Today, my wife had already made her peace and was waiting for me in the hospital visiting area.

"Don't die or I'll kill you," she said.

I explained to her that the prostate biopsy was a relatively minor procedure and since I was a healthy person, I should have no complications.

"Good, then I can expect you and your soon to be sore butt home for dinner tonight."

"Don't worry, I'll be fine."

In spite of reassuring my wife, my own worry had not improved. When I was seven, I wasn't anxious. My parents told me I would be okay and I believed them. I woke up from the surgery and other than a cast on my arm, they were right. Today was a different story. My many years of experience and training were not as comforting as my parents' gentle reassurance.

I met the anesthesiologist. He asked the standard questions before surgery. I had otherwise been healthy except for my Type A personality. My immediate family was also healthy. Neither my parents, nor my siblings had any major illnesses. I was lucky to have parents who were active, took good care of themselves, and had a healthy spirit.

Some urologists used only local anesthesia for pain control, but I was thankful Dr. Palmer offered intravenous sedation. I gladly welcomed any amnesia from the discomfort of someone sticking a camera in my backside.

The nurse wheeled me into the surgical room and transferred me to the procedure table. My anesthesiologist stuck his masked face six inches from me.

"Sleepy time now," he said. I forced a smile. I was entrusting my life with this person. Thank goodness for medical licensing and board certification.

The next thing I heard was a loud...

Crash!

Did the surgical instruments topple to the ground?

I opened my eyes and found myself sitting at my old dinner table. Juice spread out from underneath my chair and an empty plastic cup lay on the floor. My brother sat opposite me and was much younger, which meant I was about ten. My parents were arguing. Everyone became quiet.

"Jeff, go get a towel and clean that up. You need to be more careful next time," my mother said. Had I intentionally pushed the cup off the table?

The anesthesia had transported me into the past. We ate at the dinner table often, which was important to my mom. I hadn't thought of my family like this in a long time. Everyone sat at their usual places with my mom and dad at the ends and my brother, sister and I in the middle. My parents were having a typical argument. This time it was about a class my dad wanted to take, a spiritual class about finding your higher self.

"No, John, you're not listening. It's not just this class. I'm just not interested in that stuff anymore."

"I don't understand what happened, Laura. You were more involved with it than I was at one time. But now, nothing."

"I'm not interested in it right now. Maybe some other time."

"I wish you would go," my dad said.

"I wish you would let it go," my mom said.

The conversation ended leaving both feeling unheard and hurt. My dad had introduced my mom to New Age beliefs. She had become a voracious reader on the subject, but her interest had waned. He could never figure out why. The gradual decline of their relationship was the main factor. As their marriage worsened, my mom detached herself from their mutual beliefs. In response, my dad delved deeper.

After dinner, I helped my mom clean the dishes.

"I hope our arguing doesn't upset you, Jeffrey," my mom said. "Arguing is not a bad thing in a relationship. It allows two people to express themselves and work out problems."

"I don't understand why you don't want to go to that class with Dad," I heard myself saying. I was experiencing the dream, through my mind's eye, but couldn't fully participate.

"It's hard to explain. It's a personal decision and I don't feel ready to do it. I don't believe some of the same things that your dad does."

"Why not? If you did, it would make things better."

"Yes, it probably would, for now." She took a deep breath as if enduring a great weight and then blowing it away. "It's hard for me to explain, but people change, including our beliefs. I still have a deep faith in God. I think it's deeper than it's been in a long time. Everyone has to find their own way, as you will one day. "

"But it's not the same as Dad's."

"You're right. I choose to express my faith differently than your dad. Do you understand what I mean?"

"I think so."

"The important thing is that your dad and I love each other and you kids very much."

"I know."

"Thank you for helping me with the dishes."

"You're welcome, Mom."

"I think I can finish up from here. Why don't you go get ready for bed."

As he often did, my dad told us a story before putting my brother and me to bed.

"People called him the sleeping prophet. He was able to answer questions while sleeping that helped people. People asked him about their health and he would offer cures and remedies that would help them heal. He had no training in medicine. He was a photographer by trade, but he had a gift," my dad said.

"How could he do that stuff?" my brother asked.

My brother was two years younger than me and war torn from our daily battles. Our fighting was epic lore in the family, which only worsened with the divorce. The divorce devastated my brother and me and it took both of us a long time to overcome it. He was quiet, introspective and an independent thinker. He wanted to form his own conclusions especially separate from his older brother. We mirrored each other in personality, which may have been why we fought so much. Our distinct difference was that he was more methodical in his thought process while I was less bounded. As we grew older, we changed. My brother emerged from his college years more free spirited. Alternatively, I chose a conventional education and career, settling down with a family. He was living in Thailand or Cambodia. It changed often.

"No one is really sure. He wasn't even sure himself. He just slept and was able to do amazing things."

"It doesn't make sense," my brother said.

"There are many mysteries in this world that we can't explain."

"I don't know if I believe it," my brother said.

"I guarantee that it's true. Your mom and I would never lie to you. But one day you will have to choose what you believe and don't believe."

"How will we know what to believe?" I asked.

"You'll know when it feels right. You have to follow your heart."

"What do you mean?" I asked.

"That's another story for another time."

"Can you tell us another one?" my brother asked.

"No, it's time to go to sleep now guys. Good night."

My dad turned off the light. I heard my brother say good night and then silence.

"We're all done," a distant voice said.

"Jeff, we're all done." The voice drew closer. My dream dissipated as quickly as it started.

"You did fine. The procedure was successful," my anesthesiologist said, his inverted face only inches from mine. His warm breath against my naked forehead brought me back to the physical.

As the sounds and smells of the surgical suite pulled me into the real world, my memories of my once nuclear family clung with me. The feelings, faces and voices were still present. Never had a dream been so clear. A part of me didn't want to leave.

I felt a touch on my shoulder and then a kiss on my forehead.

"So how's your butt?" Sara asked.

"My butt has seen better days and I still feel a little loopy," I said.

Sara had met me in the post-op room. I was recovering from the after effects of the sedation as well as from my lingering dream. My vision was still a little hazy. If I just closed my eyes, I could still feel my brother and dad in the room with me.

"So is the medicine they gave you like truth serum? Are you going to tell me all of your deep, dark secrets?"

"No, not exactly. But if it makes you feel better, I still think your haircut looks very nice."

Sara smiled. "Okay, I'll give you that one. How long do you think you'll be here?" she asked.

"No longer than an hour or two."

"Well, since you seem to be on the road to recovery, I need to go pick up Jamie from school. Do you think you'll be okay for a while?"

"Yeah, I'll be fine," I said. "What's wrong with Jamie?"

"I'll tell you about it when I get back. Nothing to worry about. You just recover now."

During my sojourn in the post-op room, I had a chance to process my dream. When I was younger, the sleeping prophet story had always enthralled me. Someone with no medical training was able to tap into an unknown power and heal the sick. It evoked in me a belief that anything was possible when dealing with health and illness. I stayed up for hours fascinated by the mysteries of life and the many possibilities for healing the sick. I had forgotten how special and important those stories were to me. They reminded me of my father and our family as it was then.

FOUR

THE RECOVERY ROOM staff released me without complication, follow-up finalized with the pathology report pending. They would call me with results. Sara was on the road and on her way. Waiting for her, I made my way over to the small hospital cafeteria.

Most hospital cafeterias were the same with their standard fare of forgettable food. But then again, the food was never supposed to be great. Just enough to comfort the visitors and to sustain the house staff for another day on the job. However, one item always lured me back—the ice cream sandwiches. No matter the hospital, the ice cream sandwiches stayed the same. For five minutes, I could enjoy my dessert as life swirled around me. I hadn't had one since residency, when work was my life, sleep was a luxury, and an ice cream sandwich was lunch and dinner. The cafeteria was empty so I could eat my ice cream in peace.

"I've seen many pitiful faces in my time. They all come through here. There isn't anywhere else to go." An elderly woman wiping the table next to me had appeared out of nowhere. "Hunger or caffeine always lures them back."

I only heard about half of what she said in the midst of my ice cream dream.

"I'm sorry?"

"Everyone eventually ends up here," she said, moving her arms in the air as if displaying priceless merchandise.

"I agree. Patients and doctors are drawn to the hospital cafeteria whether they like it or not."

"So why are you looking so downcast?" she asked. I had no work to distract me and my pager was at the office. I was stuck. She was friendly, but I didn't want to talk.

"Bad day," I said. I diverted my eyes back to my ice cream.

She sat down at the table next to me.

"I have to rest my old bones. My knees have been killing me today. My doctor wanted to give me new ones years ago, but I wouldn't let him."

She was an older, African American woman, probably in her sixties. A starched white cafeteria uniform enveloped her heavyset form. The wrinkle lines that pulled on her skin suggested more than a few hardships in her past. Her body slumped a little as she walked. Yet, a twinkle in her eyes and her bleach blonde hair with red tips unveiled a spark otherwise concealed by her physical body.

I didn't want to be rude.

"Knee pain seems to happen to all of us someday," I said.

"So what is it you're worrying about?" she asked.

"What? What do you mean?"

"Like I said, I can see it in your eyes. You've got the weight of the world on you."

Inexplicably, I answered her. "I have an unexpected illness and I'm not ready to deal with it."

"We never are. That's why it's unexpected."

"The results are still pending. I'm here today to get more answers."

"Are you ready for the answers? They can be the hardest part."

At least I would know what it was and I could move on. Unfortunately, she was right. No matter how frustrating the unknown was, a debilitating illness was often worse.

"I don't know."

"Answers usually come when we're least expecting it. You might want to get ready."

Who was this woman? She was becoming annoying and my ice cream was melting.

"If you don't know what you want, how are you going to make decisions and move forward?" she asked.

"What do you mean?" I felt completely naked in front of this woman.

"To move forward starts the process of healing. But to move forward, I tell people to look into their past. Usually the answer is there all along."

"My past?"

"Yes—past relationships, past families. We learn a lot when we're young that we don't realize until we're old."

"What can I possibly learn from my past that will help me with my current illness?"

"Some answers have a way of sneaking up on us."

She talked nonsense and acted as if she knew me. This conversation was going to stop. I faced foreword, eyes on my half-eaten treat.

"Thank you. I'll keep that in mind," I said.

"Will you? You don't know me from Adam, but I'll tell you what, sometimes you have to remember where you come from."

First, she butted into my personal ice cream time and then offered unsolicited advice.

"Listen, Honey, I've seen too many people who come through here and make the wrong decisions."

"I have to go. My wife is probably waiting for me outside."

"You learn all kinds of things serving people. Sometimes all it takes is to open up and listen. The answers will be there for you," she said as I rose to leave.

"Have a good day," I said, leaving.

"You too, Honey."

Waiting for Sara on a hospital bench left me to my thoughts. The conversation with the cafeteria lady troubled and annoyed me. Most disturbing was that her words rang true. My anesthetic dream still hung close like a lingering smell and I couldn't help but wonder if that was what she meant when she said to remember my past.

Sara pulled up in the car. "Hey, Babe, how are you feeling?" she asked.

The lab test and prostate biopsy were stressing me out. I wasn't thinking straight. I was tired and needed some good sleep. The cafeteria lady was friendly and good at reading people. She probably had nothing better to do. She was an overqualified woman in her current vocation who in another life should be a psychologist. Or, she was crazy and I was crazier for listening to her.

"I'm fine, ready to go home," I said as I climbed into the car.

On the drive home, I asked Sara if I had ever told her why my parents divorced. I hadn't.

"When it happened, I was only concerned with trying to keep them together."

"I'm sorry."

"Don't be. It happened a long time ago."

"I know, but it was hard for you."

"Their marriage became more difficult than their love for each other. And to think that I tried to somehow keep them together. They knew to stop trying when I didn't."

"There's nothing wrong with that. You were a child trying to cope during a difficult time."

"They never stopped loving us though," I said.

My parents had grown distant and their marriage failed—a fear I had for Sara and me. I was happy for the most part with our relationship, but I couldn't always get a good read on her. Our lives were so busy that days would go by without a kiss or a hug. Such rare affection would have been unthinkable fifteen years, a career and two children ago.

"My mom did her best to keep everything as it was. My dad used to tell these crazy stories about this spiritual healer."

"Why?"

"I think he was scared to lose us, with the divorce and all. To keep us close, to keep our beliefs similar."

"No, I mean, what brought those memories to mind?"

"I don't know. Maybe my own mortality."

"Do you need some spiritual healin'?"

"Not yet, but I'll let you know when to take the voodoo doll out of the freezer." I looked at her and smiled.

"It's not a voodoo doll. They are saints and it's called *Candomblé*."

"Can-dom-ble," I tried to replicate my wife's Portuguese. "Whatever you say, Honey."

"You haven't been in the freezer for a while. And you probably want to keep it that way." Sara looked at me with a raised eyebrow.

"When was the last time?" I was stunned that she had relegated me to such fate.

"I didn't do it."

"Who? Your crazy aunt?"

"She was upset that you wanted to put her in a nursing home."

"Understandable, but she belonged there."

Sara's parents passed when she was in her early teens. Her mom's sister became her surrogate mother until she left for college. Her aunt was somewhat eccentric, but loved Sara like a daughter. She lived and died a true Brazilian.

"The freezer wasn't Candomblé. That was my aunt's own special touch. It worked on multiple occasions." Sara grinned.

"Like when?"

"Like when a boy stood me up for a date or was too *machismo* for his own good. Sometimes scolding him wasn't enough."

"I never stood you up for a date."

"I know. You were the perfect gentleman." Sara reached over and squeezed my hand. "Good thing too because you don't want to be in the freezer." She raised both eyebrows, her dark almond-shaped eyes looked at me mischievously.

"Come on, did anything really happen?"

She grinned again.

"Wait a second. When did I break my wrist? Was that before or after we moved your aunt into a nursing home?"

"I had nothing to do with it," Sara said. "You'd have to take that up with her."

"That would to be difficult now considering she's dead."

"Maybe we can have a séance."

"A séance, just to chastise your aunt. She wouldn't be amused."

"No, she'd probably try to slap you from the grave."

"It's funny that your aunt wasn't much different than my family in terms of unconventional beliefs."

"Your dad telling stories isn't that unconventional."

"Yeah, but my parents also used to hold spiritual discussion groups with other like-minded people. They would meditate, chant and discuss spiritual topics. They weren't putting voodoo saints in freezers, but they were definitely going outside of the mainstream."

"I didn't know that. I mean, I know your dad was into those beliefs, but not with your mom."

"Their weekly groups often met at our house. One time, when I should have been in bed, I snuck in. My mom was leading a meditation. Soothing music played from the corner and candles illuminated the room. It was like a dream. They began chanting and I stood transfixed, terrified and mystified at the same time. My mom then spotted me and I scrambled back to bed. We never talked about it, but that moment stuck with me. The mystery of that night was magical."

"Maybe those beliefs are more a part of you than you think?"

"What do you mean by that?"

"Just that kids are impressionable. My aunt always made me pray to Saint Joseph, the patron saint of families. I was never sure if I was praying for her or my parents so I prayed for both. And I still do."

"Maybe you're right. Maybe I should look to the past. Those bed-time stories were my first introduction to health and healing. Come to think of it, they are what started my interest in medicine. Without them, I may not have become a doctor."

"They're part of who you are."

"They're a part of who I was. Now they're just a childhood memory."

FIVE

L ATER THAT NIGHT, while rummaging through my closet, I un-
earthed several things I had thought were lost to time.
Unfortunately, I couldn't locate the one item for which I searched.
Through the years, as the girls grew, my space in the house shrank
and more of my things ended up on the floor of my bedroom closet.
Among the medical journals, old shoes and everything else, it was
difficult to find anything.

"Hey, Honey, have you seen that small chalk painting of my face
and a lot of colorful bubbles floating above my head?" Not until the
words came out of my mouth did I realize how ridiculous I sounded.

"I've never seen that painting. It sounds like a bad dream or a bad
trip," Sara said.

"I can't find it anywhere."

My frizzy haired patient had enticed my curiosity.

"Time for dinner," Jamie called out.

I was determined to find that painting, but it wasn't going to happen tonight. My closet mess had temporarily outwitted me. Tonight
was the kid's turn to make dinner. The menu usually consisted of
spaghetti. The menu rarely consisted of anything else other than spaghetti. As a result, they became quite proficient and could make a
mean bowl of noodles and tomato sauce.

"Time for dinner, Hun," Sara said as she passed by. "You can look for your trippin' hippy painting later."

"I know. It's just that I saw this woman the other day at my clinic. And I can't get her out of my mind."

"Should I be worried?" Sara asked.

"No, it's not like that. Not at all! She reminded me of an experience when I was a teenager—a psychic artist."

"Sounds interesting. Tell me at dinner because I'm hungry and I'm sure your two daughters are already eating."

Dinner was important in our family. Because of our busy schedules, it was often the only hour in the day we all convened. It should be essential in every family as I told my patients. The family dinner was crucial for a child's development especially the critical teenage years. Some studies showed that kids who ate regular dinner with their families ate healthier, were less likely to be overweight, drink, or smoke and may also score higher on achievement tests. Recently, I had missed more dinners than I wanted to admit due to work, but I wasn't going to miss spaghetti night.

The girls had prepared and served a dazzling meal including candles, linens and the better dishware on the dining room table. Our kitchen was set up as the center of the house with the dining room as an adjoining, open room as Sara had wanted. The kitchen had always been the center of her home growing up and she would have it no other way. I agreed, especially since I wasn't going to be doing much of the cooking.

"That is quite a presentation," I said to the girls as I walked in.

"Our spaghetti deserves nothing less," Jamie said. She wore one of her mom's aprons, still bright clean. Her hair was in a ponytail as usual.

"Did you leave any for your mom and me?" I asked.

"We haven't started eating yet," Anna said. Tomato sauce covered large swaths of Anna's apron. Her hair stuck to her face with what looked like grated parmesan cheese.

"We know. We learned proper manners... from Mom," Jamie said.

"And what am I, chopped liver?"

"We've learned other things from you, Dad," Anna said. I could always count on my youngest to be brutally honest.

"It looks like you outdid yourselves this time. I might have to increase your allowances. This spaghetti smells wonderful."

"Thanks, Dad," Jamie said.

I sat down at the table and the girls followed me.

"So, why did Mom have to pick you up at school today, Jamie?" I asked.

"Oh, it was nothing," Jamie said.

"She was arguing with her school vice-principal about going on your trip together and missed the bus," Sara said.

"What trip together?"

"You know, Dad. The one that I've been planning for months. The medical mission to Nicaragua," Jamie said.

"Of course." I had completely forgotten.

"The vice-principle is giving her a hard time about missing more days of school," Sara said.

"How long is the trip?" I asked.

"Three weeks and you can't back out now," Jamie said.

"What days have you missed from school? I don't remember any days you missed from school." I looked at both Jamie and Sara. "Is there something that you aren't telling me?"

"You know the days she missed because you were with her," Sara said. "You took her to the emergency room for abdominal pain."

"Oh yeah." How could I forget? I watched as my little girl writhed in severe pelvic pain. She required surgery for an ovary that had torsed, cutting off its blood supply. Among all the nights I've spent in the ER, that was the worst.

"Dad, is everything okay?" Anna asked. "You don't seem right."

"Yeah, Honey, are you okay?" Sara asked.

"Yes, I'm fine." Although, I did feel a little out of it. I had too many things on my mind. First, it was the anesthetic dream that transported me back in time and then the frizzy haired woman whose warning kept invading my thoughts, all of which were circling around my prostate problem.

"So, Dad, what do you think about our trip?" Jamie asked.

"Three weeks seems like a long time right now," I said.

"I was looking online and the group organizes everything," she said. "All we need to supply are the plane tickets. I can go as your assistant."

"I think it would be a great experience. But first, I have to work it in my schedule and then with this whole thing going on now—"

"What whole thing?" Anna asked.

I looked up and saw my beautiful younger daughter looking at me with concerned, innocent eyes. The same look Sara often gave me. She was growing up much faster than I wanted. She was almost done with elementary school, but it seemed like only yesterday she was crawling around on the floor.

"It's something that your mother and I have wanted to talk to you about. We waited because we didn't want to worry you and I still have a lab test pending."

"Well, you're worrying me now," Jamie said.

"There's something wrong with my prostate."

"What? Cancer?" Jamie said.

"Maybe."

"Dad, you can't have cancer," Jamie said. She looked at Sara. "Mom?"

"Like your dad said, we don't have all the answers so we don't know what it is," Sara said. "It may not be cancer."

"It could be nothing. But sooner or later you were going to find out because I may have to go in and out of the hospital."

"You're not going to die, are you?" Anna asked.

"No, I don't think it's that serious," I said. But cancer is cancer and in spite of trying to be reassuring, I was not reassured. Yet, how could I explain that to Anna.

"Will you be all right, Dad?" Jamie asked.

"I hope so. Besides, I'm not going to leave your mother to fend for herself with you two crazy kids."

"Everything will be all right. There is nothing to worry about. Your dad told me that this is common and most people have no problems." Sara presented a strong front.

"What's exactly wrong?" Jamie asked.

"My prostate is what is wrong."

"What is a prostate?" Anna asked.

"The prostate is a gland all males have. It helps to make babies."

"Just take it out. We don't need any more siblings. Anna can deal without the baby brother she has always wanted," Jamie said.

"That may very well need to happen eventually, but like I said, we need to wait for more lab results."

"Could this affect our trip? It's only a month and a half away?" Jamie asked.

Jamie had been planning this medical mission for a while. I had told her stories of humanitarian medical trips I made earlier in my career, which piqued her interest. She researched everything, contacted the organization and received the application materials. A couple of months ago, I consented to going, but now with everything seemingly swirling around me in confusion, it was the last thing I wanted to do. I'd have to let her down gently, but some other time. I wasn't up to it now.

"Like I said, we'll have to see about the trip. I want to go, but we may have to postpone it until I can get everything treated and sorted out."

"I understand," Jamie said, but obviously disappointed. Jamie was a model daughter. She was on the tail end of her second year in high school. As a father, I couldn't have been more proud of her. She had the intelligence and sophistication to hold her own on a difficult trip like a humanitarian mission. On some level, she understood the gravity of my situation. Some things are more important than a working vacation. I had to concentrate on my health and not on a trip to Nicaragua.

Anxiety encircled the table. We ate the rest of the dinner in silence, each with our own thoughts.

Before we finished, Anna said, "Dad, I think you'll be all right. I'll pray for you."

I wish I had that much faith.

"I think they handled that well," I said to Sara as we were getting ready for bed.

"If by well, you mean complete silence, then yes," she said.

"No tears were shed."

"I think they were a little shocked."

"How disappointed do you think Jamie is on canceling the trip?"

"She understands more than Anna the seriousness of the situation, but she has really been looking forward to that trip."

"Were you able to smooth things over at her school for the extra absences?"

"I tried, but you may have to go in and give them a better idea of what you'll be doing. Help them understand the educational value behind the trip and let the MD after your name pull some weight."

"It doesn't seem to matter now if we aren't going."

"No, maybe not. It's a shame. Jamie has worked hard to organize the trip and not going will devastate her."

"I know." I stopped putting away my clothes. "What should I do?"

"I don't know, Jeff. It seems like a risk now to go. Who knows what would happen."

"I agree."

We climbed into bed.

"So, you've never seen that painting I asked about earlier?"

"The one with your head surrounded by bubbles? Sounds like a shower scene. No, I've never seen it," Sara said.

"How weird is it that a woman who I hadn't seen in twenty-five years comes into my clinic and starts telling me about a dream she had?"

"It's pretty weird."

"Not only that, but I can't get her crazy eyes out of my head. She also made some disturbing remarks. She said I had to make a decision and if I don't I'll sink. What does that mean to you?"

"I don't know. Where are you going to sink?"

"She didn't know. Her dream ended without an answer."

"Sounds like you have a not so secret admirer dreaming about you."

"Stop. This is serious. It gave me an unsettling feeling that I can't shake."

"Obviously. You won't stop talking about it."

"I have to find that painting. Maybe there is something about it that I don't remember."

"Your head with bubbles would be unforgettable," Sara said, smiling.

I snorted off her barb.

"Well, there must to be a reason this is bothering you. You've seen unusual patients before and they never affected you like this."

"You're right."

"Just sleep on it and maybe things will become clearer. Maybe you'll remember where you left that painting and you can stare at those bubbles all day."

"Now you're just making fun of me."

"Just a little bit."

SIX

"**H**EY, HONEY, ARE you sure you haven't seen that painting?" I'd been looking all day. I couldn't get it out of my mind. Once I found it, my curiosity would be satisfied and I could lose it all over again, maybe this time for good.

"Oh, here it is. I found it," I called out. It was hidden under a stack of old medical journals in my closet. But that's weird, I'd already looked there.

The painting had aged well. It had kept its color in spite of my neglect. My face was central with four translucent bubbles floating above my head in vibrant detail.

As I studied it, my countenance seemed to change. I looked older. The hair was a little grey too. Kim Travers must have taken a some artistic license. Maybe that's the trick. The psychic artist paints the subject looking older than they are and when they look back years later it seemed like the painting had magically transformed.

"Hey, Barb, you wouldn't believe it, but this painting has changed." Wait a second. What happened to the bubbles? They disappeared. My face looked even more aged. I had a full head of grey hair.

"Sara, come look at this so I know I'm not crazy. This painting is changing before my eyes." Why hadn't my wife answered? "Sara, are you there?" Something was wrong.

"Sara, where are you?" The picture became blurry and indistinct. The shapes meshed. The painting swirled before my eyes into a vortex of colors. This couldn't be happening. "Sara can you hear me?" Then, my feet started sinking. My feet disappeared into the floor! Two eyes appeared in the painting. They were the crazy blue eyes of the tie-dye woman and they were emanating from my swirling painting.

"Sara, Sara!" I continued sinking and the floor began to swirl around me. The floor became an extension of the painting. It squeezed my legs together, then my hips, and then abdomen. It became difficult to expand my lungs from the pressure. I couldn't catch my breath. It constricted my throat tighter and tighter. I couldn't breathe. I took my last breath.

"Haaaaah!" I gasped for air.

"Jeff, are you okay?"

"What? What's going on?"

"You were moving around and talking in your sleep."

"Oh," I said, catching my breath.

"Are you okay?"

"I'm fine."

"You're soaking wet."

"Cold sweats. I'll go change." Throwing water on my face woke me up, but didn't erase those eyes from my mind. They were fixed as if etched into my brain. What did it mean? My dad always said that dreams held meaning, but of what? Could Kim Travers have been right? No, it made no sense. I was tired. I needed some sleep. I had a full day of work ahead.

"Let's go! You guys should've been ready twenty minutes ago. It takes thirty minutes to get to your grandparents."

"We know, Dad, we're almost ready. If you want us to be on time you should build another bathroom," Jamie yelled from her room.

With the family in the car, we were off. My mom lived on the other side of town in the home I grew up in. When my parents divorced, she decided to stay. It was her home and she didn't want to move. She met Tom a few years later and he had no objections of moving in. He just wanted to be with her.

I had been dreading this dinner since my prostate became an issue. I wasn't sure how to tell my mom. She would worry. I was inclined to wait until I had more answers.

"Are you looking forward to seeing your parents?" Sara asked after we were on the road for a while.

"Yes and no. When's the last time we saw them?"

"It's been four or five months."

"Really? It couldn't have been that long. I thought maybe no more than a couple of weeks."

"Jamie, Anna and I have met up with them a couple of times, but you've always been busy."

"I didn't realize it had been that long. I guess I've been busier recently."

"Yes, you have. You've been missing a lot of things recently."

I looked at Sara. The anger in her tone was absent in her face.

"Where did that come from?" I asked.

"I'm sorry. I don't know. Anyway, are you going to tell them about what's been going on with you?"

"I don't know. I was just wondering that myself."

"They would probably want to know."

"Yes, you're right, but then my mom will worry."

"Moms always worry about their kids. It's what we do."

My mom's house was a small, one-story, brick home in an older neighborhood. In its heyday, the block had been teaming with kids, but most had left home, leaving the neighborhood much quieter. My mom met us at the front door still dressed in her work clothes of a light-colored, formal blouse and dress pants over which she wore her kitchen apron. Her grey hair was short and styled in a professional manner. She smiled, waving to us. Her face lit up when Anna and Jamie stepped out of the car and Anna ran to give her a hug.

"Hey, Mom, what's for dinner?" I asked as I gave my mom a hug.

"You don't ever change, do you? Always looking for your next meal," my mom said.

"It smells good."

"It's your favorite, chicken Alfredo."

"You know how to get to my heart, through my stomach."

"It's almost ready."

Since I had moved out, little had changed in my childhood home. It had the same smell, same kitchen table, and some of the same furniture. As I watched my mom lead the girls back to the kitchen, I couldn't help but remember the dream I had of my family while in surgery. In the living room, through the hallway, was where my mom caught me spying on their meditation ceremony. Now it was a reading room. My mom had long ago replaced the candles and crystals with books and periodicals.

After my parents divorced, my mom slowly formed a new life. She finished a master's degree and became a clinical therapist. She then began working with disadvantaged young women for the city, leading a woman's center. She slowly shed her old persona, but never lost her true self—down to earth, mindful, and dignified. While at school, she met Tom. Tom was a history professor at the local college. His inquisitive mind interested my mom and they made a good match. If they weren't immersed in an obscure historical theory, then they were discussing a Dr. Phil episode.

I left for college shortly after they married. And initially, I didn't hang around much. But over time, I came to enjoy their company.

"Everyone sit down. We're ready to eat," my mom called from the kitchen.

"So how's life been, Jeff?" Tom asked.

"Things have been okay," I said.

Tom was a remnant of the past, a retired Army intelligence soldier. He joined the military after college, deployed to Vietnam and stayed for his twenty. He was happiest with a good book and a full meal, which my mom always supplied. His thinning hair was high and tight and his abdomen less so since retirement. He was never without a buttoned up shirt and dark pressed slacks.

"You don't sound too convincing," Tom said.

I didn't respond. Sara nudged me.

"Is everything okay?" my mom asked, stepping into the dining room.

"Yeah, everything is fine. It's been a long week."

"What's been long about it?" my mom asked.

"Oh, things at work," I said.

"Everything okay at home?" My mom looked at Sara and me.

"No problems, just one of those weeks," I said. I wasn't ready to tell them.

"Don't let it get to you. One week goes and another one comes," Tom said. Thankfully, Tom was good at changing subjects. "I read an article on the internet last night about research on the mind."

"What did it talk about?" I asked.

"It reminded me of a book I read a few years ago called *Bright Air, Brilliant Fire* by Edelman. Did you know he was a Nobel Laureate?"

I nodded my head, "Nope."

"Well, he discussed how the path to consciousness lies in the connections between different parts of our brain. This leads to forming symbols. And voilà, consciousness was born. It was of course a little more complicated than that."

"What kind of symbols?" Sara asked.

"Simple symbols, like animal drawings in a cave or stick figures carved into rock. These symbols progress to more complex symbols such as letters to represent sound. Eventually the symbols evolved into language," Tom said.

"I've heard this before," Sara said. "I still remember some of the theories from my linguistics courses." Sara had received her master's in linguistics studies while I was in medical school. She figured it would make her more competitive in the job market. "Linguistics is, in fact, the study of language as a system of signs or symbols for the purpose of communicating information. Primitive communication started over 1.5 million years ago with our very distant relatives. Those cave drawings were our first written language."

"Very rudimentary language," Tom said, "but language nonetheless."

"Our most primitive ancestors were as closely related to chimps as they were to humans," I said.

"Yes, primitive language for a primitive people," Sara said.

"How does the book define consciousness?" I asked.

"The book says that it is difficult to define and is unique to each individual. Simply put, the book explains that consciousness is perceiving the past, present and future relationship between oneself and the environment," Tom said. "Humans of course have the highest level of consciousness. This parallels what your mom does. Psychology is the study of human behavior and the mind."

"I like to say that it's a study of our soul," my mom said, poking her head from the kitchen.

"If I'm hearing you right, the author of your book explains that symbols helped to create consciousness?" I asked.

"For the most part, yes."

"So then to clarify, our distant chimp-like relatives were conscious? Like Descartes said, 'I think therefore I am'?" I asked.

"The author said there was a prolonged evolutionary development of our consciousness using symbols. The symbols were a path, not an endpoint. Our distant relatives were at the beginning of the path," Tom said.

"Enough talk, dinner is ready," my mom said. "Jeff, can you help me with these dishes. Tom, can you make sure everyone has a drink and utensils."

"Everyone is good to go by the looks of it. Bring on the food," Tom said.

My mom entered the dining room with the final touches to the meal. She had removed her apron. She sat down and put her napkin in her lap.

"Let's eat," Tom said.

"Finally," Anna said. Sara gave her a look, but Anna had already started gobbling up her food and didn't notice.

"Don't worry, Sara," my mom said. "I understand. Anna does have half of my son's genes in her. He could never wait either, no matter how much I tried. Sometimes his manners were closer to our primitive ancestors. I blamed it on his DNA, on his father's side."

"Like this?" I said and opened my mouth full of food. Anna giggled and Jamie said eewh.

"Jeff," Sara said. "Please close your mouth."

"Like I said, it's in the genes," my mom said.

I closed my mouth and smiled.

We passed the entrees around and started eating. My mom had cooked a charming meal to celebrate nothing in particular, but being together.

"This connection between symbols and our consciousness is interesting," my mom said. "In counseling, we use symbols. Not necessarily letter symbols to form words, but other things in a person's life that can symbolize a greater issue. We try to bring these issues into a greater consciousness or awareness to allow for healing. Uncovering the meaning of a person's symbols can lead to a breakthrough in their counseling treatment."

"Well said, Darling," Tom said.

"You could say that my patients try to understand the symbols of their life," my mom said.

"That's deep, Grandma," Jamie said.

"Yeah, that does sound interesting," Tom said.

"This talk reminds me of a psychiatrist I spoke to a while ago. He described a new study on consciousness and the brain. He remarked that conscious perception enables contact with widespread brain sources. Without consciousness, those areas of the brain are dormant. Consciousness highly activates our brain," I said.

"Well, that's a no brainer," Sara said. "I don't need some fancy study to tell me the more I use my brain the more stimulated it gets."

"Tell that to the neurophysiologist dedicating his life to it. But if what Tom is saying is true, this means that symbols in effect helped the human brain to evolve to what it is today. Follow me now; the more our ancestors used symbols, the more their conscious perception developed, the more they activated their brains, the bigger the human brain became, evolving from primate to human."

"I see what you're getting at," Tom said. "This created an evolving circle of symbols, language, consciousness, and brain activation leading up to the modern human brain."

"Yuck, that's gross," Anna said.

"Can we talk about brains and monkeys some other time while we aren't eating?" Sara asked.

"Yeah, that's gross," Jamie said.

"Okay, no more brains or monkeys, but what of symbols," I said.

"Dad, what do you mean by symbols?" Anna asked.

"I'll take this one, Jeff," Sara said. "A symbol is a word, picture, or object that represents something else. A symbol often helps to convey a certain meaning that can be difficult to express."

"So a word is a symbol that represents what we are trying to communicate?" Jamie asked.

"Exactly," Sara said.

"And by using symbols, by forming a written language and making cave paintings our ancestors evolved to who we are today?" Jamie asked.

"Yes," I said.

"When did that stop?" Jamie asked.

"When did what stop?" Sara asked.

"When did we stop using symbols to evolve?"

"That's an excellent question," Tom said. "And to add to that question; how do we use symbols to continue to evolve?"

"If by evolve you mean grow," my mom said, "I feel that my patients grow all the time through stops and starts with the help of symbols. Individually, they evolve and grow as a person."

"Languages have also continued to evolve," Sara said.

"But I wonder if we continue to evolve because of language," I said.

"You mean is our intellectual capacity growing because of language," Tom said.

"I'd say no. At some point down the evolutionary road, the evolution of our spoken language probably stopped making any considerable influence on our brain development," I said. "Our different forms of communication may continue to help humans evolve, but I doubt that spoken language has any more influence. It helps us develop from a babbling baby into an adult human, but spoken language probably does not push us beyond that."

"So if language no longer affects human evolution, than what does? It seems unlikely that after using symbols for a million years to evolve that we would suddenly stop," Sara said.

"Symbolism almost seems innate in us," my mom said.

"It appears to have been a powerful influence in our species development," Tom said.

"What does evolve mean?" Anna asked.

"It can have many different meanings, but biological evolution means that over time, individual traits change and these changes are then passed on to our children, ultimately advancing an entire group or species," I said.

"Can evolution also help someone get better?" Anna asked.

"What do you mean?" Sara asked.

"Well, maybe it can help Dad get better," Anna said.

"Why would your dad need to get better?" my mom asked.

Sara noticed it first and put her hand out as if to stop Anna from saying anything more, but the words were already at her lips.

"He's sick," Anna said.

"What do you mean?" My mom's eyes darted from Sara to me. "What's going on Jeff?"

"Oh, man. This isn't how I wanted to tell you."

"What's going on?" my mom asked, her tone deepening.

I put my fork down and took a long drink of water, gathering my thoughts.

"I found out a few of days ago that I might have prostate cancer."

"Oh no," my mom said.

"My tests are still pending."

"But that doesn't make any sense. You're the picture of health," my mom said. "How did this happen?"

"It just did."

"I don't believe it. You've always been healthy, you exercise, and eat right. And you are my son and you can't have cancer," my mom said.

"Well that doesn't seem to matter to the cancer, but like I said, we're still waiting on results."

"Do you know anything more?" Tom asked.

"Only that I have an elevated PSA."

"What did your doctor say?" my mom asked.

"They don't know any more than I do."

My mom was flustered, questions raced through her mind. Tom laid a hand on her wrist, which calmed her. She took a deep breath.

"How are you doing?" Tom asked.

"I'm doing okay. Hanging in there," I said.

"How are you doing, Sara?"

"I'm hanging in there too. Everything has happened so fast that I don't feel like I've had a chance to think about it."

"Is there anything we can do for you?" my mom asked.

"So far, everybody is coping with it well. We told the girls yesterday and they're concerned, but not distraught."

"We're a little distraught, Dad. We're just good at dealing with it," Jamie said.

"Have you thought about family counseling? Sometimes it can help you work through difficult times," my mom said.

"No, we hadn't talked about that, but it's a good idea."

"It'll help the kids express their anxieties and concerns," my mom said.

"This can be very traumatic for them," Tom said.

"We're sitting right here," Jamie said.

"Yeah, we're sitting right here. And anyway, I'm fine." Anna said.

"You may think you're fine," my mom said, "but it's hard to evaluate your emotions when you're knee deep in it. Someone else can help you with that."

"What are your options for treatment?" Tom asked.

"Until we find out what it is, I'm not certain. It could mean no treatment or complete removal of the prostate." And possibly chemotherapy and radiation, but I didn't want to cause more alarm. Both treatments implied cancer and death in many people's eyes. There was no need for that sentiment now.

"I assume you have good physicians taking care of you," Tom said.

"The best in the area. The same doctor I refer patients to."

"When will you get the results?" my mom asked.

"In about a week."

"Please keep me informed. I worry about you," she said.

"Sure, Mom, I'll keep you informed."

"Promise? Because I know that if things get stressful you'll shut down and won't talk to anybody."

"I promise."

"Remember, I'm your mother and I worry about you."

"I know."

The conversation died with no more discussion of symbols, consciousness, or evolution. I had no desire to talk and no one else seemed to either. Anna's reminder of my illness sapped my energy. Once again, we ate dinner in silence. My prostate was even able to quiet the loquacious Tom. The chicken Alfredo wasn't as satisfying as my mom's customary cooking.

I helped my mom finish the dishes as Tom entertained the girls with another one of his stories. My mom was silent as she tended to the washing while I dried.

"I'm worried about the girls," she finally said.

"I know."

"It's a lot of stress they're dealing with. They may not know how to process it all, especially Anna. She is still very young."

"You're right."

"And I know how you get. Just like when you were little. If things become difficult, you close up, put your head down and drive through. But you can't this time because you have them to think about and Sara also."

"I know."

My mom looked up from the dishes unconvinced she was reaching me fully.

"Come with me. I want to show you something," she said.

We walked to her bedroom and she searched in her old oak dresser, which was six feet high and inlayed with carvings. It was so tall the top two drawers remained empty. My mom had inherited the century old heirloom from her grandmother. She pulled out a picture from the bottom drawer.

"This was our family. Do you remember?" she asked. "I had this picture taken when we were all much younger."

"Yes, I remember."

"I know how hard it was for you children. I could see the pain in your eyes. I wanted so much to make it stop. But it wasn't meant to be."

"No, it wasn't."

"You took it the hardest, Jeff."

I raised my eyebrows in acknowledgement. It was still somewhat hard to swallow after all the years.

"Please learn from me and your father's mistakes."

"I have."

"Don't forget what's most important to you. Your family, the girls, your marriage."

"I won't, Mom."

"Don't think I don't see what's going on. We've seen a lot more of Sara and the girls than we've seen of you. That also means you haven't been spending hardly enough time with them either."

"I know. I haven't been."

My mom dug into the drawer a little further. She pulled out a plastic figurine of Daffy Duck.

"Do you remember this?" She held up the plastic toy.

"Yeah, Dad would stick it to the dash on trips."

"One of you kids grabbed it at a rest stop store. Neither your dad nor I found it until we were twenty miles down the road. Your father was so angry, which wasn't like him. We drove all the way back to pay for it. From then on, it stayed on the dash as a reminder."

"It reminds me of our camping trips to the Shenandoah Mountains."

"That's what it became. We were never happier and more of a family then on those trips." She put the figurine back in the drawer. "You need to find moments like those for your own family."

"Yeah, it's been hard lately."

"That's a poor excuse. They deserve better."

In the past, we'd have argued by now, but I knew my mom was right. I didn't have an answer for her. Thankfully, Anna saved me as she came running into the room.

"Mom says it's time to go," Anna said, huffing and puffing.

"Has Grandpa Tom been tiring you out with all of his stories?" my mom asked.

"Yes, they are long," Anna said.

As we were leaving the bedroom, "Please, Jeff, think about it."

"I will, Mom."

SEVEN

DREAMS. WHY DO they keep bothering me? I had another one last night. They were becoming more real with each occurrence. I've had vivid dreams in the past, but not like this. My senses were alive. These were real.

The night before, my dream was brief. Deep baritone chanting reverberated around me. Soft, meaningful voices offered up prayers to God. Someone drummed in the distance, vibrating beats to my core as if leading a march to an unknown place. Steam stung my skin and hard dirt cooled my feet as I sat cross-legged. The smell of sage pervaded the air and it was pitch black except for the occasional flicker of red light a few feet away.

From the glimmer of light, I could briefly make out faces in a circle. Faces I thought I recognized, but remained hidden in the darkness. An immense weight squeezed my chest. The steam seared my lungs making it painful to breathe. Then I awoke. I didn't write it down and yet all the details stuck in my memory. It wasn't as disturbing as the large eyes staring at me, but unsettling.

Medical studies showed that most dreams were re-enactments of our day, usually focused on stressful events. While some people believed dreams can predict the future, studies suggested we selectively remembered dreams that fit future events. Most dreams were our subconscious mind re-enacting our days.

During internship, which was a stressful time in my medical training, I dreamed about patients. Sara was typically the patient I would re-enact on while asleep. I remembered none of this, but she would describe a ten to fifteen minute presentation to include their problem, physical exam and diagnosis. Those were extreme examples of stress that replayed in my subconscious interrupting my sleep.

Recently, I had stress in my life especially with the prostate cancer looming, but these new dreams were different. They felt significant. Maybe my stepmother, Judith, could shed some light on it. She was knowledgeable on the topic of dreams along with other spiritual and New Age philosophies such as intuition, spiritual healing and meditation.

Her talents allowed her to see beyond the physical realm, which most people described as being psychic. She was a counselor, spiritual healer and teacher. She had been successful and through word of mouth, her clientele had slowly grown to include hundreds of people around the country. She was good at what she did. Who knows how she did it, but she was often right.

I was on my way to meet her and my dad for a meal at the local Denny's. My dad liked Denny's malt milkshakes. Judith liked to smoke. Denny's was still a bastion of smoking diehards and she could smoke without being shunned for her habit. She said it kept her grounded.

"Hey, Dad, Judith, how are you?"

"We're doing fine," my dad said. "How are you?"

He stood up and gave me a hug. He wore khaki pants and a polo shirt with loafers. Judith followed. She was about my father's height with feathery-short, pearly-white hair. She wore a flowing, light silk dress and a button up sweater.

"I'm hanging in there. Sara and the girls are doing well," I said, sitting down in the booth.

"We haven't seen you in a while. Is everything okay?" my dad asked.

"Things are fine," I said.

My father had been a patient, loving parent. I had often looked to him for guidance through life. He was a practicing chiropractor of forty years. When I became a physician, his pride was only outdone by my dutiful embrace of the spiritual medicine torch. People often said we looked and acted exactly alike except for one small detail. I was nearly a foot taller. Height skipped his generation.

"Jeff, we haven't ordered yet. What would you like to eat? I'm treating," my father said.

"I'll have a milkshake and a BLT," I said.

"There is nothing better than classics," he said.

His guidance started early with those bedtime stories, books and enlisting me in New Age classes. After my parents separated and my dad and Judith married, the spiritual medicine instruction increased tenfold. His interest led to my indoctrination. I could never fault his desire for me to follow down the same path that he loved.

"We had a little excitement this week," my dad said, looking at Judith.

"What happened?" Not much stirred my dad to excitement from his calm, collected self.

Judith extinguished her cigarette on the table ashtray.

"We were in the middle of one of my psychic development classes," Judith said. "I was leading everybody in a deep chanting meditation. You could feel the energy boiling over in the room."

"We were really getting into it," my dad said.

"When I quieted the group down, a lone, chanting voice remained. At first, it sounded muffled. Then we realized it wasn't coming from any one of us."

"I thought we had attracted some dead monk from another dimension," my dad said. "It was soulful chanting."

"So what did you do?" I asked.

"We waited about a minute for it to stop, but the chanting continued. Finally, your dad was elected to go search for it."

"In Judith's building, there is a second floor that nobody occupies. Well, that's where the noise was coming from. I made my way up the staircase with the entire class of about ten people on my heels. I peeked through the door window, but could see nothing. I jiggled the loose doorknob enough to pry it open and stumbled into the room from the weight of the others pushing against me. In the middle of the apartment among boxes and furniture was a burly Rottweiler chanting away. He stopped his howling and quizzically gazed at me. Realizing I wasn't his owner, he made a beeline for the door. Upon seeing that their monk was instead an angry dog, the others bolted down the stairs. I was too slow and the dog had a good jump on me so in a fit of insight, I spun and faced him. I held out my hand and commanded, *down*. To which the dog stopped, for a moment, so I could slip out and close the door," my dad said.

"Apparently, the dog didn't like our interruption so he barked the rest of the class," Judith said.

"You never know who you're going to inspire" my dad said.

"Or how intuition will present itself," Judith said.

"Judith now has a chanting master upstairs who happens to be a dog." My dad laughed. "Other than the dog experience, things have been going pretty well. Life is good."

Judith had been looking at me throughout my dad's story.

"You look tired, Jeff," she said. Her eyes searched mine. It was difficult to keep anything from her. She could look straight into me as if parting the many layers of defense I erected to keep the outside world from knowing my true self.

"I haven't been sleeping well lately."

"In my experience, sleep problems start and end in the mind," Judith said.

She hadn't always been a psychic counselor. In her previous life, she had worked the nightshift as an ER nurse in a busy downtown hospital. She said the night brought in the restless people—restless from pain, drugs, alcohol, marriage problems, worry, or life in general. They always had a reason for why they weren't otherwise sleeping.

"I think you're right."

"What's been on your mind?" Judith asked.

"Dreams."

"That's interesting. What kind of dreams?" Judith asked.

"Disturbing ones."

"Have you written them down?" my dad asked.

"No, I haven't needed to. I remember them completely."

"Have you tried to make sense of them?" my dad asked.

"Well, my dreams aren't like the Rosetta Stone. I wouldn't know where to start."

"First off, you should ask yourself, what does the dream mean to you?" my dad said.

"It means nothing as far as I can tell except for a sense of fear and suffocation."

"Sometimes the meaning of dreams present themselves later. As I bet in your case, they do," Judith said as if already knowing my dream more than I did. It wouldn't be a surprise. Things like that came easy to Judith. She often had premonitions for family, friends, and even patients. For many years, she didn't share them. However, things changed after a special day in the ER over ten years ago. She realized she needed to branch out and explore her gifts more. In the middle of an uncommonly slow shift, a ten your old boy walked in with his mom. He hadn't been feeling well and the mom didn't know why. The boy trudged across the ER and for a brief second looked into Judith's eyes. She sensed an absence in him as if his soul was leaving his body. Then an image of his entire person flashed in her mind like a full body PET scan. One area glowed brightly—a spot on his brain. She told the attending physician whom she knew well. He initially dismissed it, but after seeing the patient and knowing Judith, he ordered the appropriate studies to diagnoses a cerebral aneurysm—a condition that if undiagnosed would have killed him.

"Maybe you're right and it will occur to me later what the dreams mean. I just wish they'd stop so I can get a good night's sleep," I said.

"You should meditate on it and maybe your subconscious will reveal the meaning of the dreams," my dad said.

"Dad, I wouldn't know where to start with meditating on my dreams. Anyway, sleep experts say that most dreams are re-enactments of the day's events. They have studies to back up their claims."

"What about dreams that are not of the day's events?" Judith asked.

"Don't know. They are uncategorized in the eyes of science and medicine."

"Some things can't be easily described through strict studies," Judith said.

"Maybe they're trying to tell you something," my dad said.

"You know the study of dreams is called Oneirology," Judith said. "Some people in my line of work feel that there is a dream language. There are standard symbols in all dreams, which help us interpret them. Often though, the symbols are unique to the individual and only the individual can ultimately interpret it."

"Did you know that we dream about two hours a day? That equals about six years in a lifetime," I said.

"That's a lot of dreaming," my dad said.

"Even if ninety percent of our dreams are mundane daily events replayed in our mind that's still a lot time left over for other dreams," Judith said.

"At least a couple of months' worth," my dad said.

"My only question is where are the ten percent of our dreams that aren't daily events coming from?" Judith asked.

"Maybe from our higher self," my dad said.

"I believe that our subconscious pulls from our higher self," Judith said.

"Our higher self being?" I asked, already knowing the answer because I'd heard the term before. I tried not to sound condescending.

"A reflection of God. Our higher self is our connection to God," my dad said without an ounce of disdain.

"Dreams are our daily touch with our higher self," Judith said.

"And what a beautiful touch it is," my dad said.

"Tell me about your dreams," Judith said.

"They don't make sense," I said.

"It doesn't matter, just tell me."

Relenting, I started. "In my most recent dream, I sat in a dark room with shadowy faces. Hot steam filled the room and glowing embers radiated in the center. Another one of my dreams had to deal with an old acquaintance, a spiritual painting and the feeling that I was suffocating."

"That first dream sounds like a sweat lodge to me," my dad said.

"I agree. That's exactly what it sounds like," Judith said. "Do you remember anything else about that dream?

"I felt like I couldn't breathe."

"Well there is an obvious connection," Judith said.

"You're right. How did I miss that?"

"Son, don't you remember the sweat lodge? You were a teenager at the time."

"Vaguely," I said.

"My poor wayward son. Have you forgotten everything I taught you? Should I explain this to him or do you want to?" my dad asked Judith.

"You go ahead."

"A sweat lodge is a Native American ritual that's been central to the Native American way of life for as long as their history dates. The sweat lodge acts as their church for spiritual guidance and their hospital for mind/body healing. It serves as a guide for those with questions and a stepping stone for youngsters."

"What does that mean for me? I'm not Native American."

"That's a question you have to answer. Can you remember anything from your lodge experience?"

"Very little. At the time, as a teenager, it was a coming of age experience. I'm already of age so I'm not seeing the connection."

"Maybe a healing experience," Judith said.

"Why do I need healing...?" I was so caught up in these dreams and symbols my prostate had slipped my mind.

"The dream may not be about healing, but a resistance to healing," Judith said. I could tell she knew something wasn't right. She wasn't one to push a subject. My dad, however, hadn't noticed my wandering thoughts.

"Your dream does sound like a resistance to healing. When you're not ready for it, sometimes the lodge can be too powerful," my dad said.

"How much healing am I really going to get from suffocating steam?" I said.

My dad sighed. "Whatever happened to your openness for the spiritual? You used to love the subject. But now it's only a discarded memory. You don't even remember how to meditate?"

New Age beliefs and practices had been a bond between us. Eventually, after many negative comments and rebuttals, he understood that I no longer abided by them anymore.

"Sorry, Dad, I don't mean to be difficult. I've had a long day."

"That's alright. I just don't understand. Why did you change?"

"Dad, I really don't want to get into that right now."

He was speechless, staring at me as if processing where things went wrong. He then sighed and returned to eating his food.

Silence ruled the air and I realized how distant my father and I had become. We didn't know each other like we used to. Before, we would visit or talk on the phone at least a couple of times a week, now it was barely once a month. Judith had set up this lunch. The last time I'd talked to my dad was two or three months ago. He would call, but I was always busy and unable to call him back, and then a couple of days passed and I would forget. Recently, whenever we spoke, we ended up at odds. No matter how we started, we always ended up arguing.

"I should get going. I have to get up early tomorrow morning."

"When's the next time we're going to see you and your beautiful family?" Judith asked.

"Maybe next week. I'll have to talk to Sara."

And I left.

EIGHT

I PULLED INTO my driveway after another long day of work. All I wanted to do was sleep. I hadn't spoken to my father since our argument a few days ago. A nagging voice in my head kept telling me I should call, but another talk would probably result in another argument. Our relationship was what it was.

"I'm home," I called. The house was surprisingly quiet. Maybe I would get the sleep I so desperately wanted.

"How was work?" Sara said from the kitchen.

"Normal for a change."

I put away my coat and walked into the kitchen.

"Any news from the urologist?"

"No."

"Do you remember what tonight is?"

"Yes?"

"You forgot didn't you?"

"It depends on what you're talking about."

"I only ask for one night. Just one night a month for date night. The last three you've been at work."

"It's been four months since I took you out to dinner? It couldn't have been that long."

"It's been at least four months."

"I've been busy at work."

"You're always busy at work. "

I shrugged. "I work. I don't know what else to say."

"You've been a lot busier lately, but let's not talk about that." She gave me a kiss on the cheek. "We're going to have a good night tonight."

"Of course," I said. "I'll be in the study."

"Don't forget. Just you, me, dinner and a lot of lovey-dovey talking."

"I won't forget. I have some charting to finish then I'll be ready."

"That's what you said last date night and we were an hour late for our reservations."

"That won't happen again."

"Jeff, are you ready?" Sara yelled from the other room. "We have to go. We're already late."

"Almost."

"We have reservations."

"I'll be ready."

"Are you dressed?"

"Yes, I'm dressed." Sara poked her head into the room. She wore a formfitting, black dress accentuating her curves. Her wavy black hair shimmered down to her shoulders.

"You're still wearing your clothes from work."

"Do you want me to change?"

"Yes, please put something different on."

"Sorry, I didn't know that these clothes were so unacceptable."

"I knew you wouldn't be ready."

"I'm ready. Just give me a minute to change."

Sara was already annoyed. This date night wasn't starting out well. In the car, it didn't improve.

"I wish for once you would act like you wanted to spend time with me," Sara said.

"What do you mean? We're on our way to the restaurant."

"But not without me begging and pleading and practically dragging you out of the house."

"You didn't drag me out of the house."

"But it shouldn't take that much effort. You act as if you don't want to go. This is our time together amidst our busy schedule. Once a month. That's all. And still you show no desire."

"I want to go. I'm in the car aren't I?" I knew I shouldn't have said it as soon as it left my mouth. It was insensitive. I was irritated.

"Yes, you're here physically. But every other part of you is somewhere else."

"What do you want me to do? I've been preoccupied. I have a lot of stuff going on."

"I know you do, but you'd been preoccupied long before your prostate became an issue. This has been going on for at least six months. You're never present. Even the girls have mentioned seeing you less."

"When?"

"They say it all the time."

"I spend a lot of time with them."

"Well, they seem to think that you haven't"

"I don't understand what you want from me."

"We want you to be present with us and to act like you enjoy being around us."

"What would ever give you the idea I didn't want to spend time with you or the girls?"

"Your absence physically and emotionally. You don't have to take it from me, but if the girls are complaining then something isn't right."

We continued to the restaurant in silence. I was brooding. Sara was on the verge of either blowing up or crying. I could never tell which. We dined in sullen quietude until—

"Jeff, I'm not happy."

"What do you mean, you're not happy?"

"I'm not happy with us, our relationship."

"I'm happy with us," I said.

"We've fallen into a rut. We've acquired some bad habits and I think it's leading us in the wrong direction."

"Well, what are you suggesting?"

"I don't know? Can you honestly say that you're happy in our relationship, because it doesn't seem like it?"

Her question struck me like a punch in the gut. Not only was she questioning my commitment to our family, but also the foundation of our relationship. She had some nerve. But was I happy? I had been so preoccupied recently it had never crossed my mind. Was I purposefully sabotaging our date nights, trying to avoid her? I squeezed my head to relieve the tension. This was the last thing I needed. I thought I could count on our relationship; that we were strong. I knew things hadn't been great recently, but I didn't know it was this bad.

"Sara, I can't talk about this now."

"Then when?"

"I don't know."

"There's never a good time for this. There's never a good time for me. Maybe we shouldn't be together." This time it was obvious. She was crying. I tried to comfort her, but she felt so distant. She eventually calmed herself. We finished dinner and left without saying more than a few words.

We went to bed angry and woke up angry. Sara and I didn't talk until I came to breakfast. Unfortunately, the girls were around and I was overmatched.

"Jamie, tell your father what you told me the other day. How you don't spend time together anymore."

"That was it. We don't spend as much time together like we used to. You never seem to be around."

"I'm sorry I didn't realize "

"That's why I was hoping to be able to hang out more when we go to Nicaragua."

"About that. I don't think we'll be able to go."

"It's all planned out. You can't back out now."

"I just have too much on my plate to go on a third world vacation."

"I've worked so hard to plan it."

"I know, but remember, I never gave you a one hundred percent confirmation."

"I still thought we'd end up going."

"It's not going to happen now. Maybe some other time," I said.

"When? You're always busy. You come home late from work more and more. Mom's right, you're never here."

"I'm sorry, Jamie. I wish I could go, but I can't."

"Yeah, that's what you keep saying, but it doesn't feel like it." Jamie stormed out of the room.

"Why did you have to do that?" I glared at Sara.

"I haven't done anything. You heard it yourself. You're never around anymore. That's on you."

"Yeah, Dad, we never play games like we used to," Anna said. "You're not as happy as you used to be."

"Quiet." I scowled across the table at my innocent baby girl. So perceptive, she could cut straight to the point. She struck a chord I didn't know existed. A tear came to her eye, then more tears as she sat seeming so young and alone in her big kitchen chair. Sara approached with a comforting hug. Her whispered reassurance stopped Anna's tears. Anna took her cereal and whimpered to her room.

"This must stop, Jeff."

I didn't respond.

"You should apologize to Anna."

"I will."

"Something is going to have to change or this isn't going to work."

"What's not going to work?"

"What's not going to work?" Sara's face became flushed. Her eyes fixated on me and she twisted the wooden spatula in her hand hard enough that I thought she was going to snap it. "This. Our family, our marriage. The things that should be the most important part of your life."

"You don't need to yell."

"Someone has to show some passion for this relationship because you surely don't."

"That's not fair. I show passion. This family and our marriage are important to me." I took a couple of deep breaths. The urge to lash out welled up inside of me.

"I'll tell you what's not fair—a shell of a man for a husband."

I paused, shocked by the barrage of criticism.

"Don't question me or who I am!" I said. "How dare you. I'm not going to listen to this anymore!" I trembled with anger. I left. I had to get away before I said something I couldn't take back. I roared out of the kitchen and to my study where at least my computer appreciated me. I gave it plenty of attention.

How dare Sara question me like that—a shell of a man. It was so demeaning. Did she think of me as some pitiful creature? I was a doctor and a successful businessman. Most would be proud to achieve what I had. I needed a break. I put my head on my desk, closed my eyes and pretended this wasn't happening. This will go away. She was going to have to apologize, but this will pass.

With my eyes closed, I felt so drained from the fighting. I could barely lift my head from the desk. I just needed to sleep. Fatigue and a stillness overcame me. Light then peered through my lids and a cool breeze touched my face. I opened my eyes, but instead of finding my desk, I was gazing at a long, tan, out-stretched leg. Its delicate toes careened the water's surface.

"What are you looking at?" a female voice said.

I shook my head and rubbed my eyes. Those legs were familiar.

"Wake up, sleepyhead, we're almost there," she said.

I was lying face down against a hard, wooden surface. My cheek matted to a grubby sweater and my fingers intertwined within the fibers of a worn rug.

"Penelope?"

"Yes."

I examined my surroundings further. My bed was a section of the deck on a tiny sailboat zigzagging up a large river. Farms encroached on either side with desert beyond. People waded in the water, working, washing and playing.

"What am I doing here?"

She made a quizzical expression, which soon disappeared as she pointed into the distance.

"Look. There it is."

I twisted around. In the distance on the right bank was a living, undulating mass of the ugliest beasts you could imagine.

"Are those—"

"Camels."

Our small boat made another quick turn and we floated up to a makeshift pier.

"Jeff, follow me," Penelope said. She leaped onto the wooden dock and quickly climbed up the sandy bank. "Can you believe this?" she asked as I caught up with her. "We are in the midst of thousands of camels herded hundreds of miles from all over Egypt, North Africa and Arabia."

"They're ugly animals and stink," I said.

"I heard they taste good too."

"What do you mean, 'taste good'? Camel meat?"

"Yes, I was told it's delicious. It's either that or another dinner of pita bread. I'm sure we can find somebody to cook it for us."

Penelope was a little more adventurous than I was. She was an Australian girl who I had met during my travels through Europe while I was in college. We made a pack to meet in Egypt the following summer for more traveling adventures. Somehow, the pack held and we ended up back together on the other side of the world. I would have been stupid to refuse a beautiful Australian girl with long, reddish blonde hair and spunk to back it up. If I had a choice of one dream, this one wasn't bad to have. We lost touch after Egypt. The vast ocean was difficult to overcome in a relationship.

She dragged me to the craziest places. This stop was in the middle of our cruise up the Nile. Our cruise ship was more like a dingy. The two of us along with four other travelers and two young Egyptian crewmen crammed onto a small vessel for one week. We made several stops along the way including the camel bazaar.

Camels crammed into every space of the unorganized market. If I was lucky enough to dodge one of the lumbering beasts, it meant that my foot had found its pile of feces left behind. Butchers interspersed themselves among the large mass of camels, selling slabs of said meat.

"I think this is the place the English couple was talking about," she said.

"What place?"

"The place we heard about in Cairo. When we were watching the Whirling Dervishes, the English couple wouldn't stop talking about this amazing Sufi mystic. They said we should see this guy."

"Weren't we going to get some camel meat?"

"That can wait. The Egyptians have held this camel bazaar for a thousand years, and the camels aren't going anywhere soon. There will be plenty of meat when we get back."

She darted in-between two camel stalls and emerged behind the main thoroughfare. In front of us, hugged in between two large mounds of sand and the Nile behind, was a small thatched hut. It looked like every other thatched hut in Egypt.

"This must be him. The Sufi mystic they were talking about," Penelope said.

"How do you know?"

"See the symbol." She pointed to a nine-sided star above the door. "That's the symbol the English couple said to look for. Let's go in."

"Are you sure—"

Before I could finish, she ducked under and disappeared into the darkness of the hut. I wasn't too keen on going into strange huts, but she was a beautiful girl. I had to follow her. I folded my body for the five-foot door and made my way in. When I unfolded, Penelope sat cross-legged on a carpet in front of an old man who looked about one hundred and fifty years old. He was thin with long, gray hair and a full, white beard with whiskers dangling down to his chest. His vision appeared poor and he moved his stiff joints slowly.

"This is Mr. Yusuf," Penelope said.

"How do you know that?" I asked.

"Because, he told me," she said.

"Sit down please," the man said in perfect Queen's English.

"Oh, I see." I sat. Penelope looked at me and shook her head.

"My friend here would like his fortune told," Penelope said.

"What? You're the one who wanted to come here."

"Tell me your name," Yusuf said. He looked at me with his cataract eyes, his countenance stern.

"Jeff."

"Jeff, I don't tell fortunes."

"That's okay, because…" I hoped this was going to end soon.

"But sometimes I can help people along in their lives."

"That sounds interesting," Penelope said.

"Would you stop. If you're so interested, why don't you have your fortune told?"

"No, you first."

The Sufi looked at Penelope and me. "Jeff, may I proceed?" he asked.

"I guess. Yes, please do."

"Now let me look at your hand," he said.

He took my right hand, then my left. He turned my left hand over and back. He studied it for a few seconds. Then he looked up, straight at me.

"Do you know how to read palms because I do not know what I am doing?" He gave a big, toothless grin. Penelope snorted out in laughter. I couldn't help but chuckle. I must have found the only Sufi mystic comedian.

"Jeff, do you know what it means to be a Sufi?"

"No," I answered, unsure of where this was leading.

"We turn away from everything, but that which is God. Did you see the Whirling Dervishes?"

"Yes, we did."

"They are amazing, yes?"

"Yes, they are."

"Their spinning is their devotional act towards God. Jeff, how do you look towards God?"

"Uh, I don't know." I wasn't expecting to be quizzed.

"We all express our intimacy with God in different ways. Sufism believes that life is a spiritual journey toward God."

"I've never thought of how I looked toward God."

"Since you do not, then I will." He took both of my hands and pulled me closer, peering into my eyes for what seemed like eternity. His beard was only a couple of inches from my chin. He smelled of earth and incense. His eyes no longer hazy, but focused intently on mine. He let go and grabbed a smooth, weathered stick sitting next to him. It looked like a walking stick, but was too short even for his stature. He swiftly rolled up one of the carpets in the center of the floor revealing soft sand. He started to write and talk at the same time.

"Back in the time of the ancients, thousands of years before Muhammad and Jesus, my people, the ancient Egyptian mystics, used symbols. They used these symbols in their religious practices to communicate with the dead and grow in knowledge. Symbols such as the cartouche that you are wearing around your neck." A travel trinket I had bought from a street vendor in Luxor. "These symbols can be powerful tools. The first symbol I will show is your present self, otherwise known as *nafs* or ego."

With a couple quick flicks of his wrist, he formed a simple image in the sand of a circle with a central dot.

"Now I will show you what you have to overcome." With a few more movements of the stick, he created a second symbol in the sand, which looked like a horned animal like a bull. "And finally this is what you strive to be, your soul or *ruh*." He was more deliberate with the third symbol. He slowly traced an upper case *T* and then on top placed a downward pointed teardrop.

"What do those mean?" Penelope asked.

"Hey, quiet, this is my fortune," I said.

"I know, but it's so exciting."

"The second symbol is a challenge that you face in the world. It is the symbol of the bull. The bull has a symbol of duality. Light and dark, good and evil. Two opposing forces. You have a conflict inside of you that is unresolved. The third symbol is the *ankh*. It is the staff of life and a symbol of rebirth. It means that you might have a chance of resolving your two opposing forces."

"What about the first symbol?"

"This is the symbol of Ra, the sun God. He is the most powerful of all gods."

"That is who I am?"

"No, this is actually a smiley face." With a few swipes of his stick, he completed the symbol adding two eyes and a smirk. "You are too serious. Don't worry, be happy." His face lit up into another toothless smile with a twinkle in his eye.

"What a comedian," I said.

"I leave the first symbol up to you. Only you can know who you are."

"He tricked you," Penelope said, laughing. "That was funny. The last two symbols are interesting. A challenge and then a rebirth. Very exciting."

"But wait, there is more. I also see that you have a special gift."

"What is it?"

"But, unusual."

"And why is that?" I asked.

"I have only seen this attributed to Egyptian mystics."

"What is it?" both Penelope and I asked together.

"Wake dreaming. Ancient Egyptian mysticism viewed dreams as actual occurrences. Real life that occurred while they were asleep. What happened in their dreams was no less real than what happened while they were awake. This took on further meaning for enlightened mystics who were able to dream while awake. This was in effect a dream in a dream, but since dreaming for them was no different from real life, it was real life within real life. While wake dreaming, they could talk to their dead ancestors and learn the mysteries of

heaven and earth. Egyptian mystics even used dream temples as healing sanctuaries for the ill. Dreams were very powerful in ancient
Egypt."

"I've never had a wake dream."

"Regardless, the potential is there for wake dreaming."

"Okay, anything else?" I asked.

"No, that is all I see. That will be forty Egyptian pounds."

"Forty! How about twenty?"

"Thirty it is."

I reluctantly handed over my lunch and dinner money.

"Now it's your turn, Penelope," I said.

"I'm getting hungry. Let's do it later," Penelope said.

"Are you for real? I can't believe you."

"Thank you, Mr. Yusuf, for your time," Penelope said. "We have
to go because Jeff is hungry."

"Now my hunger's important. Alright, let's go."

"Jeff, please do not forget what I told you. It is important for
you."

"What, the smiley face and the bull?"

"No. Don't forget to look toward God." As he said this, he
grabbed my cartouche hanging around my neck and looked into my
eyes, no longer the comedian, instead grave, "Listen to your dreams."

"Okay, I won't forget."

We ducked through the door and escaped the small hut.

"I can't believe you didn't get your fortune after forcing me to get
mine."

"I didn't force you. You did it on your own. I can't believe you
bargained with a holy man."

"I was thinking with my stomach. Now you can buy me a camel
sandwich since I paid for our entertainment," I said.

"Sounds like a deal."

And we both jumped back into the milieu of people, camels,
spices, animal feces and cooking meat.

"Jeff? Are you awake?"

I was back in my office, head down on my desk.

"How can you be sleeping?"

I took a second to collect my thoughts and then peeled my face off the veneered surface and rubbed my eyes free of the dream. Sara stood in the doorway.

"I'm awake, I'm awake. What do you want—to criticize me again? I need my sleep since I'm so weak. I'm a shell of a man remember."

"I'm sorry, that was mean. I shouldn't have said that and I don't mean it. You are not a shell of a man."

"Why are you back? Do you want to keep fighting?"

"No, I'm tired of fighting."

"Then what do you want?"

"I want some indication that you're willing to contribute to this marriage."

"Like what?"

"We need marriage counseling. I didn't realize how angry and unhappy I was. Things have to change or else."

"Or else what?"

"Or else I don't even want to think about it."

"Fine, counseling." I was tired of fighting and actually becoming scared I was going to lose my wife. "Now, can I have some time alone?"

She left without saying a word.

NINE

THE FOLLOWING MORNING, I awoke with the Sufi mystic on my mind. The look in his eyes when he took hold of my cartouche was troubling. My memory of that experience was different from my dream. At the time, the Sufi and his sand symbols were an amusing side trip. And I had no recollection of the Sufi foretelling a special gift for dreaming. On the other hand, I was too busy ogling Penelope to pay anything else much attention. If the dream offered one positive, it was the fleeting feeling of the freedom I once had while traveling.

My next trip was a little closer to home and not as exciting. My urologist was expecting me for follow-up. In spite of the visit's importance, my office assistant had to remind me of it. If there was ever a time I needed a rebirth as the Sufi said, it was now. My entire life was in conflict with nothing certain and no change in site. My wife practically wanted a divorce. Nothing I said or did with my girls was right. The last place I wanted to be was in a doctor's office waiting on lab results.

The urologist entered with a smile, but his next expression told me I had cancer. We discussed treatment options to include prostate removal or radiation therapy. I tried to wrap my brain around the idea of having cancer, but all I could think about was what I was going to tell Sara and the girls?

Suddenly, the room dimmed. As if someone turned up the radio dial, a familiar chanting, praying and drumming reverberated in my head. I found myself back in the sweat lodge I participated in as a teenager.

I sat in a circle of indistinct faces with a Native American leader in the center. Light and shadows played on his leathered skin and his voice reverberated through the lodge. The leader first prayed to the East, the rising sun, representing new beginnings and awakenings. During his invocation, he connected to his surroundings as if he was an extension of the earth looking to the heavens in prayer. The leader prayed to the West, representing the setting sun and the foundation for life ahead. He commanded the ceremony, directing the rituals and summoning the glowing red rocks from the fire pit outside. He then prayed to the South, representing love, trust and emotions. With each cardinal direction, he ordered new stones for the fire tenders to haul into the lodge. When they opened the flap, cool air rushed in. After the fire tenders deposited the stones and closed the flap, the heat quickly accumulated. Lastly, the lodge leader prayed to the North symbolizing wisdom, thought, and logic.

We finished the ceremony and closed the lodge. On the way out, a boy accidently stepped into the pit, burning his foot on a smoldering rock. I was closest and so I helped the boy exit and tended to him while the lodge leader fetched a parent who was a doctor. The doctor patched him up as I assisted. This was my first experience as a caregiver. I was awestruck as he treated the boy with care and knowledge. The boy and doctor then faded away.

I woke up from my dream with my urologist still talking as if nothing had happened. It was as if time had stood still. The clinic slowly refocused in my vision. The urologist asked me a question and my thoughts then quickly returned to cancer. The visit ended with my indecision on treatment.

I drove home unsure of what to make of my sweat lodge dream. Treating the boy was a life changing experience that had faded in my memory. I had resonated with the power of healing and the caring for another. Even as a young assistant, the healing connection had moved me. I didn't understand the importance of the experience at the time, but it set my life down its current path. My dad's stories started the interest, but that event set my focus.

Even more inexplicable was that the urologist acted as if nothing had happened. Either I was losing my mind or my urologist was a terrible listener and didn't notice me snoozing. Could it have been a dream without sleep? Were the dreams important and if so, what was I missing about these long forgotten experiences? But most pressing, I had cancer and how was I going to tell my family?

I made the long drive home in an unfocused haze. The confirmation of cancer numbed my mind. I was not yet ready to face what it meant or face the fear welling up in my gut. Regardless, I had to embrace the unpleasantness because Sara and the girls would be looking to me for direction.

"How was your day?" Sara asked as I walked in. Sara and the girls had been talking in the kitchen, but stopped their conversation as I entered. The fighting from yesterday was still fresh on everybody's mind.

"Long. Very long."

"What did the urologist say?"

"Not good. I'm glad all of us are here because we need to talk."

"That sounds terrible. Is it that bad?" Jamie asked.

"It's bad, but it could be worse. I have prostate cancer."

"Oh, Jeff." Sara came over and gave me a hug. Then both girls hugged me. Sara was speechless.

"Dad, what are you going to do?" Jamie asked.

"That's what we have to talk about. The urologist gave me options for treatments, but I wanted to talk to your mom before I gave him an answer."

We all agreed that my best option was to remove the prostate. Their support and love was uplifting, but I knew our previous argument was not over, rather on the backburner. We established an unsaid truce. I told Sara I had to finish some notes and drove to my clinic. But I didn't do any work. Instead, I sat and stared off into space. My mind was so tired. Every decision from closing the door to getting a glass of water took a momentous amount of energy to accomplish.

I sat for hours. Shadows and darkness reflected off the clouds outside my window. My phone rang a couple of times, but I let it go to voice mail. It was probably Sara wondering where I was and why I wasn't home. Then a spark of anger ignited inside of me. It was a faceless anger. It was anger for anger's sake. What was I doing? Where was I going? Why this damn cancer? The anger grew quickly threatening to overtake me. Maybe I'll call Sara and tell her why I wasn't home. Then she'll be sorry and probably angry too.

The phone rang again.

"Who is it that keeps bothering me?" I asked my empty office. I looked at my phone and Anna's picture had popped up. Ashamed, I answered it.

"Hi, Anna."

"Mom wants to know when you'll be coming home."

"Tell her I'm leaving now."

"Okay, I will." She hung up.

What I wouldn't give to be healthy again, which was a relative term at the very least, but something you don't cherish until it's beyond your grasp.

Within days, I had settled into my diagnosis. My numbed brain had transformed into a vague tension headache. It became less shocking. I had an appointment next week with the urologist for the pre-surgical visit. Today, Sara and I had an appointment with a marriage counselor. I wasn't looking forward to it.

I frequently referred patients to counseling as studies showed it could mend marriage problems. However, my personal experience with counseling was less than optimum. When my parents divorced, they corralled my siblings and me into family counseling. I often left angrier with issues unresolved. I didn't need someone to analyze my feelings. I knew how I felt. I was mad because of their divorce. I wasn't accepting of counseling then as I was in my practice.

I envisioned our appointment going one of two ways. We could focus on an aspect of our marriage that leads to openness and reconciliation or we could inflame unhealed wounds further fracturing our delicate relationship. Every marriage had challenges. Some things remained unsettled. The key was to be open and respectful and discuss the dispute as little as possible. Problems started when resentment developed. A counseling session invariably brought these unresolved issues to the surface.

The car ride to the counselor was quiet. The radio played, filling the silence. Before we arrived Sara said, "I love you."

"I love you too," I said. It went downhill from there.

We met the counselor and exchanged pleasantries. She directed us to her office with a cushy love seat, an oversized desk chair, and her credentials plastered on the wall. We both sat on the couch and she faced us in her chair. She was small in stature and thin. She had long red hair and a little too much make-up. Her presence was calm and inviting. She reclined back into her chair letting her feet dangle off the end and resting her chin on her propped up hand.

"So why don't we get started. I spoke with Sara on the phone for a brief moment to get an idea of what brought you here today. I understand that you are having problems in your marriage. Sara, can you please tell me more," the counselor said, enunciating each word. She leaned forward in her chair and shuffled her fingers on her chin.

"Sure." Sara took a deep breath. Her long dark hair shimmered as it hung over her shoulders. As she collected her thoughts, her big brown eyes trailed off in the distance. She sat on the edge of the couch, her back straight and proud, but not haughty. Her hands gently folded over her legs with ankles crossed. Her posture learned from many years in Catholic school. Her upbringing contrasted so differently from mine. While she experienced life as a diplomat's daughter with exposure to different cultures, I grew up in suburbia playing basketball on my local school team. Her parents passed away, throwing her life into complete turmoil and forcing her to grow up.

My parents divorced and moved across town from each other and I gained a car out of it due to the commute.

How could I ever be angry with her? We had a good marriage or at least I thought we did. I wonder if she would say differently.

"We're not as close as we used to be. I feel distant from him. He is always busy at work, comes home late and is often preoccupied when he's home. He doesn't seem to want to spend time with me or the kids—"

"That's not true," I said.

"Please, Jeff, let Sara finish, then you can speak," the counselor said. Her enunciating quickly became annoying.

"He's not present in our marriage or with our kids anymore and he's detached. I guess I haven't been happy for a long time. Longer than I realized," Sara said, her cheeks flushed. Her voice quivered.

I felt a terrible sadness for my wife. We had worked together through countless obstacles that life had thrown at us. We had many good memories. Somehow, over time, our intimacy had degraded. Instead of enjoying each other's affection, we were discussing our unhappiness. My marriage was slipping away from me.

The silence, as my wife composed herself, unnerved me. Speechless, I transfixed my gaze on the counselor hoping that she would save me from a response. Instead, my wife continued.

"My family, our family is all I have. I've put everything into it. I gave up a good career, something that I enjoyed doing. But I'm not resentful. I always wanted to be a wife and a mother. Every day I try to be a supportive partner and a great mom. But now, I feel like our family is slowly crumbling. Everything that I've worked for…" Her voice trailed off and she slumped into the back of the couch.

The counselor waited for a moment. "Are you done Sara?"

Sara began again, her voice just above a whisper. "Everything I worked for feels like it was for nothing."

The counselor leaned forward and patted Sara's hand.

"Thank you for your honesty, Sara," she said. "Okay, Jeff, your turn." The counselor waited for my response. She stared at me as if she was goading me to answer. A thick layer of make-up concealed her expressionless face.

"I'm not sure where to begin. I'm here for my wife," I said, stumbling over my words.

"Tell me how you feel about what Sara just said."

"I didn't know she felt that way. I've been working a lot, but it's not because I don't want to spend time with my family. That's the furthest thing from the truth."

"Then why are you spending more time at work?" the counselor asked.

"Because I have to. I built my practice and now it's busy and I have to see patients." That was a weak excuse.

"So you're saying that you feel the need to work and provide for your family. Do you feel that if you stop working as hard, your medical practice might falter?"

"It's always in the back of my mind, but the practice would probably be fine if I worked a little less."

"Then why are you working more?" the counselor asked.

"Yes," Sara said. "Why are you working more if you don't have to? Don't you want to spend time with the girls, with me?" Her eyes began to gloss with tears.

"Now, Sara, I know you are upset, but let Jeff finish," the counselor said.

"I don't know why I'm spending more time at work."

"Why not?" Sara asked. "Just give me some kind of answer."

"Okay, I guess… I'm not getting the same satisfaction out of my work as I used to. Something is missing, but I don't know what. I used to feel completely happy with working a full day, completing my notes and then coming right home. Now I linger at work almost as if I'm waiting for something to happen."

"Why? That makes no sense," Sara said. "Why not come home to your family?"

Anger suddenly rose up inside of me.

"I don't know."

"Okay, now this is good communication, but, Sara, if Jeff does not know then we have to respect that."

"He has always put his work ahead of his family," Sara said. "It's worsened recently. We've had many talks about it, but I never thought it would get this bad."

"I've worked because I had to. Someone has to provide for the family," I said. "What do you want me to do, not work?"

"I want you to spend time with us. Like we used to. Over the last six months we barely saw you." Tears rolled down her face.

I wasn't happy either. I was lost and struggling to find a way back to normalcy.

"Well, it's not that I don't want to. It's just that, I guess I haven't been happy with myself. Not depressed. Just not happy with where I am. And now I have this damn prostate cancer and I don't know how to deal with it any more. I'm searching, but I don't know for what. I feel like I'm fighting for my life."

"I didn't know you were unhappy."

"Well, I am. And I didn't really know either."

"Sara, how do you feel about that?" the counselor asked.

"Surprised."

I heard Sara's response, but as if from a distance.

"Dr. Handling, the patient's blood pressure is eighty-five over fifty. Dr. Handling, do you hear me? The patient's blood pressure is eighty-five over fifty."

My wife and the counselor's office slowly faded away. I found myself surrounded by white coats and scrub tops in a small hospital room. It was noisy and frantic. The only thing louder than the alarms and anxious voices was the sound of my own voice.

"Yes, I heard you. Eighty-five over fifty. Okay people, let's stop chest compressions after this round and see what kind of heart rhythm we have. Mrs. Satou, can you tell me what medications the patient has received today."

Another dream. I had dropped into a code blue. From the look of the pink hospital and the beaming sunlight, I was back in my residency years while in Hawaii. I was reliving another experience. The code blue eventually ended with the patient still alive and stabilized. Mrs. Satou, an old seasoned nurse who had lived her entire life on the island, found me in the hall. She was a small, stump of a women and barely came up to my waist, but she never missed a moment to remind me and every other resident that she had been treating patients when we were still getting our behinds wiped.

"Be careful with this patient," she said

"Why?"

"Her name is Elikapeka Ho'ohanohano Smith. She's a Hawaiian kahuna, a medicine woman."

Nurse Satou came closer and whispered in my ear. "She lives by the traditional Hawaiian ways."

Mrs. Smith had chronic lung disease, not from smoking, but from poor genes. And she was dying. Her last request was to die at home with her family. They were flying from the Big Island to take her back to her ancestral lands. She also requested to take Hawaiian herbal medications for treatment.

"That might be a problem. I'll have to talk to my attending before I can give the okay. The policy in the hospital is that patients can't take any outside medications, but let me see if we can work around that for you," I said.

"Thank you. It was nice meeting you, Dr. Handling," Mrs. Smith said.

"I'll be back later today to see how you're doing. You let the nurse know if you need anything."

"Mahalo and aloha."

I met Nurse Satou outside the door.

"He won't like that request."

"I know."

"She can sign out against medical advice or better yet be discharged with home hospice, but that Hawaiian medicine won't fly with him."

"It probably wouldn't hurt her as long as there weren't any interactions with her other drugs. It may even have a placebo effect. Modern medicine doesn't have all the answers."

"Try explaining that to him."

I grunted, too tired to think of my game plan when confronting my attending. Some described him as serious, others languished his severity. He was meticulous in his treatment plans to the highest medical standards and never missed a detail behind his wire-rimmed glasses. He was an institution at the hospital, renowned for his medical care and notorious for his temper. He had failed one of my colleagues for not returning his call promptly, while the resident was in the bathroom. There was no excuses for him. Rarely did he conform treatment beyond the gold standard of modern medicine.

"In my experience, which is quite possibly longer than you've been alive, some people respond better to treatment that is more harmonious with their culture. But what do I know, I'm just a lowly nurse," Nurse Satou moseyed down the hall. "Good luck," she said before entering another patient room.

I presented Mrs. Smith's request to my attending as the last wish of a dying woman who wanted to remain true to her cultural beliefs.

"That is nonsense. I can't believe you even considered this. A rule is a rule. If the patient desires to leave, she can leave and be treated as she sees fit, but I will not allow her to take her supposed natural treatments," my attending said, glaring at me.

"I didn't think it would hurt her and it might improve her spirits," I said.

"I'm trying to treat her with modern medicine and you're trying to pawn off some voodoo. Now you make me look like the bad guy. Don't ever do that again."

"Sorry, sir. That was not my intention."

"I don't care what your intention was. You will explain to the patient that her natural treatments are unacceptable and will not be allowed in this hospital. It's laughable to even think they would help her. What were you thinking, Dr. Handling?"

"I was trying to do what was best for the patient."

"I know what's best for the patient. You need to worry about what's best for you. Fall in line or repeat this rotation."

"Yes, sir."

"Mr. Handling." A voice called from the distance. I was still standing at attention, watching my attending and his flock of residents march away while I remained near the closed door of my patient's room.

"Mr. Handling?" The voice was closer now and female. "Did you hear what your wife just said?"

"What? Um...no."

I rubbed my eyes. The counselor's academic achievements framed on the wall came into view. I tried to focus on the woman sitting opposite me in her large chair.

"Your wife has been talking."

"How long have I been out?"

"You've been right here. Did you hear what your wife said?"

"I must have missed it."

"I was talking for about five minutes. How much did you miss?" Sara asked.

"All of it," I said.

Sara threw her hands up in the air.

"I'm sorry. I'm not feeling very well all of a sudden. Can we pick up where we left off at our next session?"

"Sure, whatever," Sara said.

Back in the car, Sara fumed, upset and confused about our appointment.

"I can't believe you zoned out like that. We were finally talking about something real and then poof, your mind disappeared."

"I'm sorry. I don't know what happened."

"How can we work through things without you paying attention?"

"I don't know. I can't explain it. All I know is that one minute you were talking and then the next I was transplanted back in time to my residency."

I explained to Sara my dream with the Hawaiian kahuna.

"She died two days later from overwhelming infection and pulmonary failure. She had IV lines and machines keeping her alive. Some of her family visited, but not all. She never made it home and she never received her traditional Hawaiian medicine as requested. At the time, you and I were at the beach on my one day off for the week. I didn't find out until the following day. How ironic that a haole was taking in a beautiful Hawaiian sunset while a kama'aina woman lay dying in my hospital. Her medicine may not have helped her, but it couldn't have worsened her."

"I don't remember that."

"I never told you or anybody. I was so ashamed and frustrated. I pushed it out of my mind."

"When was it?"

"It was about one month before Gary died. Remember he called somewhat frantically and he died a month later."

"I remember when Gary called. That was a tough time."

"It was. I failed them when he and that Hawaiian woman needed me most."

"No you didn't and you know that. You were trying to do what was right and survive internship."

"I turned my back on them."

"You didn't turn your back on them. You loved Gary like a brother and you fought for that patient."

"I turned my back on a lot of things after they died. I wanted to be a doctor more than anything else."

I lost part of myself with the Hawaiian kahuna. My residency and my experience in Hawaii changed after her death. A month or two later, Sara became pregnant and my focus changed to Jamie's impending arrival. The kahuna woman slowly faded from my memory. However, I was never the same doctor.

TEN

I NEEDED HELP. I either was going crazy or had a brain tumor. Any other explanation for my dreaming while awake would be too outlandish to consider. My primary physician had ordered a sleep study and a neurology consult. I had completed the sleep study and was awaiting the results in the doctor's office. Dr. Arnold Ling was the attending physician. He was board certified in psychiatry and sleep medicine and also offered hypnosis. He had plenty of education to put any normal person to sleep.

"Hi, Jeff, my name is Arnold Ling. We actually met last night, but you were asleep."

"Hello, Arnold, nice to consciously meet you."

Arnold Ling was a small, thin man of Asian descent in his fifties. He was composed, gentle and deliberate. He took everything with perfect balance, which was in stark contrast to how I was feeling.

We sat in his office in opposing high-back chairs as if we were having tea in an old lady's living room. He sat with legs crossed, my study results on his lap and a pen in his hand.

"Tell me a little bit about the sleep problems you're having."

"I've had recurring dreams in the past usually dealing with my time in the military, but my more recent ones have been different."

I explained my dreams and the fact that they were interfering with my life. I was afraid to fall asleep because I wasn't sure what would happen. The dreaming while awake was even more unsettling.

"Besides the prostate cancer, is anything else going on in your life that could be instigating these dreams, such as increased stress at home or work?" he asked.

"Work is always stressful, but no more than usual. The other day I saw a patient who brought up an experience from my past."

"Tell me about the patient."

I explained Kim Travers, her prediction, painting and her crazy eyes. He shook his head in acknowledgment and continued on.

"What about your family?"

"My family is okay."

"You don't seem very enthusiastic."

"My wife and I have been working through some tough times and my kids have been a little distant."

"Why do you think they're distant?"

"Probably because I haven't been around much. I've been busy at work."

"We're doctors. We're always going to be busy."

I nodded in agreement. "I know, a poor excuse."

"Do you think these dreams could be a way for you to work through your stressors in a safe, controlled environment?"

"Possibly. Probably. But I also feel like they are trying to tell me something."

"What are they trying to tell you?"

"I'm not sure."

"Could it be that your dreams are trying to tell you that your life is out of balance?"

"Maybe."

"You love your wife? And your kids?"

"Yes, of course."

"But you said that you are having difficulty in your marriage and that your kids are distant."

"Yes."

"Then something isn't right." I had no response. He was right. My life was amiss.

"You said it yourself. Your dreams are trying to tell you something. Maybe they're trying to help you reconnect with your family."

"Maybe."

He put his pen and paper down and took off his glasses. He uncrossed his legs and leaned back in his chair.

"Jeff, there is a saying. 'I hear and I forget. I see and I remember. I do and I understand.' I believe that dreams allow our minds to escape our conscious self. Dreams allow us to escape the day-to-day stressors, conflicts and challenges that typically take up a lot of our energy. By escaping our daily thoughts, our minds our able to make new creative thoughts."

"I've heard of that theory. We spend about six years of our lives dreaming, but most of our dreams are re-enactments of the day's events."

"Most dreams are, but not all. Recent studies have shown that some dreams are creative thoughts unrestrained from our conscious mind. I also believe that dreams not only allow us to make creative thoughts, but also creative connections between ideas, relationships, challenges, etc., outside of our concrete conscious mind."

"What are you saying?"

"I'm saying that dreams can be a catalyst for creative thought and a vehicle for creating connections. So, I would listen to your dreams. Don't be afraid of them. They may lead you to a greater understanding."

"Any understanding would be better than what I have now."

"Are the dreams leading you in a direction that is unsafe or dangerous to you or your family?"

"No, it doesn't seem to be."

"Then what harm is there in following it?"

I shrugged. No harm at all except that I felt like I was going crazy. But a psychiatrist should know. He hadn't thrown medications at me yet.

"Otherwise, your sleep study was normal. You exam was normal. I don't think you're psychotic nor have a sleep disorder."

"Well, that's good to hear."

"Sometimes all you need is a little reassurance."

"Yes, I know. It's just different being on this end of the reassurance."

"I would like for you to follow-up in a couple of weeks and we'll see how you're doing."

The psychiatric appointment was a relief. I didn't have narcolepsy or schizophrenia. Unfortunately, it didn't explain the dreams.

I returned home and quickly hid in my study. I needed to be alone. Sara opened the door without entering.

"Have you apologized to Anna yet?" she asked.

"Not yet."

"You should."

I nodded in agreement. Later that night, it was my turn to tuck Anna into bed.

"Dad, can you tell a new story tonight."

"Sure, but I want to talk to you about something else first."

"Okay."

Anna pulled her stuffed animal from behind her pillow, wrapping her arms around it. She wore Disney pajamas, which matched her Disney bed sheets.

"I'm sorry for yelling at you the other day."

"That's okay."

"I was angry, but it wasn't from anything that you did."

"Were you angry at mom?"

"Yes. Mom and I had an argument."

"Why."

"It's complicated."

"Why."

"Sometimes it's not always easy being with somebody."

"I get angry at Jamie for taking forever in the bathroom, but then mom comes and tells her it's my turn."

"I wish it were that easy."

"Why isn't it?"

"I don't know."

"Do you still love mom?"

"Of course I do."

"So you're not going to get a divorce? A girl's parents at my school got divorced and her dad had to move away. I don't want that to happen."

"I don't want that to happen either."

I moved to the window to secure the lock and close the shades, trying to force out the thought of Sara leaving me.

"Are you angry at Grandpa also?"

"Why do you ask?"

"Because I heard you and Mom say that you never talk to Grandpa anymore."

"No, I'm not angry at Grandpa. We just have different ideas about things."

"What kind of ideas?"

"Life in general."

"What do you mean?"

I stumbled for an answer.

"Is it complicated?" Anna asked, smiling.

"Yes, it's complicated. Your Grandpa has always wanted me to be like him, but I'm not. And now I'm afraid I disappoint him.

"How do you disappoint him?"

"Good question."

"Dad, do I disappoint you?"

"Of course not. I'm very proud of you."

"Okay, good," she said.

"I don't want to worry him either."

"Is he worried about the cancer?"

"I haven't told him yet, but he probably will be."

"Dad, I'm scared." Her small hand grabbed my arm. "I don't want you to go away."

"Don't worry, I'm not going anywhere."

I reached out and squeezed her in my arms. I'm not going anywhere.

"How about we go on a trip. Just you and I," I said.

"Where?"

"A baseball game."

"Without Jamie?"

"Yep. She'll probably be at swim practice or doing something else anyway. It'll just be you and me hanging out."

"Sounds fun." Anna smiled. After a second of thought, she gave me a serious look. "Make sure you tell Mom."

"I'll get the okay from Mom. Don't worry."

She smiled again.

"Now what story would you like tonight?"

"I don't care. Just a new one."

"I'm sort of out of stories. I could tell you one that Grandpa used to tell."

"Yeah, tell one of Grandpa's."

"Okay. Let me think."

I pulled the covers up to her chin and she snuggled in.

"There was a man who was called the sleeping prophet. He could answer questions while asleep…"

After work, I picked up Anna from school and we went to our baseball game. She wore a baseball cap with her ponytail slung through the back, jeans and a t-shirt of our local team.

"I'm ready," she said, hopping into the car. "I couldn't wear this at school," pointing to the hat, "but I put it on as soon as my teacher let us out."

I reached into the backseat and pulled out my old, beat-up glove.

"Try it on. We can catch fly balls hit toward us."

She slipped it on. The glove dwarfed her small hand. I explained how the batter might hit a foul ball toward us so we had to be prepared because if we caught the ball, we get to keep it. She looked at the glove on her hand and then gave it back to me. She said she was going to duck if the ball came her way and I said that was all right also.

When we arrived at the stadium, the starting pitcher was still warming up. I found my regular seat behind home plate halfway up. I wedged in my long legs. Anna jumped into the seat next me. We settled in and surveyed the sights. The stadium was normal size for a minor league team. The city had recently renovated the grandstand with a fresh, fun look to it. Vendors stationed themselves behind the field level seating as well as roamed the aisles selling food and paraphernalia. Since it was her first baseball game, the field with its gleaming green grass and glowing white chalk lines mesmerized Anna. The plush infield dirt looked soft enough to sleep on. An untouched, manicured baseball field was like a work of art.

"It's pretty cool, isn't it?" I said.

"Yeah, it's awesome," she said, unable to look away.

I couldn't have been happier spending the day with Anna. A little father-daughter time was good. She was growing up fast and I wasn't spending hardly as much time with her as I wanted to. But this was more than a day at the park. This game was an annual ritual I had followed since Gary's death. I always attended one game alone around the anniversary of his passing. It used to be one of our things to do. Gary was a huge Orioles fan so naturally when our local minor league team joined the Orioles organization we became regular visitors. Gary liked to sit behind home plate to see if the pitcher had his stuff for the night. The seats were also close to the beer and the local girls who hung around the team, which was their real appeal.

I bought hotdogs, popcorn and sodas from the vendor.

"This is where my friend Gary and I would always sit."

"Why is that?"

"You have a perfect view of the whole field and the pitcher."

"Would you also get hotdogs and sodas?" Anna asked.

"No, we'd get beer and hotdogs, but we'll stick with the sodas. Your mom wouldn't approve."

"Jamie says Gary was your brother."

"He was a close friend. He was part of my family and like a brother to me. Your aunt thought he was her actual brother until she was about five or six. He even looked a little like me—tall and lanky."

"Do you wish he was still alive?"

"I sure do. Then we could all go to the games."

Gary and I grew up together. We played sports together. If he wasn't at my house, I was at his. He would pitch and I would hit or catch. When we were still young, his mom died. He had a rough time afterwards. He ended up eating many dinners at my house while his father worked. He became part of the family.

"You know, Gary could have played for this team. He was a pretty good pitcher."

"Wow, he must have been good."

"He would take his long arm and whip the ball around with such speed that it sizzled all the way to the catcher's mitt. But then an injury stopped him from playing."

"How did he get hurt?"

"He made a bad decision," I said. Anna look perplexed.

"He drank too much alcohol, which is not a good thing and which you're mom and I will impress upon you and your sister not to do."

"Okay," she said. She was about to ask another question, but then the mascot jumped onto the visitor's dugout and started to dance. Anna laughed and clapped along forgetting her question.

Gary's weakness was always alcohol and girls usually in combination. The summer after high school, at a party, a girl dared him to swing from the top of a house into a pool. He landed in the pool, but blew out his arm. He never recovered his baseball form after that. He could have, if he put the time in for rehabilitation, but he lost focus. He had signed a contract straight out of high school to pitch in the rookie league, but he never played a game.

The umpire called the start of the game. The home team trotted out of the dugout and positioned themselves in the field as the crowd cheered. Anna smiled and clapped along. I had always thought of my annual game as being a sacred ritual, shared and endured with no one. Anna's presence made the game less of a gloomy memorial. Maybe I had found a partner with whom to actually enjoy this tradition.

"Dad, I just remembered. I have to tell you something." Anna turned to me and her ponytail flipped to the other side. She sat with her legs folded under her in the seat.

"What is it?"

"I was watching TV and they said you could treat cancer with happiness. So I thought that all you needed was to smile and you would be better."

"Really? What show was this?"

"I don't know. Jamie changed the channel before I could find out and she wouldn't change it back."

"I'll remember that," I said. "I'm smiling now because I'm having a really fun time being here with you."

She grinned and turned around to face the game. Play had started. Halfway through the second inning, the first batter in the rotation came up and hit a ball that curled backwards over the netting. Anna screamed and ducked. The ball careened off the press box behind us and ricocheted back toward our seats. I made a whiff at the catch and it landed into Anna's popcorn sitting on her lap. She screamed again in excitement and scooped the ball up. I put her on my shoulders as she held the ball overhead and received a roaring applause.

The game continued. We finished the hot dogs and popcorn and started on some cotton candy. Anna told me about her schoolteacher and the boy who sat next to her. The boy was still having problems at school and Anna thought it was all due to his father. And the boy needed to talk to his father, but wouldn't because he was scared. She was probably right. She always surprised me with how intuitive she was. She also told me how she didn't really like her violin teacher, but she liked the violin. After more discussion about her school and friends, we refocused on the game as the opposing team started getting a couple of base hits.

We had been sitting quietly for a while.

"Dad, how did Gary die?"

"He got sick."

"How?"

"He had cancer."

"The same cancer you have?" She looked at me with worried eyes.

"No, a different cancer. And don't worry, that won't happen to me."

"Okay. That's good."

As roommates in college, Gary and I did everything together. We had the same major and took the same classes. We partied when we had time. His father then died in the middle of our four years and afterwards, our paths began to diverge. He partied more. He missed class frequently. He joined the motorcycle club in spite of not having a motorcycle. He had thought about being a doctor as well, but didn't have the passion for it. I carried the flame for the both of us and he looked up to me after getting into medical school. At our graduation, my parents were his only family at the ceremony.

We grew apart while I was in medical school, mainly because I was busy and he was jumping from one girl's apartment to the next. Shortly before I moved to Hawaii for residency, he was diagnosed with testicular cancer, the most common cancer for young men. I recommended that along with removal of the cancer and chemotherapy, he try certain alternative therapies and eat a diet rich in antioxidants. I thought he would be okay and I told him this. Most testicular cancer was treatable.

"Dad, how do you know...that it won't happen?" Anna asked.

"Because I love you, your sister and mother too much for it to happen," I said. Thankfully, my answer appeased her for a good question to which I didn't have a good answer.

The crack of a bat quickly distracted us and we turned our heads around. The ball traveled over the fence for a home team score. We stood with the crowd and cheered. The batter rounded the bases and the inning ended shortly afterwards. We remained standing for the seventh inning stretch. Anna jumped onto her seat to dance with the music and sing along with the crowd. The game then continued and we relaxed back into the benches. With the sun setting, the big stadium lights flickered on, and the cool night air moved in.

"Dad, Gary died a long time ago. Why are you still sad?"

"He was a good friend."

"Mom's parents died a long time ago and she isn't sad. She says she just misses them. But she doesn't have sadness in her eyes like you do."

"It's hard to explain. Sometimes things take a long time to heal." Anna was unwilling to ignore what I wanted to forget.

After the start of my residency, Gary and I hadn't been in contact for close to a year. And it was surprising how fast the time had gone. I was knee deep in my training. When he called, he wasn't his normal happy-go-lucky self. His cancer had spread and the doctors didn't know if he would live. It was shocking since most didn't die from testicular cancer. He explained that he never received chemotherapy treatment and didn't have the cancer removed. Instead, he stuck to my recommendations. "I don't like those doctors anyway, Man. Their waiting room gives me the creeps. All those patients look like death when I go in there. I would have called earlier, but you are so far away. I didn't know where to turn. You're all I've got."

He died a couple of months later. He believed in me and I let him down. My alternative treatments were ineffective for a treatable cancer. They were only supposed to be complementary, but I still felt responsible.

I took a deep breath and sighed loudly. Anna looked at me somewhat concerned and then held my hand resting on the bench. I had lost my best friend and the emptiness had never healed.

The game ended. Our team won and we left with a gameball and plans to return for another game sometime in the future. Anna couldn't stop talking about how much fun she had. I had endured another game—the first one I had enjoyed in fifteen years.

ELEVEN

IT HAD BEEN a long week. Other than seeing the sleep specialist, I visited the neurologist and had a brain MRI, which was normal and ruled out a tumor. I also had a normal EEG, which measures the brain's electrical activity searching for a seizure disorder. In spite of my normal exams, an uneasiness had settled within me, not related to my prostate.

My dad and Judith had invited the family over for dinner. It was time to tell them the news about my prostate cancer. They would find out one way or another, most likely from Anna if not from me. There had been no good reason to keep the news from them.

The drive out always took surprisingly long. My father and Judith lived on the outskirts of town on a large plot of land. This allowed them to perform various outdoor activities such as nature chanting or meditative drumming without disturbing or scaring the neighbors. Their home, secluded in large pine trees, was like a big yoga studio, light, airy and open. Anna and Jamie were always interested in how Judith was going to arrange their collection of sparse furniture.

We entered the house to the smell of someone grilling. My dad met us at the front door.

"Hey, Dad, what's for dinner?"

"We're cooking on the grill."

"The grill? Good. I brought a lot of hungry mouths with me."

"What are you trying to say? You don't like what I make in the kitchen."

"No offense, Dad, your cooking doesn't compare to your superb grilling."

"Hello, Sara, Jamie, and Anna. It's very nice to see you. I feel like we haven't seen each other in a long while." My dad gave each a hug.

"It's has been a couple of months," Sara said.

"Time flies when you're busy," I said. Sara sent me a disapproving look. "But we should all get together more often."

"Where is Judith?" Sara asked.

"She's upstairs. She'll be down in a moment. You guys take it easy. There are drinks in the fridge. I'll be outside finishing the chicken."

I followed my dad outside. Their oversized deck dwarfed the grill. The forest surrounded their backyard with tall trees looming over-head creating large swaths of shade and shadows. The grass adjacent to the deck seemed to keep the trees at bay. The forest was an ever-present entity at their home. Today, it was quietly foreboding.

"Hey, Dad, I need to talk."

"What's on your mind?"

"I went to my doctor the other day for a regular check-up and they found I have prostate cancer."

Seeming unperturbed, my dad continued grilling. He wore his typical polo shirt with khaki shorts and sockless loafers. He remained still except for a swift flick of the wrist to turn the food. My dad made few extemporaneous movements, only ones needed to complete the job. As a chiropractor, he performed quick, violent, but controlled maneuvers to realign a patient's spine. His skill now demonstrated by the speed of his spatula as it flipped the chicken and vegetarian burgers. The burgers I assume were for Judith. My dad could never convince his appetite to accept vegetarianism no matter how hard he tried.

"It's a low grade cancer and the urologist recommends treatment sooner rather than later."

"Your grandfather had prostate cancer and the doctors just watched it. He died well before it caused him any problems."

"Grandpa was eighty years old when he was diagnosed and died at ninety. I have a few more years to go before I get to that point."

"Well, what are you trying to tell me, Jeff?"

"I'm telling you that I have prostate cancer. I'm going in the beginning of next week for my pre-op visit for a prostatectomy."

"Will you need any other treatment?"

"Maybe chemotherapy?"

"Chemotherapy? You didn't say anything about chemotherapy. How serious is it?"

"Serious enough that I may need chemotherapy if the prostate is more cancerous than we thought. I won't die tomorrow, but it needs to be treated."

He flipped a couple pieces of chicken.

"Have you told your mother?"

"Yes, I told Mom."

"How are Sara and the girls taking it?"

"They're doing okay. I still think it hasn't fully registered with them yet."

"You should consider complementary treatments along with the chemotherapy."

"Dad, I don't want to talk about this now."

"Chemotherapy is toxic to the body."

"I know. That's the whole idea. Give me enough toxic medications to kill the cancer, but not me."

"There is a reason you have cancer. Your body is telling you something."

"What is it telling me other than I'm a forty-year-old with cancer?"

"Cancer is a sign that your body is out of balance."

"Dad, I really don't want to get into this now."

"Why? Isn't your health important enough to consider alternatives to modern medicine?"

"Modern medicine is all there is. It's all I've got."

"Jeff, when did you stop believing there are other possibilities? You've become very close-minded. What happened to my son who saw the world with open eyes?"

"I've changed, Dad."

"Why?"

"I don't want to get into it."

"What happened that made you so close minded?"

The anger from the many years of unfinished arguments and suppressed frustrations unfurled in my gut.

"I killed Gary, alright. Gary died because of me."

"What do you mean, Gary died because of you?"

"I gave him treatment advice for his cancer that he used instead of following the oncologist's recommendations and he died. He trusted me more than anyone. We were like brothers and I let him down."

"You can't blame yourself for that."

"Gary is dead and I could have prevented it."

"You don't know what the outcome would have been if he had received his treatment as recommended."

"It doesn't matter. I stopped buying into all that stuff a long time ago." My dad just nodded. "I had to choose and I chose to be a doctor not someone subscribing to voodoo healing."

"I'm sorry you feel that way."

"Well, I do and now you know."

We stood silent for a few moments. I was worked up, but regretted immediately what I had said. My dad looked down on the grill. I had nothing more to say. That was the first time I had told anybody about my involvement in Gary's death. I'm pretty sure Sara knew, but we never talked about it.

My father's spiritual medicine led Gary down the wrong path and abandoned me when I most depended on it. After Gary's and then the Hawaiian kahuna's death, I had to give it up. I was in residency for a reason—training to be a physician who used empirical knowledge and good science for medical treatment. Any thoughts of alternative treatments or spiritual medicine were out of the question.

"Can you tell everybody that the chicken is ready, Jeff?"

"Sure."

As I was leaving, "I wish things were different," I said

"I just worry about you, Jeff."

We gathered for dinner. Judith had reappeared in her usual flowing dress. Her pearly-white hair feathered and brushed from her face. She skirted across the floor as if she were floating as she made the final preparations for the dinner. In spite of her inconspicuous nature, she always had a strong presence whenever she entered the room. My dad returned with the chicken to complete the meal.

As we began eating, my dad and I remained silent while Judith caught up with Jamie and Anna.

"I was planning this trip to Nicaragua, but we can't go now."

"Why can't you go?" Judith asked.

"Because Dad has prostate cancer and he needs treatment."

"Maybe you can go some other time."

"The group we were going with doesn't have anything planned for at least six months. This is their big trip for the year and who knows if I'll have time in six months. It was hard enough to plan this."

"Maybe your dad will reconsider."

"No, I think he's made up his mind. I saw the look in his eyes. I understand. He needs treatment. I don't want him to get sick."

"I don't want to alarm you, Jamie, but with the treatment, I might get sicker from the side effects before I get better."

"I know that. I meant that I don't want your cancer to get worse, like spread."

"I don't want that to happen either," I said with a nervous pit in my stomach.

"Sara, how are you doing with all of this?" Judith asked.

"Hanging in there. It was difficult at first when Jeff told me the news, but from what he's said, he has a good prognosis and the cancer is treatable."

"Anna, you seem to be taking this in stride. What have you been up to?" Judith asked.

"I've been praying for Daddy. I don't want him to die."

"I'm not going to die, Honey." I hugged Anna who was sitting next to me.

"I'll pray for him too," Judith said.

The dinner table became quiet, the anxiety palpable.

"Jeff, you've been quiet over there," Judith said, breaking the silence. "What have you been up to this week?"

"Except for dealing with this prostate cancer, not much. Although, I keep having these weird dreams that occur while I'm awake."

"What do you mean?" Judith asked.

"Remember when we spoke the other week about my vivid dreams, well now, in the middle of the day, I'll have a dream. It's happened twice. I was concerned enough that I saw two specialists, but everything has come back normal, except for the prostate cancer of course."

"Did you say 'awake dreaming'?" Judith asked.

"Yes, I'll have a dream right in the middle of a conversation."

"I wouldn't call that a dream. I would call that a vision," Judith said.

"What's the difference?"

"Dreams only occur when you're asleep. Visions can occur when you're asleep or awake. Visions have more of a focus and direction. They may also have a purpose to accomplish."

"I'm just happy I didn't have a brain tumor to go along with my prostate cancer."

"Please don't say that," Sara said. "It's hard enough dealing with your prostate cancer."

I nodded, "Sorry."

Judith continued. "What were your visions about?"

"My first vision occurred at the urologist's office. He had just told me about the cancer and then poof, the vision started. I was transported to the sweat lodge I participated in as a boy."

"Sweat lodges are vehicles for visions in the Native American culture," Judith said.

"But I didn't have a vision in the sweat lodge. It was an experience outside the sweat lodge that was significant. It detailed an event that sent me on the path toward being a doctor."

"But obviously an important moment in your life. What about the other vision?"

"My other vision took place in Hawaii while I was in residency. I was having a difficult time surviving in residency. It was around the time of Gary's death." I looked at my dad, but couldn't catch his gaze.

Judith noticed this. "Something you two have already discussed?" We both nodded. "It must be a touchy subject. Visions are powerful tools and a true gift for the person having the vision. You shouldn't ignore them."

"What else can I do with them?"

"It's interesting that both visions were actually events in your past. Your past is trying to tell you something," Judith said.

"I wish my past would go away so I can deal with the present."

"Maybe that's exactly what it's trying to do—helping you deal with the present."

"It only seems to be distracting me. I went through the medical ringer this week to make sure nothing was wrong because of these visions."

"They are such significant events. I wonder if they symbolize anything," Judith said.

"We talked about symbols the other day with Grandma and Grandpa Tom," Jamie said. "A symbol is a word, blah, blah, blah, that represents something else. A symbol often helps to convey a certain meaning that is otherwise difficult to express."

"Well said," Sara said.

"Dad, these visions are symbols of something that is difficult for you to express," Jamie said.

"Thank you, Jamie."

"Yeah, Dad, they seem pretty important. Maybe you shouldn't ignore them," Anna said. "What do they mean to you?"

"I can tell you've been spending too much time with your Grandpa," I said.

My dad smirked and the mood lightened. The conversation shifted with Anna and Jamie talking about their violin and swimming activities.

Judith looked over at me in the midst of the girl's conversation. "You shouldn't dismiss them," she said.

I nodded in agreement, but said no more.

After dinner, my dad played a board game with the girls and Sara. The tension was still obvious between us. They were having a good time and I didn't want to disturb them. Judith had stepped outside to smoke. I followed her. She sat at the end of their long deck. The tall imposing trees surrounded her and approached from all sides swaying with the breeze in unison. I plopped into a chair next to hers looking out into the trees. We sat quietly for a while as Judith finished her cigarette.

"Your dad and I saw a fox the other day creep out from over there." Judith pointed to the tree line.

"Looking for food I bet," I said.

"Probably, but usually the raccoons get to it first."

"What about the peacocks?"

She laughed. "The peacocks are long gone. We haven't seen them for a while."

One of my father's eccentric friends, who happened to raise peacocks, gave him a pair as a gift. It's still unclear why he accepted, but insists he just couldn't decline the gift. Regardless, my dad had no experience raising peacocks. One day, one of the peacocks escaped from its cage and ran into the forest never to be seen from for weeks. That was until a terrible squawking arose from the woods. Apparently, the male had escaped and wanted its mate. Judith couldn't

stand the noise from all of the squawking so she freed the other one
and the peacocks lived happily ever after. My dad spotted them a few
weeks later on the side of the road a couple miles from their house,
but hadn't seen them since.

"Your dad liked those peacocks. I think he hoped they would
walk around all day with their feathers out. Instead, all they did was
make a lot of noise."

We both chuckled. It was one of many instances when my dad
had taken life by the horns only to find the horns taking him. His
misadventures were always amusing entertainment. My father and I
used to have many laughs when we were closer. But that was a lifetime ago. We laughed less now and were more likely to argue.

I looked over at Judith. She seemed content, sitting peacefully,
apparently impervious to my internal ramblings. So we sat and let
the changing evening sky and noisy woods fill the quiet. Unfortunately, I couldn't relax. Silence in general had become
uncomfortable. The need to talk pressed on my mind, but I didn't
know how to say what was in my head. I couldn't put form to my
diverging feelings.

Judith finally broke the silence. "Your dad really loves you."

"I know."

"You shouldn't be so hard on each other. Your relationship is
stronger than it seems."

"It hasn't felt strong lately, but I think that has more to do with
me than him."

"You have a lot on your mind."

"I do." I rubbed my forehead in an attempt to dispel on oncoming headache. "I wish it would all go away."

"You're too tense."

"I need a vacation."

"You need more than a vacation. You need to open up."

"What do you mean?"

"You're in the weeds. When you're in the weeds, all you see are
the obstacles right in front of you. Expand your horizon. Take in
more than what life throws at you."

"How?"

"Use your senses. The sounds, smells, and energy of those around you."

I laughed a little. "That sounds like what you do. I can't do that."

"Sure you can. You've probably done it before, you just didn't know it."

"How can I sense someone's energy? I wouldn't know where to start."

"Most people do it all ready. It doesn't have to be New Agey. It's having an understanding about a person. It's sensing their presence. It's a first impression with enhancement and you build from there."

"Build what?"

"Your intuition. It's a muscle and you need to exercise it. You doctors do it all the time. You're gut feeling. Just give a different word to it and add the sounds, smells, pictures and intent. Your intent is the most important."

"How is this going to help me?"

"You'd be surprised."

I gave her an unconvinced look.

"What are you worrying about right now?" she asked.

"Among the many things, I guess my prostate."

"Okay. We'll start there. What was your first impression of your prostate cancer? If you met your prostate cancer for the first time, what would it be?"

"I have no idea."

"What does your gut tell you?"

I sighed heavily with the load of my cancer back in my mind. "Fear, guilt."

"Good. That *was* from the gut. Spontaneous and without your mind getting in the way."

My answer was surprising. The fear I could understand, but the guilt was a new feeling.

"Now what does it sound like?"

"What? That makes no sense." I snorted. If my prostate started making noise, cancer would be the least of my worries.

"Yes. What does it sound like? If it had a sound, what would it be?"

I looked at her to check if she was joking, but she wasn't. She waited for my response. I thought about it for a second and then I stuck out my tongue and blew a raspberry.

"That sounds about right," she said.

"I'm not good at this kind of stuff."

"You need more practice."

I needed a lot more than just practice. Judith had a gift. She knew from a young age she was different. When her playmates were people others couldn't see, she realized not everyone viewed the world as she did. In high school, her friends would ask her what grades they would receive on future tests. It left some more upset than others, but she always seemed to know. Her teacher asked her to stop because she thought Judith was somehow affecting the scores.

She became a nurse because that's what her mom did. As a nurse, her gifts flourished. Her premonitions grew stronger and more vivid. She began to understand her true calling. The health flashes, as she described them, became more detailed, but she felt restricted having to hold back at work. The ER was not always the best place to unload a psychic health reading onto an unassuming patient. She needed to find a better way and so she set out on her own taking clients by word-of-mouth until she built her business. When I was young, she amazed me with her abilities. But with time, I was less clear on what to make of her talents.

Judith was right. I was reacting and I didn't have a good sense of which direction I needed to proceed.

"Why is this happening to me?" I said.

Judith didn't say anything.

"I'm frustrated. I have no good answers. I can't do anything."

"Well, at least you have the question right," Judith said. "First you form the right question and then the answer will come to you."

I huffed. I had all the answers in the world, but none of them worked for me.

"Only you can know. In my many years of experience dealing with people's illness and spirituality, I have determined one thing. It's up to you. If you're ready, you being your ego, your body will follow."

"Ready for what?" I asked.

"Spiritual healing, growth. Whatever you may need. That reminds me. Your dad and I are having a medicine wheel ceremony next month. You should come," Judith said.

"You have a medicine wheel?"

"Yes, we built it about six months ago, maybe more. We have a local shaman come over and lead the ceremonies. I think it would be good for you and who knows, you might even enjoy it."

"I'll have to see if I can fit it into my schedule," I said. A medicine wheel ceremony was not the answer I had in mind.

Sara opened the deck door behind us. "Jeff, I don't mean to interrupt, but Anna is about to fall asleep on your Dad's lap. I think it's time to go home."

I thanked Judith for the talk and we said our good-byes. I continued to ponder our conversation on the way home. Maybe opening up and acting instead of reacting would be more positive and beneficial. But a lot of that was just talk until I actually did something. It was still difficult to wrap my brain around using my intuition as a further way to escape the minutiae or cope with my prostate cancer. I may have used my gut in some patient interactions, but never as Judith proposed and definitely not like she did.

"What were you and Judith talking about?" Sara asked.

"Not much. She said I look stressed."

"You do."

"Yeah, I need to do something about it."

TWELVE

THE NEXT WEEK was a blur of unfocused energy. I forgot to pick up Jamie at her swim practice and one of her teammates took her home. I had gotten behind in my paperwork and medical notes. My nursing assistant kept commenting on how tired I looked. I had accomplished only the bare minimum, but felt exhausted. I sat in my office, head in my hands. I wanted to vanish from it all. The argument with my father reverberated in my mind. He had to know why I stopped believing in his spiritual medicine. It was always a thorn in our relationship.

I needed to return some books I had borrowed from Tom a few months previous. At his suggestion, I met him at his work. He wanted to show me something that he'd discovered. He described it as an interesting historical nugget. His passion for historical tidbits often far exceeded anyone else's.

His office was in the old section of our town's local college. He liked it that way. He was a tenured professor and the most senior historian at the college. He had moved into his office over twenty-five years ago and never left. The room was small in floor space, but large in dimensions with sixteen-foot ceilings and one large window. A small desk and two chairs barely squeezed into the room, but he had books stacked to the ceiling, on the floor, and desk.

"Hi, Tom, how are you? Here are your books. Thanks for letting me borrow them."

"No problem. Come sit down. I have something to show you."

I moved a pile of papers occupying the chair.

Tom slowly weaved through the stacks of books and eased back into his desk chair. His office space had stayed the same, but Tom had changed over the years. An old army photo on his desk showed a svelte young man, with thick hair and Army issue glasses. Now as he sat back, his enlarging abdomen was what displayed prominently. His thick hair was conspicuously absent and replaced with a few white strands.

"Oh, these old knees always give me trouble."

"You need let me take a look at them," I said. "Stop by my clinic sometime."

"I will, I will," he said. "But you know I'm busy."

Tom sat up in his chair. He sifted through the myriad of papers and books on his desk. Behind him, I caught a glimpse of a framed picture.

"The *Vitruvian Man*," I said.

"What about it?" Tom asked, distracted from his search.

"Behind you. I see that picture all the time as a sign of good health."

"Oh yeah." Tom looked up from his paper. "A colleague gifted that to me many years ago. It's a Leonardo da Vinci masterpiece. I've been meaning to get rid of that thing. I'm no art history buff. It was never my forte," Tom said. He swiveled his chair around and picked up the picture. "Too stuffy. Boring people. Art historians are not my crowd." He wiped the dust from the painting. "But alas, the *Vitruvian Man* has stood the test of time and has become quite a fixture in our popular culture. No doubt a symbol for many things"

He swiveled back around. A glee appeared in his eyes.

"But that's why I brought you here. Our discussion the other night on the relationship between symbols, language and human evolution aroused my mentation," Tom said.

"Yes, that was interesting," I said with much less enthusiasm.

"I agree. In my musings, I realized that symbols have advanced humans in other aspects beyond language."

"In what way?"

"In the way of health. I was teaching my students about North American religion in my two hundred level history class. One of the topics was Native American beliefs. The discussion turned to a common Native American ritual called the medicine wheel."

He opened a large book and pointed to an aerial picture.

"Look, here it is," he said.

The picture was taken hundreds of feet in the air of an oversized spoked wheel overlaid onto the ground.

"A medicine wheel is made by positioning rocks in a large circle with two crossing rows aligned in the cardinal directions. It can be huge. Seventy-five feet in diameter."

"I'm familiar with them. Somewhat similar to a sweat lodge with the cardinal directions."

"Yes, in a sense, but the medicine wheel actually forms a symbol. Native Americans believe this medicine wheel can be used for healing among other things."

"So a specific symbol used for healing."

"The unique characteristic of the medicine wheel is you can actually stand within the symbol. It is life size. This also led me to investigate other cultures that used symbols for healing."

"What did you find?"

"The snake is a common symbol for health." He paused looking at me for affect.

"Please expound." I waved my hands to proceed as if I had the power to overcome his conviction, which I didn't.

"It may have multiple origins. The Mayans used it as a symbol of rebirth and as a connection between the earthly and spiritual planes. The ancient Greeks worshiped a demigod by the name of Asclepius. He was a doctor for the Gods known for medicine and healing. His symbol, a snake coiled around a staff, is the current modern symbol of medicine."

"I know that symbol. You see it on the back of ambulances," I said.

"Heck, even Moses in the Book of Numbers talks about a snake on a pole pulling disease out of those bitten by it."

"Humans and symbolism seem to be intricately linked."

"Your mom was right when she said that symbols are innate in us. Just as the monkeys used the first tools, humans have used symbols as tools since the beginning. They have been indispensable in human development and evolution." Tom smiled and held his hands behind his head as he leaned back in his chair, which exposed his prominent midsection. He was in his element. Very little excited him more than the past and making historical connections.

"Modern medicine has many symbols as well. This reminds me of the placebo effect, which could be considered a modern day symbol of healing. The placebo treatment is given in medical research trials to imitate the real treatment. It has been shown that when people are given a placebo they do better in the study than no treatment at all."

"I've heard of the placebo effect. It's fascinating, but I don't follow how it works."

"The medical establishment is also unclear how it works. There is a mind-body connection that we don't understand. Yet, doctors use the placebo effect even in their clinic to treat everyday patients. It is not just a research phenomenon."

"So we have ancient and modern day symbols for healing. But where does the healing power come from?" Answering his own question, "Maybe it's not necessarily the symbol, but what we bestow upon the symbol that gives it its healing power."

"So you think that we empower the symbol giving it the ability to heal."

"What do you think? You're the subject matter expert."

"I think the power ultimately comes from the individual."

"I would agree."

"Maybe you can tell that to some of my patients—healing comes from within."

"I don't think it would be that easy."

"Neither do I. If it were, my job would be a lot simpler. I should be going. Thanks for the info."

"Thanks for dropping off the books."

Later that evening, the phone rang. I was in my study and Sara was getting ready for bed.

"Who could that be?" Sara asked from the other room.

"I have no idea. Maybe somebody from work. I'll answer it."

It might be a patient, but my partner was holding the beeper tonight. Nobody else would be calling this late unless it was an emergency.

"Hello."

"Dr. Handling? Is this Jeff Handling?" The voice was pressured and anxious.

"Yes, this is Dr. Handling. Who is this?"

"This is Kim Travers."

"Who?"

"Kim Travers. I saw you the other day at your office. I had the dream about you."

"Yes. I remember you. How can I help you?"

"I need to talk to you?"

"If this is a medical question, we have a beeper system and my partner is on call tonight or you can make an appointment—"

"I don't need an appointment."

"Okay, then how can I help?"

"I need to talk to you."

"About what?"

"About you?"

"About me?"

"Yes, about my dream. Don't you remember?"

"Oh, the dream. I didn't put much stock into it. It seemed farfetched, honestly."

"Did you ever find that painting that I made of you?"

My hesitation betrayed me.

"No, I…I couldn't find it," I said. "What does the painting have to do with your call?"

"No matter, I have a new painting."

"Of what?"

"Not of what, of whom? You need to meet me tonight."

"Why tonight?"

"I'll be leaving tomorrow on business for at least three weeks. I'm going to a big canine grooming show in Florida."

"Can't this wait till after you get back?"

"No, it can't."

"Why not?"

"I feel that if I explain this over the phone details will get lost. You need to see the painting."

"It's late."

"It could mean life or death."

"What do you mean life or death? That's pretty extreme."

"I need to show you this painting."

"Fine. Will you stop bothering me after this?"

"Well, at least for three weeks."

"Where do you want to meet?"

"Let's meet at the Cracker and Barrel parking lot on Marini Boulevard. I'll be in a blue station wagon."

"Okay. By the way, how did you get my number?"

"Oh, never mind that."

"I'm unlisted."

"I have a lot of friends who work in high places."

"Where?"

"Well let's just say there are a lot of dog owners out there who owe me favors. My shirts are very popular. Especially the limited editions."

"That doesn't explain it."

"I know someone who works with the city water and sewage department. They gave me your number."

"Oh, well that explains it." But it doesn't begin to explain her.

"I'll meet you there in forty minutes," I said.

I told Sara I needed to go to the office for a patient. She was half-asleep anyway so I didn't need to do much explaining. In the morning, I would tell her the truth when things weren't as confusing. I wouldn't normally go out in the middle of the night to meet a patient, but I was desperate for answers and I didn't like it when someone talked about my life and death.

I spotted Ms. Travers in her late model, blue Ford station wagon sitting in the middle of a deserted Cracker and Barrel parking lot. I knocked on her car window.

"Get in," she said.

I hesitated. The world was crawling with lunatics, but my gut told me she was harmless. Her car was a mess of dog toys, milk bones, and tie-dye clothes. She had three barking shiatsus in the back each wearing tie-dye cardigans.

"So where is this painting?" I said, my voice lost among the yelping dogs.

"Quiet back there!" she said. The barking eased.

Her frizzy, blonde hair rubbed against the car roof and invaded my side. Her blue eyes gleamed in the darkness. She reached in the back, flinging a few plastic toys to the side and pulled out a small, six inch by six inch chalk painting. It was fantastically bright, surprising for its size. The painting was of a man standing in a valley surrounded by distant, cloud-covered mountain peaks. He radiated light. A path led to the mountains and another led away from them.

"This came from another dream?" I asked.

"No, a vision. I was sitting on my couch watching the *Dog Whisperer*, my fave'. At first, I thought it was a commercial, but then the vision leapt out of the TV like 3D, but I don't have a 3D TV. I was freaked. I thought my TV was possessed, but then I saw you. I saw you standing in this valley surrounded by mountains and you were glowing. The road behind you was dark, but the road ahead was illuminated."

"What does it mean?"

"You need to find this path." She pointed to the painting.

"This could be anywhere."

"I told you on the phone. This is in Central America."

"No you didn't."

"Well, I meant to."

"Regardless, how do you know this is Central America?"

"I saw this little jaguar creep up into my vision far in the distance. It only made the slightest movement, but it was there." She pointed to a small animal in the painting.

"How do you know this represents Central America? There are jaguars all over the world."

"I flew to Costa Rica about a year ago with a very special friend at the time if you know what I mean."

"You don't need to give me the details."

"I'm just trying to explain. Anyway, he was an amateur zoologist and we spent days looking for wild creatures all over Costa Rica. The hardest one was this jaguar. They are easiest to find at sunrise, which meant I had to get up at dawn on my vacation. We spotted him on the last day. I'll never forget him. He peeked out of the forest to sniff a puddle of water. He was so sleek and powerful. My friend was very happy. The trip was a success on multiple levels if you know what I mean."

"Okay, I get it," I said.

"It might signify somewhere else in the world, but I only know of jaguars in Central America.

"So you think Costa Rica?"

"It could be. It felt like somewhere in that region. Sorry, I can't give you more details."

"So you're suggesting that I go somewhere in Central America to find this path. This is the important thing you needed to tell. I was getting ready to go to sleep. I had to drive all the way out here because I thought it was some emergency. I can't believe this."

"Fine, don't believe me. I'm doing this for you. I didn't have to call you," she said, flipping her head, her hair flicking my face.

"I'm sorry. It's been a long day."

"Isn't it always?"

I shrugged. "I suppose so. Is there anything else that you can tell me about the painting?"

"You're not alone. You have a companion." She pointed to a shadow of a person who was not in the painting. "I wonder who that could be?"

"I don't know." Who would go with me to find some path? Surely, Sara wouldn't with all of our fighting. "I was supposed to take my daughter to Nicaragua. She had planned for us to go on a medical mission."

"There you go. Damn, I'm good. When I'm on, I'm on, just like the old days. No one appreciated my talents so I have to make tie-dye clothes for stupid dogs." The dogs yelped. "No, no. Mommy didn't mean that." She reached under her seat and fumbled around until she produced a couple of dog bones, which she tossed into the back. "I still love you Tooty, Pooty, and Mooty."

Ignoring what just transpired, I persisted.

"Central America couldn't be the answer."

"Why not?"

"I cancelled my trip."

"Why? You have to go. Don't you see how important it is?"

"I can't go because of... personal reasons."

"Nothing can be more important than this," she said.

"It's life or death."

"Now that's not fair. That's what I said."

"I have cancer and I need treatment."

"I'm sorry to hear that," she said, the first sane words she'd spoken.

"And I'm terrified of the possible outcome. I don't want to leave my family." I was on the verge of some embarrassing emotions as I opened up to this stranger.

"My painting doesn't show you leaving them. You could be returning to them. It's an open path."

I composed myself.

"Thank you, Ms. Travers, for your concern. Do you mind if I take the painting?"

"Of course, take it. That will be fifty dollars."

"Fifty dollars!" I couldn't help but laugh at the absurdity. "How about forty? That's all I have in my wallet."

"That will do. Momma needs a new pair of shoes, doesn't she sweeties?" Tooty, Pooty, and Mooty responded with a chorus of barking, which was my cue to leave.

I sat in my car unsure of what to do next. I wanted to believe this woman and I was trying to figure out why. Every medical instinct in my body told me she was disturbed. But I could feel myself being pulled toward what she said. I looked down at the painting. Why did I spend forty dollar on this thing? It was worthless, but I didn't want to let it go. I felt connected to it. This painting and Jamie's Nicaraguan trip couldn't have been mere coincidence.

I would be foolish to delay cancer treatment for a vacation. My urologist would think I was crazy and refuse to treat me again. I thought of the talk Judith and I had on the deck. When I was younger, if I had a question with an unclear path, sometimes I would go to her for intuitive counseling. She always said that she didn't tell the future, but she could see the result of your current course. I hadn't spoken to her in years about such things. She was a night owl and probably still awake. I needed help with all this.

"Hi, Judith, sorry to bother you."

"No bother at all. It was nice seeing Sara and the girls the other night. You should bring them by more often."

"I know, I should."

"They seem to be coping well with your illness although they are obviously worried, especially Sara."

"Yeah, she's working through it."

"So, why did you call? What's on your mind?"

"I was wondering if you could help me. I'm struggling with a course of action and I don't know which way to go with it."

"Tell me about it."

"I'm trying to decide what to do with the cancer treatment and a trip I was planning with Jamie."

"The Nicaraguan trip?"

"Yes, that trip. On the one hand, I need to start treatment for the prostate cancer. The sooner the better. But, maybe going on the Nicaraguan trip is where I need to be. I feel like I am being pulled toward it."

"Jamie would be happy."

"I wish I was just told the right decision."

"It sounds like you already have been. Don't ignore your intuition."

"Do you see anything intuitively?" I asked. I was desperate and at the end of my rope. My family was falling apart, my wife was unhappy and our marriage was on the verge of collapse, my relationship with my dad was severely damaged, and I was struggling to cope with a potentially life changing cancer. I would take any advice to improve things.

"Okay, hold on for a second and let me get in the right frame of mind."

I waited in the phone's silence. The parking lot was eerily empty, the lamp light over my space burnt out. My car was cold and the night was still. How had life led me here? Where had I gone wrong?

"I see a path that you follow while on the trip. It's not the route that you initially planned. It's a different path that presents itself as long as you're open to it. If you do find it, you should follow it. It may seem a little out of the ordinary or even extreme, but everything will be okay. You may even find answers on this path."

"What if I don't go?"

"If you don't go, you continue with your life here. You continue along your current course."

"No death or dying?"

"I usually can't see death. I just see an unhappiness that continues to follow you. Others around you are unhappy. You seem to be stuck. I hope for you and the family this is not how things end up."

"Me too."

I rubbed my eyes. It was late. Now was the time to make the decision. "Do you think I should go?"

"On the trip?"

"Yes, to Nicaragua."

"Only you can know that, but if you ask me, you already have your answer."

Sara popped up on my phone

"Judith, I have to go. Sara is calling."

"Okay, but let me just say this; if you need to make a difficult decision, take a moment to quiet yourself. It always seems to clear things up for me."

We said our goodbyes and I clicked over to Sara.

"Hi, I'm on my way home."

"What took you so long?"

"Long story. I'll tell you when I get home."

"Okay," she said, sounding suspicious.

THIRTEEN

BY THE TIME I arrived home, Sara was asleep. When I awoke, she was already up and in the kitchen. However, at breakfast, she was waiting for me.

"Where were you last night?"

"I can explain."

"What do you have to explain? Were you at work or not? Are you having an affair? Is that what this is all about? Is that why you're so distant and spending less and less time with me?"

In the past, we would have been able to absorb small arguments like this, but now everything escalated well beyond where it began.

"No, I'm not having an affair."

"Then where were you? I called your office, but no one answered."

"Do you remember that woman who I saw in my office a couple of weeks ago?"

"I knew it was a woman!"

"Please listen to me. She was the patient who came in saying that she had a dream about my death. She made that painting of me twenty-five years ago."

"I remember the discussion."

"It was her. She called me unexpectedly and wanted to talk. She said it was life or death, my life or death! She wouldn't give me any details until I met her in person so we convened at the Cracker and Barrel on Marini."

"Why would you even meet her? That's not what a normal, married husband does. If you're not having an affair than what are you doing meeting a woman late at night?"

"I guess I'm scared. This woman keeps saying that I'm going to die and she doesn't even know I have prostate cancer. I've felt lost recently and I'm searching for answers."

"Does she have answers?"

"Maybe. I don't know, but what she says rings true. It feels right to me."

"So what did she have to say? What was her name again?"

"Kim Travers. She had a vision and she saw me going to Nicaragua."

"She actually saw you in Nicaragua?"

"Well, not exactly. She was a little more cryptic than that, but she said if I didn't go, death would follow."

"What's that supposed to mean? I thought the urologist said your cancer was treatable."

"You're right. That's basically what he said." However, prostate cancer still kills, but bringing that up wouldn't help the situation.

"So are you going to believe this woman instead of your urologist?"

"It's not necessarily who said it. It's that it felt right to me."

"You're not making any sense, Jeff. You're a physician trained in critical thinking, but a woman with no medical training is influencing you. What does she do again?"

"She used to be a psychic artist, but is now a tie-dye clothing designer for dogs."

"She makes clothes for dogs?"

"I know it sounds crazy, but she made another painting for me. It's of Jamie and me in Central America. Now how could she know about our trip?"

"I don't know. I hear those dog clothing designers are all know-ing." Sara rolled her eyes.

"She said I needed to go to Central America to find the right path."

"I'm sure there are plenty of paths in Nicaragua. There are paths all over Central America. Heck, you can step outside and find a path."

"Finding the right one is the key."

"I don't understand what's going on with you and it worries me."

"I don't understand myself lately."

"You really believe this woman?"

"It sounds crazy, but yes."

Sara took a deep breath as she scanned my face.

"It looks like you've made up your mind."

"I think I have."

"Jamie will be excited."

"Yes, she will. I hope we aren't too late."

"Are you sure this is the right thing to do, Jeff? This is your health and you are the doctor, but I hope you aren't making any rash deci-sions, because this is impulsive."

"This feels like the clearest decision I've made in a long time."

I told Jamie the news shortly after talking with Sara. She was ecstatic and gave me a hug. She ran off to make sure the trip was still on and we had our spaces reserved. I then called to cancel my appointment with the urologist. He called back shortly afterwards.

"Jeff, what's going on? My clerk told me you cancelled your ap-pointment and you didn't make a follow-up. I was ready to start with your treatment. Why the change of heart?"

"I need to think about it more."

"I can't recommend delaying your treatment any further."

"I know. I understand. This is my choice."

"When will you make a decision?"

"I'll be back in a few weeks and things will hopefully be clearer then."

"If you don't mind me asking, where are you going?"

"Nicaragua, with my daughter. We're volunteering for a medical mission."

"Nicaragua. That's admirable, but that doesn't sound like the safest option for someone with cancer. What if something happens and you need medical treatment. You'll either have to get local care of unknown quality or medically evacuated which can be a big hassle and pricey."

"Thanks for your concern, Mike. You're right, I'm taking a chance, but it's something I need to do."

"I understand. Everyone deals with cancer differently."

"I'll call your office when I get back to make a follow-up appointment."

"Have a good trip."

"I'll try."

My urologist took it pretty well. It would be easy to regard my dismissal of his treatment plan as an affront to his medical capabilities, but he didn't. I'm probably not his first patient to make an unusual life decision after he had diagnosed cancer.

"Hey, Dad?" I heard Jamie call from the other room. "They gave our spaces to someone else."

"Oh, that's not good."

"But," she said, entering the room. "Someone called this morning to cancel and two slots opened up. They're ours now."

"That's excellent." I said.

"Dad, are you sure you want to go? I don't want you to do this for me. I want to go on the trip, but it's more important to me that you're healthy. I don't want your cancer to get worse."

"You don't worry about me. I'll be fine."

"We'll be gone about three weeks counting travel."

"We're going to Nicaragua," I said.

"Yaaay! We're going to Nicaragua. Thank you soooo much, Dad. I have to go to school. The vice-principal is a stickler. I may need your help getting my absences excused for this trip."

"That shouldn't be a problem. You let me know."

"After school, I'll call the trip coordinator and get all of the info including our travel itinerary. I love you, Dad."

"I love you too."

I hope I'm right with this decision. I hope the cancer hasn't metastasized on my return or even worse, I drop dead while on some Nicaraguan goat path.

We sat down for a real dinner for the first time in a while. A liveliness enveloped the dinner table, which hadn't happened since the girls were little and had energy to bounce off the walls. Jamie's enthusiasm for our trip was almost boiling over. Her excitement had apparently rubbed off on Anna who sang and danced while setting the table.

"So, I called the trip coordinator. This is how it's going down," Jamie said.

"Give it to me on the down low."

Jamie cringed. "Dad, please don't say that in public, it's embarrassing. Anyway, I'm trying to be serious."

"Sorry, sorry. Go ahead and explain."

Jamie thoroughly explained the details. We would fly to Miami to meet with the group. Then the group would fly to Managua, the capital city, where we would link up with representatives from the Ministry of Health who would drive us to our destination town, Matagalpa. Matagalpa was a small town north of the capital, surrounded by mountains and scattered hilltop villages. Most of the people were poor and couldn't afford routine medical care, often going without medical help.

Jamie's excitement was beginning to rub off on me. I was looking forward to a change of scenery. Maybe a little inspiration would help rekindle my passion for medicine. Jamie's enthusiasm was obvious. We were a week out and she had already packed.

"It sounds like you have everything worked out. You've done a wonderful job. Now all I have to do is pack and we'll be ready," I said.

"Yes, except one thing. I need for you to talk to my vice-principal so he doesn't fail me out of school."

I met Jamie's vice-principal, Mr. Buford, the next morning at her school. My understanding from Jamie was that he was the disciplinary vice-principal and absences fell under his realm. When I entered his office, he snapped to attention.

"Good morning, Mr. Handling, I'm Mr. Buford. How may I help you?"

Mr. Buford was no doubt an Army man. His clothes were impeccable on a wiry, medium height frame and his face clean-shaven with a gleaming baldhead. His office was austere with no pictures of family on the desk presumably guarding his personal life from the students he supervised. Few decorations adorned the white walls. Hanging behind his desk was a poster of the word "Discipline" with a soldier standing obediently in uniform. He also had the Army's core values framed on a sidewall slightly out of view. He reminded me of my time in the military.

I served for seven years after medical school. They were some of the best years. It wasn't fun being owned by the Army, but the possibilities for adventure were endless. Whether it was deploying to a war zone or traveling on medical missions to a third world country, the Army always offered excitement. Sara's opinion was a little different. She wasn't thrilled with me joining, but consented nonetheless. The moves and my time away were difficult for her. She made many sacrifices then, ones that our marriage was still paying for.

Mr. Buford held my gaze with a stern look behind unforgiving eyes.

"Nice to meet you. I'm here on behalf of my daughter, Jamie Handling."

"Yes, I know Jamie. She is a good student. Please take a seat."

I sat in the captain's chair directly opposing his desk.

"If you don't mind me asking, were you in the military?" I asked.

"Yes, for thirty years as an enlisted infantry soldier. I was a sergeant major for ten of those years, the highest enlisted rank in the Army. What about yourself? Did you serve?" He raised a cynical eyebrow.

"Yes, I did. I served for seven years. I was honorably discharged a major."

"Where were you stationed?"

"I did my medical training at Tripler in Hawaii, then I served in Germany before I deployed to Iraq."

"So you're a doctor?"

"Yes."

"I deployed to Iraq as well. Three tours including a fifteen-month sand party and one tour in Afghanistan."

"Where were you in Iraq?"

"Baghdad twice and Mosul once."

"I was stationed in a small southern Iraqi border town for a year. We helped the Iraqis monitor their entry point into Iran."

"I'm sure it was paradise," he said.

"It was a memorable experience, but that's the problem. Some of those memories I'd like to forget. It was a year I'm glad is over."

"I know the feeling. There are a lot of things that unfortunately stick with you."

He cleared his throat.

"So enough chitchat, what brought you in today, Mr. Handling?"

"I want to take Jamie on a trip with me for three weeks."

"That's a lot of time off and a lot of missed school work. She already missed school earlier in the year from illness. If I recall correctly, I spoke with her and your wife a couple of weeks ago about additional absences and I said no. Jamie is an excellent student and

it was a shame that she missed school for being sick, but school policy only allows a certain number of absences and Jamie is already
over her quota. I treat all of my students the same."

"That's why I'm here today."

"Why do you think I should change my mind?"

"This opportunity is once in a lifetime. Something that can never
be taught in a classroom and I know you understand the value of life
experiences. When I was in the Army, no matter how much training
I gave my young medics, I could never teach them what it was like
to treat a wounded soldier with mortars exploding around them,
rocket-propelled grenades flying overhead and gunfire pinging off
the pavement. They had to face it for themselves. I don't want her to
miss this experience. I think she will grow tremendously from it."

"Tell me about this trip she's to accompany you on?"

"It's a medical mission to Nicaragua. I will be one of the doctors.
She will be my medical assistant and effectively my nurse. We will
treat the local population of a small town."

"You are making things difficult for me, Mr. Handling. I don't
normally give three weeks off for a student even as gifted as Jamie."
He paused and rubbed his clean-shaven chin as he squinted at me.
"On a side note though, I am a little concerned about Jamie."

"Why is that?" Jamie was the epitome of a good student.

"I'm afraid she may be too serious, if that is possible."

"Really, well she has always had a certain focus in life, but I never
thought of it as being too much."

"Recently, I've been hearing things from her teachers. I don't
think it's anything to worry about now, but if it continues, then
maybe down the road she'll have difficulties. Life is not all work," he
said.

"I see." Was my recent withdrawal from my family the cause?

"Maybe a change in perspective would be good for her. I also
understand the importance of real world experience."

I nodded in agreement.

"If she goes, she will need to get assignments from all of her
teachers and complete them by the time she returns."

"I will let her know."

"She will have a lot of coursework to make up when she gets back. She should be prepared to work hard on her return."

"I'll give her the news."

"I don't normally do this. Don't go telling the other parents about my leniency."

"It is safe with me."

I left feeling as if I had won a small victory. My time in the Army was still producing dividends and I was able to convince Vice-Principal Buford of our trip's importance. Jamie and Sara would be happy.

FOURTEEN

THE LAST WEEK prior to the trip was a blur of planning and packing. My partner was gracious and would cover for me. I considered taking a sabbatical to concentrate on the trip and the future cancer treatment, but decided otherwise. I couldn't leave my life's work.

I had managed to stuff my necessities in a newly bought Eagle Creek traveling backpack. I hadn't completely forgotten my packing skills from my Army days. Jamie had no such luck and we had to pare down the vast quantity of clothing she had set out to bring. She wanted to be prepared, but I didn't want an extra seventy pounds on my back when I ended up carrying both of our bags.

We arrived in Miami without incident and met the group including the trip coordinator, Brenda Shivo. It was my first interaction with her and after our meeting, I hoped there weren't many more. She was tall, overbearing, and had a shrill voice. I let Jamie deal with her as much as possible. Jamie had been doing a good job so far. Nevertheless, Brenda deserved a lot of credit. She had planned things well. All equipment and people had made it to Miami without problems.

The group consisted of two plastic surgeons, two anesthesiologists, and couple primary care doctors including me. We also had a few nurses, two medical assistants including Jamie, and Brenda's team of assistants to help set up, run errands and undertake other various logistical tasks. We formed a large group which entailed hours of work to organize as Brenda explained to me.

"Got it?" Brenda said.

"Yes ma'am," I said.

Apparently, Brenda was a former nurse who found that she was much more successful coordinating such trips instead of taking care of patients. Her personality had a certain effect on people, but her organizational skills were bar none and her trips were always a success. At least that was what the other volunteers reported.

"Alright, group. When we get to Managua, we all need to stay together. The airport is small, but I don't want anyone getting lost or kidnapped. From the terminal, we will proceed to baggage where our contacts should meet us. Are there any questions?" Brenda asked.

"Did she say, 'kidnapped'?" I asked Jamie.

"Shhh, Dad, I don't want to get in trouble."

Brenda looked over at us with an irritated eye, but then continued. "From there we will be driven to our hotel, The TransAmericana Hotel Managua, and stay for two nights before heading to our destination. So if for some reason we get separated in the airport and you can't find any of us, then get your bags and proceed by taxi to The TransAmericana Hotel. However, that shouldn't happen because no one is getting lost. The hotel is an elegant, five-star accommodation. Let me reiterate, please do not get separated from the group. That never looks good. Any questions? All right, let's get on the plane."

"Quite a pep talk," I said to Jamie.

"She was easier to deal with on the phone."

"What if we lose her?" I said.

"Dad, that's not nice, but it would be more pleasant."

"If I'm sitting next to her on the plane, you have to switch with me."

"No way, Dad, you're on your own, but I'm switching if she's sitting next to me."

Thankfully, neither of us sat next to Brenda. Jamie secured a window seat and I sat in the middle next to one of the other physicians on the trip. He was a plastic surgeon and would be working on facial deformities with cleft palates being his specialty.

"This is my fourth trip with this group," he said.

"How have the other trips gone?"

"Everything is well run. Brenda makes sure things go smoothly. This is my first time to Nicaragua, but the other plastic surgeon was here for a previous mission. He says that there should be no surprises. Both of us worked in Honduras last summer."

"How many patients are you expecting," I asked.

"About fifty. We sent someone early to scout out the area to get an idea of whom we'll be treating. We already have people lined up. This thing will run like clockwork, especially with Brenda behind the wheels."

"It sounds like you'll be busy."

"Twelve hour days, but it's rewarding work so the fatigue doesn't set in as quickly."

"I hope so. Do you know how many non-surgical patients we will be expecting?"

"I'm not sure. I heard about nine-hundred."

"That's not too bad. Nine-hundred for four doctors over two weeks is okay."

"No, that's nine-hundred per day. In my experience, these people are so poor or live in such a rural area they've never seen a physician before. Once the word gets out, they'll come from all over to visit the American doctor. They think we're miracle workers. It's true in my position. I give them a new face, which completely changes their world. Some even become local celebrities from the dramatic change. That's the beauty of surgery. I can permanently fix the problem. On the other hand, you will find that you're only handing out

Tylenol and vitamins. I question what we can do medically in such a
short time period without consistent follow-up."

No doubt, this surgeon was confident in his ability, but he did
pose an interesting question. How many people will I be able to help
in such a short time period?

"I'd like to think that out of nine-hundred patients I should be
able to aid someone for the day."

"You'd think, but you'd be surprised. It can be difficult treating
people from another culture and belief system. They can have very
different ideas on health and healing."

"I won't give up hope just yet. I didn't come all this way just to
give vitamins."

"You'll find somebody that clings to your heart strings and then
you'll get hooked. That's what happened to me. A little boy, about
five, who reminded me of my son, came in with his pregnant mom.
She needed prenatal care. The boy, on the other hand, had a large
cleft lip and palate. We had already filled our slots for the entire trip,
but I couldn't say no to this little boy. We worked into the night for
him. He never showed any fear. After the surgery, he was so happy
because for the first time he looked like everybody else. I get pictures
from him every so often. He should be going to high school pretty
soon."

"How old is your son?"

"He would be twenty, but he didn't make it to see twelve. He died
of leukemia."

"I'm sorry to hear that."

"Life is precious."

"I agree. I brought my daughter, Jamie, with me. Actually, she
brought me as she was the one who planned this whole thing."

"You're a lucky man to have a loving daughter to spend time with
on a trip like this."

"Yes, I am."

The plastic surgeon fell into silence and we said no more. This
trip obviously meant more to him than treating an indigent population. We probably all had ulterior motives for starting on this journey.

Jamie was asleep. I gave her a small kiss on the head and tried to sleep myself before our arrival.

We landed safely in Managua. We mazed our way through customs and baggage surprisingly quickly in a relatively empty airport. The group remained intact without any lost souls. We rendezvoused with our local transportation and were on our way.

The road we started on was a newly paved, multilane boulevard, but as we left the main airport complex, it became a narrow, one-lane street lacking any markings. The occasional car careened by our convoy. Our overloaded minivan passed at death defying speeds numerous dilapidated lumbering pickups loaded with farming supplies. The land was open and rural, covered with farms and overgrown vegetation. Along the highway stood the occasional ramshackle house made of plywood or aluminum and painted in bright neon colors.

As we approached the city, the homes grew closer together and the street became more populated with taxis, people, and buses. Kids played outside, chickens and dogs milled about with old folks. The smell of burnt trash pervaded the air.

We raced around a few more turns in the city and finally arrived at our hotel. It was luxurious—a five-star hotel for a three-star price.

"Does this place cater to tourists?" I asked our driver.

"Business men," he said with a thick accent.

We all piled out of the minivans.

"Gather around everybody," Brenda said. "Welcome to Managua. This is our hotel for the next two nights. Take advantage of it because our accommodations don't get any better. Why don't we check in and then meet for dinner in a couple of hours in the hotel restaurant. There, I will give you more details of our mission."

"Dad, come and look at this room." Jamie poked her head from outside the hotel room door. I was more than halfway down the long hall. She crinkled her eyebrows. "You're slow. You should have let them carry our stuff."

I was lugging both of our bags. The hotel offered a bell service, but I insisted. I didn't feel comfortable leaving my belongings with a stranger in a foreign country. I was just as capable of carrying them to the room, maybe less capable of carrying two, as I found out.

"Hold on, I'm almost there."

"Wow, look at all of these different soaps, shampoos and lotions. Mom would love this."

"I'm going to need to use them after carrying these bags."

I unloaded the luggage in a nook of the spacious hallway leading into the suite. Light glistened off the stone and marble that covered the floor and countertops. We each had our own cavernous bedroom that opened into a central TV and bar area. The tap water was even drinkable, unlike the rest of the country, because the hotel filtered water on the premises.

"The bathroom is bigger than my bedroom and the towels are so soft," Jamie said from the bathroom. "They even have bathrobes with slippers!"

"You never wear a bathrobe at home."

"Maybe I should start."

"Well, let's get cleaned up and eat dinner. Then you can wear the bathrobe."

The restaurant was a continuation of the hotel's extravagance. Large chandeliers illuminated a vast dining room while silver and crystal sparkled on the table. Three waiters covered each table and as soon as a crumb hit the bleached, white tablecloth, one of the three darted over to expertly brush it off.

I ordered the *churrasco*, a delicious Argentinean steak, which melted in my mouth like no steak ever had. Somehow, heaven was captured in this slab of meat. This place would cost a fortune in the States, however, in Nicaragua, it was like going to an inexpensive, but gourmet Denny's. The dollar went a long way.

Jamie and I sat with a couple who were part of Brenda's team of assistants. They had been on the scout and planning squad that found a suitable town for the mission to set up shop. This was their third trip to Nicaragua.

"The place we're going to is quiet and charming," said the woman whose name was Lilly. "The surrounding area is rural and many people don't make much money."

"What's the town like?" Jamie asked.

"It's a quaint mountain town. But one of the bigger towns in Nicaragua"

"What you really need to worry about are the guerrillas," Lilly's husband, Buck said.

"Oh, stop that Buck. There are no guerrillas, at least not where we're going."

"Guerrillas? I thought they'd laid down their weapons years ago," I said.

"That's what CNN tells you," Buck said, raising an eyebrow with a menacing look.

"The Contras gave up their weapons long ago," Lilly said. "We shouldn't have any problems with them. Their hideout was normally in the mountains to the northeast."

"In what direction are we going?" I asked.

"Northeast, but we'll probably only have at most one kidnapping," Buck said. He then raised both eyebrows. Buck was a large man. He was well over six feet tall and two hundred and fifty pounds. Lilly on the other hand was a wisp of a woman. Small and thin, quiet and pleasant, but that didn't stop her from keeping Buck in check. They complemented each other well.

"Do we have any security?" I studied Buck who was deadpan.

"No, just local guides. Don't listen to my husband, he's kidding. The threat is low and we've been there before without problems."

"How long have you been working with Brenda?" I asked.

"A few years now. We've been all over Central America and the Philippines. We're planning a trip to Indonesia next year."

Brenda stood up and clanged on her glass.

"Okay group, I would like to get started," Brenda yelled over the rumbling voices in the restaurant. "I can see that you all are enjoying these wonderful accommodations, which is good because the work will start soon. Tomorrow will be a free day for some of you as we assemble all of our supplies and confirm it's transportation to Matagalpa. The following day we will be traveling to Matagalpa. When we get there, we'll have a walk through, set up and then start seeing patients. Any other questions? No? Okay, get ready folks. This is not going to be a vacation. We will be working hard, but at the end of the three weeks, you'll be proud."

Brenda's speech continued with facts about Nicaragua and Matagalpa, warning us about getting lost, travel safety in a foreign country and so forth. I looked over at Jamie who had zoned out midway through the talk. We had made it. Now what? If the excitement of the trip centered on Brenda's safety briefings, my disappointment would be limitless. I began to have the sinking feeling we would complete the trip and although it would be a success, it would be a failure. Waiting for the unknown to present itself was a test of faith.

FIFTEEN

WE WOKE UP early excited to discover the city. I was decked in my travel gear—khakis from head to toe. I had more pockets on my pants and shirt than a billiard hall.

"Dad, please do not wear that hat with the chin strap," Jamie said. Jamie was a little more fashionably dressed in light capri pants, shirt and sneakers.

"I like this hat. And what if there's a gust of wind?"

"Dad."

"Okay, I won't wear the chin strap."

Everyone else must have been sleeping late because we were the only ones at breakfast. It was worth the early wake-up call. Every conceivable tropical fruit lined the tables, carved into an array of shapes and sizes. A chef manned a made-to-order station of ome-lets, crepes, waffles and pancakes. A pastry counter beckoned that covered an entire wall.

"What do you want to do today?" I asked Jamie.

"Let's go explore Managua."

"Good idea. I saw an advertisement for an exhibit at the National Museum about the *Vitruvian Man*." Tom's photo had piqued my in-terest.

"That sounds very boring, Dad."

"We'll just take a quick look."

We enjoyed the breakfast. Jamie talked about her swim squad and the classes she liked. It was great, but also disheartening. When she was younger, the two of us were a team. I would take her to practices or after-school activities while Sara took care of Anna. She would greet me at the door with a drawing from school and a hug. That changed as work consumed more of my time. I didn't know my daughter like I used to and now she was nearly a woman.

We finished breakfast and stepped out from our secluded hotel onto the humid Managua streets. A taxi drove us to the downtown tourist area and dropped us off near the Presidential Palace and from there we made our way around town. We visited the remains of the Santiago of Managua Cathedral also known as the Old Cathedral. Once the main church in all of Nicaragua, an earthquake had badly damaged it and it had fallen into disrepair. No visitors were allowed inside, since it was unsafe, so we looked at the skeleton of the building from behind a metal fence.

Across the street was the central park and beyond the park was the Simón Bolívar Avenue. Large and expansive, it was the kind of street you would expect to see besieged with large military processions or festive parades. Today, it was eerily empty. The Simón Bolívar Avenue led to Lake Managua, a large fresh water lake crucial to the Nicaraguan fishing industry.

"Are you ready for the museum?" I asked.

"If we must."

The National Museum was on the other side of the Old Cathedral.

"There it is. See the advertisement for the *Vitruvian Man* exhibit. It covers half the museum wall. They went all out for this one."

The museum had other exhibits besides the *Vitruvian Man*, which mainly covered Nicaraguan history and selected artists. Jamie's interest was already waning so we made straight for the Vitruvian exhibit after acquiring the necessary electronic English tour guide. Jamie declined hers so I was kind enough to narrate much to her discontent. We proceeded to the entrance of the exhibit.

"It says Vitruvius was a Roman architect during Julius Caesar's time. He was famous for writing one of the first books on architecture called *On Architecture.*

"How original," Jamie said. "Dad, aren't you hungry? I saw a cute little place around the corner."

"No, I'm still full from that big breakfast. Thank you for asking." I continued, to her chagrin, as we entered a small room detailing the beginnings of ancient architecture. "From Vitruvius' book, came a theory of proportions which led to the proportions for the perfect man."

"So Vitruvius is the perfect man? Too bad he lived two thousand years ago."

"What's that supposed to mean?" I wasn't ready yet for my daughter to be a woman.

"Nothing. Mom says the perfect man doesn't exist."

"At least not in our house, apparently."

We continued through a hallway detailing Vitruvius' contributions to architecture, photographs and old manuscripts that lay enclosed behind glass display cases. The hallway opened up into a large room exhibiting multiple drawings and pictures. Each piece resembled the *Vitruvian Man,* but not the picture itself.

"The recording goes on to say that there were many artists and architects who tried to recreate Vitruvius's dimensions of the perfect man, but they all came up lacking. It wasn't until Leonardo da Vinci created his drawing that the riddle was solved."

"What was the riddle?"

"Vitruvius believed that the perfect man could at once be touching the edges of a square and circle. Prior to da Vinci, no artist had created such a man without him looking oddly misshapen. Da Vinci placed the circle just right to allow the man to touch both edges of circle and square. This in effect squared the circle or circled the square. That's at least what this electronic guide says."

"So all of these drawings must be failed attempts at drawing the perfect man."

"The perfect *Vitruvian Man*," a voice said from behind us. "I'm sure some would argue that we have yet discovered the perfect man." He was small, almost slight in stature with a large goatee and a graying head of thin hair. He looked to be in his sixties.

"Hello, my name is José Vallejos. I'm an organizer of this exhibit. How do you like it?"

"It's interesting. I had no idea that so many other Vitruvian men were created," I said.

"Yes, there were many attempts to make the so called perfect man according to Vitruvius' proportions. It wasn't until Leonardo da Vinci literally thought outside the box that Vitruvius' theory was brought to life."

"What's so great about it?" Jamie asked.

"At the time, his drawing was scientifically advanced. It was a fusion of art and science."

"In what way?" Jamie asked.

"No one had ever viewed the human body in such a relation to science and nature."

"It seems pretty obvious now."

"It wasn't back then. People still believed the earth was the center of the universe and man held dominion over all of nature instead of living within it."

"There are those that still believe that," I said.

"Unfortunately, you are right. But to prove his point, some people even believe that da Vinci based his *Vitruvian Man* on the golden ratio."

"What is the golden ratio?" Jamie asked.

"It is a number that is found over and over again in nature. It is found in the pattern of leaves on a tree, the nautilus shell you find on the beach, and even the trajectory a falcon takes to hunt its prey. The ratio can be applied to rectangles called the golden rectangle. Pythagoras, the famous Greek mathematician, discovered the golden ratio in triangles and called it the golden triangle. It is also even found in the frequency of our brain waves. The one common denominator among all of these examples is the golden ratio."

"Why is it important?" Jamie asked. "It's just a number."

"It is thought to be the perfect number. Some even believe it was handed down by God. In nature, the golden ratio is the most efficient way to grow. Artists and architects use the golden ratio to create perfect proportions, which are thought to be more aesthetically pleasing. A good example would be this drawing over here by Heinrich Agrippa."

The image was of a short, stocky man encircled in the center of a pentagram with hands, feet, and head touching the sides where the pentagram and circle met.

"Agrippa attempted to draw a man within a pentagram, which also represents the golden ratio, to show man's relationship to the golden ratio," José said.

"That one is not very aesthetically pleasing," Jamie said.

"That's not my favorite either," José said.

"You seem knowledgeable on this. You said you helped to organize this exhibit. Are you a curator here?" I asked our unexpected tour guide.

"No, I'm only an interested volunteer. I'm a professor of mathematics at the University of Nicaragua. Previously, I trained and worked at the University of Virginia where I came to appreciate the interplay of mathematics and history at Mr. Jefferson's University."

"What are your thoughts on da Vinci's *Vitruvian Man*?" I asked as we walked up to a display of da Vinci's drawing.

"I think it's a clever masterpiece. Here, let me show you. I am very proud of this, our most modern exhibit. It's interactive," José said.

In front of us was a large LCD display mounted on the wall and connected to a small horizontal LCD monitor in front. On both screens was da Vinci's *Vitruvian Man*.

"The *Vitruvian Man* was otherwise known as the Canon of Proportions. Da Vinci believed in the *cosmografia del minor mondo*. In other words, the human body represents the greater workings of the universe."

"You said that da Vinci used the golden ratio in his *Vitruvian Man*. Can you show us where he used it?" I asked.

"It is truly only speculation as no one really knows if he intended to use the golden ratio. Da Vinci himself never described the *Vitruvian Man* in terms of the golden ratio. However, there are too many instances of the number in the *Vitruvian Man* to attribute it to mere coincidence. Let me show you on this touch screen."

He pressed the stylet to the small LCD monitor and deftly drew three rectangles over the body of the *Vitruvian Man* dividing his head, torso and limbs. He was quite skilled and must have given this talk many times before.

"These three rectangles of different sizes are all golden rectangles representing the golden ratio."

He then cleared the screen and drew lines from the shoulder to fingertips with a line through the elbow.

"The ratio of the length from shoulder to elbow and elbow to fingertips is the golden ratio."

He cleared the screen again. And then drew a vertical line from the baseline of the square through the navel to the top of the head.

"Dividing this vertical line at the navel and then taking the ratio will give you the golden ratio. There are other examples of the golden ratio in the drawing. I don't think it was mere coincidence. Leonardo da Vinci was truly trying to exemplify the perfect man in nature, which could only be done by utilizing the golden ratio in man's proportions."

"That's cool," Jamie said.

"Now let me show you my favorite *Vitruvian Man*," he said.

We walked to another exhibit gallery entitled, *Intentos Fallidos*.

"These are failed attempts by other artists using Vitruvius's guidelines to create the perfect man. Instead, they created the imperfect man. This is the one." José pointed to an oddly shaped human bounded by a circle and square. The picture gave the impression the man was tied down and stretched by his arms and legs. "It was drawn by Cesariano in the fifteen hundreds. Note how the legs are too short and the arms and feet are too long for the torso."

"It looks like a torture device," I said.

"If it's so imperfect, why do you like it?" Jamie asked.

"For the very reason that it is imperfect. To me, this man looks like he is reaching for perfection, but unable to obtain it. It is a more accurate representation of humans. I believe we are all striving for perfection, but most fail to achieve it. A discouraging thought, I know. However, not all is lost as the path to perfection is more interesting than perfection itself. At least that's my opinion."

"Is the golden ratio in this painting?" I asked.

"Not that I'm aware of."

"What about those triangles?" Jamie asked, pointing to the triangles within the painting.

"I believe those are right triangles and do not have the golden ratio. But good thought."

"You said that the golden ratio is found within the frequency of our brain waves. Do you know any more about that?" I asked.

"No, I don't. Only that it seems that the golden ratio is as much innate in humans as it is in nature.

"Hey, Dad, that's up your alley."

"I bet the golden ratio is exemplified in humans in other ways as well," I said.

"That would be beyond my specialty. Do you have any other questions?" José asked.

I looked at Jamie and she shook her head. "No, but thank you for your time. I think we need to be going," I said. While fascinating, we were losing precious time to see other parts of the city.

"No problem. Glad to help. I hope you enjoyed it."

"We did," Jamie said.

"So you enjoyed it after all?" I asked.

"Yes, once that nice old man joined us. He was a much better tour guide than you were, Dad."

"I suppose you're right. He did organize the entire exhibit. He should know a thing or two about it. Hey, let's go upstairs. I think there are some exhibits about Nicaraguan history that I'd like to look at."

Jamie made a displeased face.

"Only for five minutes and then we'll leave. I think the steps to the second floor are around the corner."

As I was rounding the corner, I heard Jamie yell out, "Hey, that's mine." Out of the corner my eye, I saw a person flash by me and exit a side door. As soon as he vanished, Jamie was after him.

"Wait. Where are you going?" I asked.

"He stole my purse," she said.

My daughter was surprisingly quick and made it to the door as it was closing. I was right behind her. We exited into an empty ally. On the ground in front of us was her travel purse with the straps cut.

"He took the money you gave me, but left the map."

"You didn't have anything else in there?"

"The camera is in my pocket and you have the rest of the stuff."

"At least we have the camera," I said.

"Hey, Dad, look." Jamie pointed to a poster advertisement for the *Vitruvian Man* exhibit hanging on a building across the alley. It was graffitied with a large "X" over the middle of the perfect man.

"Some people just don't appreciate art," Jamie said.

I had to laugh over the change of heart Jamie had for da Vinci's masterpiece. We returned to the front of the museum and reported the theft to museum security. They then called in the local police. Since the police had no leads, there wasn't much else we could do and we left it at that.

"I'm getting hungry. Let's skip the rest of the museum and get something to eat," I said.

"Sounds good to me."

SIXTEEN

THE NEXT DAY, with sightseeing over, we pressed on to Mata-galpa. Our journey took us on the main highway north hitting potholes so frequently our driver must have been aiming for them. Lake Managua passed us on the left, its water lazily moving with the breeze. The population density decreased the further we drove from Managua. The houses and cars were less numerous with greener, more open land.

Most of the houses were the same small, simple dwellings we witnessed on arrival. Scattered among the homes was the occasional fruit stand selling fresh produce and juice smoothies. The people, in spite of their meager living conditions, took pride in their homes and land, nurturing their small plots.

The locals studied our vehicles as we passed. The dogs barely flinched in their heat-induced siesta. Some kids waved as we zipped by. Our train of white minivans racing down the road looked out of place in this sleepy tropical country.

The drive to Matagalpa was about two and a half hours. During that time, my thoughts wandered. I hoped Sara and Anna were doing fine. We called them last night from the hotel and reported our successful arrival. They were enjoying each other's company and were going out on daily excursions to the zoo, park, and children's museum. All places Anna had happily selected without any input from her older sister. Our marriage was still strained. Sara was relieved we arrived safely, but we didn't have much else to say. Jamie spoke for twenty minutes and I spoke for less than two. A large gulf separated us and I was as confused as ever on how to cross it.

I was dreamless again last night. My last dream or vision was over a week ago. They had invaded my life for weeks and then abruptly and without reason stopped. Maybe, finally, I was on the right path. The trip had also diverted my thoughts from the prostate cancer. I dismissed a good treatment plan on a hunch by an odd, eccentric woman. I hope I hadn't made a mistake.

As we continued on our trip, the mountains, previously in the distance grew closer until we reached Matagalpa, the Pearl of the North, as Lilly called it. Matagalpa was a small city nestled in a valley offering beautiful mountain views. The town possessed a large church, a small public hospital, restaurants, businesses and outside markets. Most buildings were one or two stories. As many as a hundred thousand people lived in the town and many more scattered along the countryside. The average worker made less than two dollars per day.

We stayed in one of the few hotels in town, which was a three-story, concrete block structure. The small reception was a victim of sparse decoration. A single employee checked us in while swatting flies away. The hotel was actually more like a large *pension*. It was nothing compared to our previous night's accommodations, but it had all of the necessities with its biggest attraction being the air conditioning unit.

Our room had two, worn, single beds with the advertised air conditioner grinding away in the corner blowing out coolish air. The bathroom had a toilet sitting nearly underneath a showerhead and a small sink in the corner. If need be, I could use all three fixtures at once. We dropped off our bags and left to inspect the clinic in our white minivan cavalcade.

The hospital was on the northern fringe of town. It spread out over a small campus, fenced in by the natural overgrowth of the jungle. Our caravan stopped out front. Few other cars were in the parking lot.

Brenda introduced us to a hospital administrator who would be our hospital contact and tour guide for the day. He was a short, stocky man with a thick, dark mustache that touched his large eyeglasses. He wore a brown suit nearly sweated through in the morning humidity. The first order of business was the tour and he directed us to follow. The hospital was a small building with open walkways, which allowed for the occasional pleasant breeze in the stifling heat. We proceeded first to the clinic.

"This will be your clinic." Our tour guide motioned to a long row of doorways down an expansive hallway. "We have a clerk at the front. There is a room for each of you doctors to see patients. I also understand that you have brought medications with you. You can set up a small pharmacy at the end of the hall. Let us take time to look in the rooms to see if there are any things that you need."

They were simple rooms with a small desk and a couple of chairs. Absent from each room was an exam table and a computer, which were standard in a typical clinic in the U.S. The surgeons and anesthesiologists inspected the surgical suite and were satisfied.

We wound our way through the rest of the hospital. Older equipment outfitted most of the rooms, but everything was clean and well taken care of. A few patients milled around with the occasional nurse or doctor. Our guide concluded the tour back at the clinic area by lunchtime.

After lunch, Brenda discussed patient flow, the pharmacy and the interpreters. We then unloaded two, large trucks filled with medical supplies, medications, a few tables and chairs among other things. We locked up all of the supplies in our pseudo pharmacy and headed back to the hotel by dinnertime.

I was hungry and eager to explore Matagalpa. From our hotel, Jamie and I along with Lilly, Buck, and the surgical nurses strolled about in search of food. We headed for a restaurant around the corner that served excellent local *típicos* cooking consisting of chicken, beans and rice.

The weather was warm with a gentle breeze so we sat outside. I ordered a cold cerveza and Jamie enjoyed a juice smoothie, a local drink sold everywhere including restaurants and street vendors. They were delicious.

"Dad, what did you think of the hospital?"

"It was adequate. I don't need much to be able to do my job."

"I'm excited about tomorrow," Jamie said. "I wonder how many people will show up."

"I wonder too," I said.

"I'm betting they will be lined up out the door," one of the nurses said. "And by the next day, they will snake down the street. We'll have to turn people away. That's usually how these things go."

"Unfortunately, we can't treat everybody, but we try," Lilly said.

"What do you know of the people of Matagalpa?" I asked.

"They will probably have the typical ailments of knee pain, back pain, and headaches that are characteristic in a rural country where manual labor is the norm," one of the nurses said.

"That makes sense since they are predominantly farmers. This part of Nicaragua is a huge coffee growing center," Buck said, "which was started no less than by a group of Germans."

"What are the people like? What is there culture?" I asked.

"Actually, the Matagalpan people have a pretty distinct history in Nicaragua," Lilly said. "The migration of people into this area came from the Andean population of South America and possibly from the Mayans of the north. These people melded into what came to be known as the Matagalpan Indians."

"Why do you say possibly Mayans? Isn't Nicaragua close enough to the Mayan civilization to suggest they lived here?" I asked.

"They haven't found any Mayan ruins in Nicaragua yet, but there is still a lot of unexplored country especially as you go further north. They also made a recent discovery of pre-Mayan ruins on the eastern

2

JEREMY B KENT

part of Nicaragua that may have been settled by a group of people that influenced and melded with the Mayans."

"What gives them that clue?" I asked.

"The way they built and designed their temples out of earth and rock."

"What part does the Spanish play in Matagalpan history?" I asked.

"Due to their location in the highlands of Nicaragua, Matagalpa was largely left alone by the Spanish for hundreds of years and it wasn't until the eighteen hundreds when they were finally conquered and assimilated into the Hispanic culture. The Matagalpans acquired a reputation for bravery and skill in battle. They were known as fierce fighters and resisted the Spanish until they were nearly wiped out."

"I wonder if we will come across any tomorrow," I said.

"You probably wouldn't realize it. Most people are now a mixture of local Indian and Spanish," Lilly said.

"What about their language? Will our interpreters be able to understand them?"

"The Matagalpan language is basically extinct, but there are a few people who still speak it. Language shouldn't be a problem. Nearly all speak Spanish."

"What are their beliefs?" I asked. "Sometimes understanding their religious values will help in forming treatment plans and enabling compliance with those plans."

"I heard they used to make human sacrifices to their sun god," Buck said.

"That's terrible," Jamie said, making a face.

"That hasn't been true for hundreds of years," Lilly said. "But makes for a sensational story, doesn't it, Dear?" She frowned at Buck. "The Matagalpan Indians had a polytheistic nature theology that centered on the worship of the rain, sun, fire, wind, seasons, etc. Basically, things they depended on to grow their crops to survive. They also had a touch of the mysticism."

"What kind of mysticism?" Jamie asked.

"Apparently, while Nicaragua was still being settled thousands of years ago, a group of mystics emigrated from the Caribbean coast of Nicaragua. They are known as *sukia* soothsayers."

"That does sound mystical," one of the nurses said. "What do you know of these soothsayers?"

"They are part healer and part priest. I had heard their practice still exists. The Nicaraguan government has tried to incorporate them into the local health infrastructure by giving them classes on modern medicine and health care."

"Where are they now? Do they work in the hospital?" I asked.

"I don't know. I don't think they work in the hospital. I think they are located predominately further north in the mountains and work among the people."

The conversation veered as Buck insisted he knew the exact location of a hidden Mayan temple. We ordered our food and it didn't disappoint.

After dinner, the sun was still out so Jamie and I parted from the group to explore the town. We meandered along the sidewalk on a busy street passing small stores, internet cafes, *farmácias*, and eateries. We came upon a large, open market of stalls bunched together jutting up to the sidewalk. Peering into the darkness beyond these initial stands, we found hundreds of booths assembled in rows under a makeshift canopy of blankets, plastic siding, and aluminum roofing. This false roof was no more than six to seven feet off the ground in some places. It blocked out the light making it eerily dark. The market was like a cave of retail. I couldn't resist the temptation to explore. Jamie was rightfully a little hesitant, but she followed along closely.

Our eyes adjusted, unveiling the ultimate mall of handcrafts. A cobbler sold shoes and would make them on the spot. Next to him was a seamstress who fashioned fitted, traditional Nicaraguan shirts. Spanning the rooftop were intricately woven hammocks in a rainbow of colors. I had to habitually hunch over to duck the various articles of clothing or merchandise that draped along the path. My head often found something to hit, making a large racket, which caused an ire look from the attendant. A couple stalls sold huge, ornately carved rocking chairs that were lacquered up to an astonishingly shinny finish.

"Hey, Dad, I found you something. This little boy is selling wallets and you need a new one. Why don't you buy one from him?"

The boy couldn't have been more than ten, was alone, and guarding what was probably his family's merchandise and life's savings.

"He says they are handmade."

"You make them?" I asked the boy.

"Yes, I make them with *mi papi*," the boy said.

"How much?" I asked.

"Fifteen dollars, but for you, ten."

"Wow, already an entrepreneur. Okay, it's a deal."

We continued walking deeper into the market finding more hammocks and rocking chairs. The merchandise morphed into food, with bags of multicolored spices and herbs, dried goods, fruits and vegetables. Arriving at an intersection, we turned the corner coming face-to-face with a large lifeless eyeball.

"Ahhh!" I yelled and jumped back.

"Dad, that's just a dead fish."

"That dead fish almost gave me an eyelash kiss."

Jamie sighed. "Dad, you're being loud and now everyone is looking at us."

"You weren't eye level with it," I said. Jamie shook her head. "Okay, can we keep moving?"

We entered the seafood and meat section of the market with hanging pieces of fish, cow, and pig along with crabs and octopus on ice.

"Let's keep walking. This place smells and it creeps me out," Jamie said.

"See, it is creepy in the bowels of this market."

We walked further beyond the meat stepping into a slightly more open area. Rays of sunlight broke through the tin roof. Among the few stalls, vendors displayed rocks, crystals, and religious charms. The end booth caught my eye. It wasn't a stand at all. It was a little

hut made from blankets and tent material. On the outside in big blue
English letters read, *Psychic Readings*, no doubt advertising for tourists.
Underneath were the words, *Sukia Adivino*.

"Jamie, look." I pointed to the tent.

"Yeah, what's the big deal? She's a psychic who gives readings. It
looks like we are in that part of the market with these crystals and
stuff."

"No, look at the words underneath. I think that's what Lilly mentioned. The sukia soothsayers. Do you know what adivino means?"

"I have no idea."

"Let's go talk to him."

"I'm ready to get back to the hotel."

"It'll only take a minute and then we'll leave. I'm interested in
how they treat the sick."

The hut had no door, only a blanket that covered the opening. I
threw it aside and we both stepped into a foyer that was no bigger
than the two of us. From further inside the hut, a female voice called
out.

"*Entre, por favor.* Come in please."

I pushed another blanket aside, which uncovered the inner sanctuary of this woman's business. The lighting was subdued with light
coming from a few burning candles and rays of sunlight that found
its way in through cracks in her hut. The woman was actually a young
girl, no more than fifteen. She sat on a folding chair with a small
table in front of her. Her long, straight, black hair fell over the back
of chair. She closed a book as we entered.

"English?" she asked.

"Yes," I said.

"What question do you have?" she asked with a thick accent.

"I saw your sign outside. Are you a sukia soothsayer?"

"I do not understand what a soothsayer means."

"A priest or a mystic," I said.

"Oh, *místico.* Yes, I am a místico. I tell your future. What do you
want to know?"

"I'm not here for my future. I was interested in your medical practices."

"No medicine. I am not old enough. I need more training."

"Who does the medicine?" I asked.

"There are other sukia adivino who can do it."

"Are they here in Matagalpa?"

"No, they are in the mountains. North."

"How come you are here?"

"My father sent me. I can speak English and make money for the family."

"Is your father a sukia?"

"No and yes. My father does not practice the sukia ways anymore."

"Where do you get your training?"

"My grandfather teaches me."

"So your grandfather is a sukia?"

"Yes, he does medicine the sukia way."

"Where can I find him?"

"You cannot find him."

"Why not?"

"He only treats Matagalpans. He also does not live here. He does not like the city. Now what questions do you have of your future?"

"I don't have any questions."

"What about your daughter? She looks like she has questions."

I looked over at Jamie and she did seem interested. Her initial aloofness had vanished.

"I do have a question." She plopped down in the chair in front of the girl. I continued standing hunched over in the corner. "My dad and I came a long way from America to treat people at the hospital. He is a doctor. Will our trip be a success?"

The girl reached in her lap and pulled out a metal object; a silver rope coiled on itself. She held it under the light. On closer inspection, the rope was in fact a snake. It was about four or five inches in diameter and appeared to have some weight to it. It looked to be made of solid silver.

"What's that?" Jamie asked.

"This is my animal *amuleto*. It helps me with my sukia powers."

"It's very pretty," Jamie said.

"Thank you. I am not old enough to use the powerful snakes. The poison is very dangerous and it takes many years to learn how to use it. Only snake sukia can use them."

"What is a snake sukia?" Jamie asked.

"They use the powers of the snake to heal. My grandfather is one and he is teaching me."

"When will you be done?"

"In many years. My father wants me to work and go to school so my learning is slow. I have a gift. I can tell your fortune and so I can make money."

"I have to go to school to. But I like it."

"I like school also. I want to be a doctor."

Jamie turned and looked at me. She smiled. It was something Jamie never voiced, like it was a secret, but she had always wanted to be a physician also.

"How are you learning to be a snake sukia?" Jamie asked.

"I have my lessons with me." She reached around her chair and lifted a cloth basket onto the small table. Uncovering it she said, "Look inside. This is my homework."

The dim light in the room prevented us from peering into the depths of the basket, but I could decipher faint movements and flashes of brightness off smooth surfaces. Jamie was hesitant. She leaned back. I could only guess what was in there, but I had a good idea. All of a sudden, a smooth moving head poked out of the dark bag and slithered. Jamie jumped up almost knocking the table over. She had never been a fan of snakes.

"Do not worry, it is not poisonous." Jamie didn't budge and wouldn't move closer to the table.

"I will put it away. Now, back to your question."

"Yes, will our trip here be a success?" Jamie said, pulling the chair a little further from the table.

"It will not be as you thought it would be," the young sukia said.

"What do you mean?"

"Your trip takes… how do you say, an unknown way. I do not see you in Matagalpa."

"That can't be. We're only working at the hospital for two weeks and then we leave for home."

"I see you at the hospital a small time and then you leave."

"That doesn't make any sense."

"I also see that your father is keeping something from you."

"He is?" Jamie twisted around and glared at me.

"But yes, your trip will be a success."

"Oh," Jamie said, whipping her head back to face the girl. "That's good to know."

We paid the girl for her services. On the way out, she handed Jamie a gift, wrapped in a leather swathe.

"You will need this."

"I can't take this," Jamie said.

"No, you will need this. Take it."

"Okay, I guess."

We exited the hut and reappeared into the market. The evening darkness had nearly set in.

"We better get back to the hotel before we get lost in this maze in the darkness," I said. Jamie was still clutching the object in her hand. The market had turned into a vast space of shadows and blind spots. Using the streetlights shining through the roof as our beacon to the outside world, we eventually escaped returning to the sidewalk.

"What is it?" I asked. Jamie opened up her hand and unfolded the leather wrap. The streetlight gleamed off the object, setting Jamie's fingers aglow and revealing the perfectly coiled silver snake.

SEVENTEEN

THE CITY BECAME much more difficult to navigate on the darkened street. Cars blinded us as they whipped past. Their headlights illuminated the otherwise invisible pedestrians we dodged as they walked by. We didn't talk, instead our attention focused on safely returning to the hotel.

"So, Dad, was that girl right? Is there something you haven't told me about this trip?" Jamie asked when we arrived at our room.

"I haven't kept anything from you except for…" I stopped, remembering I hadn't actually told her about my run-in with Kim Travers who painted Jamie accompanying me on the trip.

"What? So she was right. There's obviously something."

"I had forgotten." I was bumbling. I should have told her in the beginning, but it all sounded ridiculous.

"Dad, it's not fair to me if you're keeping things from me on a trip I planned."

"The girl may be right about a few things. I spoke with someone else before we left who had a similar premonition."

"What was the premonition?"

"That our path may change, but more importantly that I should follow it."

"What path are we going to follow?"

"I don't know. I figured it would present itself. Things have been so weird and unpredictable recently. I would have told you, but at the time, it didn't seem like a big deal. It's probably coincidental that this girl even brought it up."

"Coincidence or not, it looks like I've been officially initiated on this path as well." Jamie held up the coiled, silver snake. "This must have been priceless to her, but she wouldn't take it back. It's beautiful and will make a nice keepsake. I didn't want to take it, but she absolutely insisted."

"You're right. This is probably worth more than she makes in a year. Keep it on hand. We may find her again and you can give it back. We'll come up with some excuse of why we can't keep it, like you're allergic to silver."

We collapsed into bed, exhausted after a long day of traveling. I just wanted a peaceful, restorative sleep. I slid under the bed sheets. The old, worn mattress succumbed to my weight, wrapping it's amazingly comfortable springs around my body. I laid my head on two, thin, well-used pillows and closed my heavy eyelids.

At the heels of my feet, I felt a large, silky smooth mass. The mass stirred and began to undulate. It then curled itself around my ankles. The creature unwound, slithered up my leg, over my stomach, and sat lengthwise on my sternum with its tail tickling my toes. The head of the slithering beast was no more than a few inches from my imperiled chin. His tongue flicked at my unshaven whiskers. The snake lingered on my chest, eager to strike. I couldn't move. Fear paralyzed me. Only my mouth worked, but no sounds formed when I yelled out. The snake watched me, studied me. His eyes bore into my soul as if he knew my every thought.

How did it get in? The window. We left the window open! Jamie! Jamie, are you awake? Check your bed for snakes. Jamie, can you hear me? No sound. Had the snake already attacked her? I had to move. I had to get out of bed. Rapidly, the snake tensed up. It could sense my fear. It coiled back and lunged for me neck. The fangs punctured my skin, sending a stinging pain radiating into my head and shoulders. Blood ran down my neck and poison entered my veins.

Then I awoke, jumping out of bed, tearing off the covers, and flicking on the lights to find nothing. No snakes. No bite marks on my neck. Jamie was still asleep in bed. It was just another dream. I closed the bedroom window nonetheless.

"What was that all about last night? Why did you turn on the light?" Jamie asked. We were on our way to the hospital to start the first day of the mission.

"I had a bad dream."

"Yeah, I could tell. What was it about?"

"Snakes."

"Why snakes?"

"I don't know."

"Maybe that girl affected you more than you think."

"Maybe."

I never had a fear of snakes although I had close encounters with them in the past. When I was young, my family lived on the outskirts of town and we would often get unannounced creatures into our warm house. A small yellow-bellied snake peeked its head from underneath a closet door while I played nearby. My mom was more alarmed than I was and the local animal control whisked the creature away. Another time, I crept by a six-foot water moccasin while playing in the backyard before it was blown away by our shotgun toting neighbor. None of them caused frightening dreams, yet a young girl mentioned snakes and I lost sleep over it.

We arrived at the hospital, but it looked like a different place. Instead of an empty parking lot, throngs of people, cars, bicycles, mopeds, animals and children had materialized.

"Are all of these people here for us?" Jamie asked.

"Yes," one of the assistants said from the front seat.

"I guess the word did get out," I said.

The crowd made room for our train of minivans and we filed into the hospital. Brenda gave us a short pep talk and another walk-through of how patient flow was going to ensue. We found our rooms and the mission was officially underway.

I had already instructed Jamie on how I wanted her to screen the patients. She caught on right away. My interpreter, Juanita, was a college-aged girl who spoke good English. She was short with a slender frame and dark features. She kept her long hair tied into a bun. Although I had an initial difficulty in communicating medical instructions through Juanita, we eventually worked out the kinks. Soon patients were streaming in.

We treated the typical issues of knee pain, back pain, and headaches. Occasionally, we saw old traumatic amputations most likely from land mines, fractures that never healed correctly, and large goiters on the neck. Most of the time, I couldn't help them as their window for proper healing had passed. Every so often, I caught an infection that I could treat with antibiotics. Sometimes whole families would fill my exam room from grandmother to baby each with their own problem.

We treated people who were from town. Others were from the countryside. Juanita pointed out the differences. Those outside of town had features that were more indigenous while those from town looked a little more Hispanic. From the look of their strong, callused hands, weathered skin, and lean bodies, many of them had known a life of hard work. No wonder they had joint pain. Their knees were knobby and crackled like cereal and their knuckles were the size of walnuts, men and women. This land allowed no weak or weary. These people were survivors.

Patients came and went. They were all smiles and very grateful. They listened intently to what Juanita and I said nodding their heads with few questions. We broke for lunch and had a filling meal of plantains and thick tortillas washed down with a fruit smoothie. Nearing the end of the day, a long line of people still tethered to the back of the parking lot. I had already seen over a hundred patients, which was a staggering amount considering I treat about twenty to twenty-five patients during a normal day in the States.

We closed the doors asking the rest to return tomorrow. A few patients remained in the waiting room. Jamie picked up the screening sheet of an eight-year-old girl and her mom who looked like she was fifty. She was actually thirty and had knee pain from working in the fields. Her daughter was her youngest of six children. The mom was concerned about her daughter's leg pain. She had scraped her leg while playing and it had become infected. She visited a local healer who gave her a home remedy ointment, but the infection was only getting worse.

I looked at her leg and it was red, swollen and hot, which were obvious signs of a bad skin infection called cellulitis. Except for limping from the pain, she otherwise looked fine. Untreated cellulitis could be fatal, but we caught it just in time before it spread to her blood. This was a clear indication where good, old antibiotics would treat her well. I wrote the prescription for the mom to pick up at our pharmacy and asked her to follow-up the next morning. Juanita gave the instructions. The mom thanked me profusely on her way out.

"Do you think we'll see them again?" I asked Juanita.

"Probably not. They live high in the mountains. It took them a long time to get here and they probably have nowhere to sleep. They will most likely not return."

With the clinic closed, Brenda spoke commemorating the completion of our first day.

"We saw a total of 620 patients today including the surgery cases. You did a wonderful job and we helped many people. I only saw smiling faces leaving the clinic. Our first day has been a great success. You should pat yourself on the back. Now, let's not lose our focus or energy. We still have two weeks ahead of us. Keep up the good work."

I didn't need a pat on the back. This was a good change of pace from my daily routine. The clinic offered a freedom to practice medicine away from the constraints of home. I was helping the people as they needed to be helped. We all packed into the minivans and returned to the hotel.

Jamie and I revisited the restaurant from the night before. We found a seat on the outside porch, sipped our fruit drinks, and ate our típicos food. The night was warm and comfortable. After a busy day, we happily relaxed into our seats and watched the Matagalpan people go about their daily lives; teenagers returned from school, a woman carried groceries from the local market, and a couple lingered about a store window. Routine activities not much different from those done in the States.

Occasionally, a scene would remind me this wasn't the U.S., such as a man no more than five feet tall carrying a large, fifty-gallon wicker basket filled to the top with apples. He had strapped the basket to his back and slung another rope around his forehead for added assistance. His head jutted out straining his neck muscles to withstand the load. It looked like his legs were going to buckle and the basket would crush him, but he slowly plodded past our table and down the street out of sight.

While we were eating, a little girl no more than seven approached our table.

"Do you want to buy?" She shoved two black ceramic bowls in front of me. She was barefoot and wore a yellow dress with ruffles and stitching that was typical of the Nicaraguan style. Her feet were dirty and her dress soiled, but she had a pretty smile. She was another child similar to the market boy selling her family's goods.

"How much?" I asked.

"Five dollars." I handed her the money. She smiled again and then solicited the next table.

"Jamie, do you still have the silver snake?"

"Yep, right here in my bag."

We watched the barefooted girl in her yellow dress as she skipped across the street to sell her wares at another restaurant.

"Let's go see if we can find the sukia girl and give it back to her. That's worth too much for us to keep"

We finished eating and walked toward the market. On our way, we passed the Matagalpan Cathedral, a white baroque style catholic

church. Built in the eighteen hundreds, it was one of the main land-
marks of Matagalpa.

"Dad, can we go in the church?"

"Sure, but not for too long. It'll be getting dark soon."

It was a standard Catholic church. Prayer candles waylaid us at
the narthex. The nave was long and slender with vaulted ceilings and
chapels along either side aisle. Jamie walked down the central aisle
and slid into a middle pew. She pulled out the kneeler and began to
pray. This was more than just a sightseeing mission. I sat in the empty
pew behind her and flipped through the hymnal. Jamie resembled
her mother so strikingly with her ponytail that I did a double take. I
had never seen Sara pray on a kneeler, but I imagine Jamie was a
spitting image.

"What did you pray for?" I asked as we left the church.

"Dad, that's private."

"Okay. You don't have to tell me."

We continued walking along the slender sidewalk. Jamie looked
down, letting her feet guide her.

"You better watch out. You might run into something," I said.

Jamie looked up. Her eyes were worried.

"I don't want anything to happen to you," she said. "Do you think
this *path* might help you and you know, the cancer?"

"I'd feel crazy if I said yes, but then again I'm here." I put my
arm around her. "I know you're concerned, but rest assured, I will
be getting good treatment when we return. You don't need to worry
about me. And we're on vacation and having a good time. Let's not
think about." We continued on, but I could tell Jamie still had a head
full of churning thoughts.

"Do you have anything else on your mind?" I asked after we had
been walking a bit.

"No, I'm fine."

"Is school going okay?"

"Yeah."

She was going to make me work for it, but Mr. Buford's comments did concern me. Ambition and focus were good traits, but too much could cause problems.

"I want you to know that if you want to talk about anything, we can. I'll listen. I'm a pretty good listener."

"Okay, Dad."

Still silence as we strolled along. The day was pleasant with a slight breeze and not too many cars or pedestrians, which made it quiet.

"You know, I was thinking the other day how we used to do a lot more things together. We were a team. And now we've been reunited for a reunion tour."

Jamie looked at me and smiled, partially amused.

"When we get back, I'm going to spend more time with you, whether you like it or not. I've missed our team."

"That sounds good."

We found the market and peeked into the darkness. My eyes adjusted and I slowly contorted my body to maneuver under the low roof. Jamie and I weaved our way through the different stalls. We moved quickly. I didn't want to be stuck in this place under darkness for a second time. Only by sheer luck, did we escape previously. Skirting by shoes, bags, meat, and seafood booths, we finally made it to the rear of the market. The stand with crystals and rocks were as we had left them, but the sukia tent had disappeared.

"Are we in the right place?" I asked.

"I'm pretty sure. I remember the rocks and crystals being right there."

"She must have left," I said.

"It was only yesterday. I wonder what happened." Jamie was disappointed that weren't able to reunite with her new friend. We asked a woman, who was selling crystals, if she knew where her neighbor had moved, but her English was limited to vending and not locating lost sukia girls.

"Let's get back to the hotel before it gets too late." We were getting nowhere with our questions.

"This low roof is dangerous for my skull in the darkness."

"Good thing you're hardheaded," Jamie said.

"Your mom would probably disagree."

EIGHTEEN

THE SECOND DAY was a repeat of the first and so was the third. Streams of people flowed in and out. Brenda announced the daily patient stats and we felt good about how many people we were helping. Similar to my clinic, I enjoyed talking with the people, discovering small bits of their life, and receiving smiles for my help.

The fourth day rolled around and apparently, the news of our clinic had spread because people filled the parking lot and were lining up down the road. My team of Jamie and Juanita and the other teams had labored into a good rhythm of treating patients. Although daunting, seeing such a large number of people was not impossible. We opened the doors and they surged in.

"Dad, that girl is back," Jamie said. We had been working for about one hour. "The mom is asking for you."

"Which girl? The one with the skin infection?"

"Yeah, that one. The mom wants to talk to you."

"Good, I'm glad they came back. I hope everything is okay. Please bring them in."

The mom and the girl entered the room. The girl was without a limp, but the mom looked troubled.

"*Como estas?*" I asked in my gringo Spanish. The mom spurted out words at lightning speed. I looked at Juanita for assistance.

"She says she needs your help. That someone is sick."

"Is it your daughter? She looks better," I pointed to the little girl sitting in the seat next to her mom.

The mom shook her head. "Someone else," Juanita said.

"Is this person here now?"

"She says the person is not here. He lives in the mountains."

"Who is this person?"

"*Mi esposo*," the woman said.

"Her husband."

"Why couldn't he come here today?" I asked.

"Because he is too sick. She is afraid he is going to die," Juanita relayed to me after much discussion with the woman.

"What does she want from me?" I asked.

"She wants you to come with her to her home to treat her husband."

"That's a little bit beyond the scope of what we're doing here," I said to Juanita who was having difficulty interpreting this to the woman. Finally, I think she understood. In consolation, I wanted to at least look at the little girl's leg.

"May I?" I asked the little girl. The leg had significantly improved. It had minimal redness with no pain or swelling. The antibiotic was working. I listened to the girl's heart and lungs and gave her a full checkup being much more thorough than I had been with the previous patients due to time constraints.

"She is healthy. Continue taking all of the medications," I said. Juanita explained this to the mom.

The woman looked at me unsure of what to do next.

"I'm sorry I can't help you," I said.

In desperation, the mom reached out and took my hand.

"Please help," she said in her broken English. I heard a gasp. Although her gesture surprised me, the gasp wasn't from me. And it wasn't from the mom, who looked straight into my eyes. The gasp came from Jamie.

"Dad, look!" Jamie pointed at the woman's hand. It was callused and strong with dirt packed under the fingernails, but I saw nothing surprising. Then I noticed where Jamie was pointing. It was not her hand, but her wrist, which she had exposed when she seized my arm. From underneath her worn blouse just below her palm, she had etched a tattoo, simple and colorless of a coiled snake.

"The path, Dad. This is it." Jamie smiled with an expression of one who has had a simple but convincing revelation.

I was again speechless. The woman continued to hold my hand. I stared at the tattoo. It held a striking resemblance to the silver snake we had unsuccessfully been trying to de-gift.

"Dad, that's the snake, the one the girl gave me. This all fits into place."

Logically, it made no sense. It sounded crazy to even consider it, but maybe this was the sign I had been waiting for.

"Dad, don't you see? The silver snake that we can't return. Your dreams of snakes. This fits. This is our alternate path. We should follow this woman."

"I don't know if we can. It would mean leaving the mission."

"We would probably only be gone for a day. How long is it to your home?" Jamie asked the woman.

"About two and a half hours," Juanita said.

"We could drive up there and be back by tomorrow night."

Jamie could be right. I could hear Judith's voice, "Follow your intuition."

"We'll have to talk to Brenda first."

"I'll talk with her," Jamie said.

"Juanita, can you figure out where exactly she lives?" I started to think of the things that we would need for a one-night trip. "But wait, we'll need Juanita as well. How else will I figure out what's going on? Juanita do you mind going with us?"

"I will go. I am familiar with where she lives."

"Jamie, go and ask Brenda for use of Juanita's service's for the day and this list of medications. No, wait, I had better talk with her myself to explain. Brenda won't be happy."

I was right. Brenda was not pleased.

"I cannot condone this. This is beyond the objectives of our operation much less it being dangerous."

"I'm trying to help these people. This patient sounds like someone who is seriously ill. He can't travel the distance because of his illness. I may be able to help him instead of only giving vitamins," I said.

"If you leave, then you are no longer my responsibility. You are ultimately a tourist here."

"I understand. This is my decision."

"Wait, I want my assistant to witness this as well."

"That's fine." Although, I didn't see the need since we were standing in the middle of our makeshift pharmacy with three assistants lingering around, eavesdropping on our conversation.

"How do you plan on getting there because you're not going to take one of our vans?"

"I'm not sure. We haven't figured that out yet."

"And you can't take my interpreter either."

That was a blow to my overall plan, but I wasn't going to argue because I really needed just one thing before I left.

"You want to take what?" Brenda said.

"I need to take some medications. I'm not sure how sick this person is, but I bet it's an infection. I need to take some antibiotics."

Brenda gave a big sigh. "Well, I don't want you to go out there unarmed. Go ahead and take the meds you need."

"Thank you, Brenda. You've been very gracious." I was laying it on thick, extolling her positive qualities while leaving out the many others. "You'll see me in a day. I promise."

"I hope so for your sake."

I returned to our small office.

"I have the meds, but I have some bad news. Brenda would not release Juanita to come."

"Why not?" Jamie asked. "We'll need her."

"They still need her here."

"I am coming. They do not need me if you are not here. There are no other doctors to interpret for."

"True. Well, it's your decision," I said. "If Brenda finds out, you might not get paid for your absence."

"I do not care. I am coming. I think you will need me and I want to be there to help."

"Then it's decided."

"Good," Jamie said, smiling at Juanita.

"Now, how are we going to get to this woman's home?" I asked.

"She lives in the mountains past Jinotega. The only way that I know is by bus," Juanita said.

"By bus it is then."

"Buses leave for the north all the time from the center of town. We will need to catch one there," Juanita said.

"Then let's pack and we'll meet at the bus station in one hour."

We made it back to the hotel via taxi. Our fellow mission workers gave us weird looks as we left the hospital. They had no idea where we were going much less the many reasons why we were going. Brenda wasn't going to be happy when she found out her interpreter left, but she would get over it.

I filled my daypack with toiletries, medications, my stethoscope, a fleece and a change of socks along with all the water I could carry. Jamie was surprisingly efficient with the packing of her bag. We met Juanita at the local bus station and bought tickets for the next trip to Jinotega.

The Jinotega line was among a sea of other buses, taxis, people, and street stalls. It wasn't like a Greyhound back home. It possessed a unique character all its own. The body was an old school bus painted green and black, with yellow and orange swoops and splatter designs. It looked like a huge, mutated Venus flytrap, sporting a buffed out chrome grill as its mouth. To complete the look the bus also featured chrome side mirrors, blinking Christmas lights around the roof and tassels around the windshield.

"So this is our bus?"

"They call this a chicken bus," Jamie said.

"They went all out on the paint job. Why do they call it a chicken bus?"

"You'll see." Juanita smiled.

The interior was drastically different from the exterior. There was no paint or chrome, only worn, tattered cushions on seating reminiscent of grade school buses. We found seats in the middle with Juanita across the aisle. Passengers continued to file in. They loaded the roof with dry goods, fruits, vegetables, luggage, water, and the occasional live animal and packed more stuff under the seats. Standing passengers, children and personal effects littered the aisle. Everyone crammed together leaving no inch of space. The bus growled to a start and we were off.

The mechanical giant lurched its way through the city until we hit the main road to Jinotega on the outskirts of town. The driver switched gears causing a terrible scraping sound as if the transmission was going to fall out, then a sigh from the large diesel engine and soon we were cruising down the highway. The chickens on the roof clucked. A pig somewhere inside squeaked and snorted. Pieces of luggage and other possessions skirted along the floor. Most likely, the pig was one of those things.

We had a family of four seated in front of us. Their two young boys hung over the seats and were entertaining Jamie by making faces. A standing passenger's hip rested against my shoulder. Another passenger pushed up against my outstretched leg. Thankfully, we had the windows open. The breeze snatched the potpourris of smells from under my nose so only a hint of my fellow passengers' aroma and their cargo disturbed my sensibilities. I fully came to appreciate the chicken bus. It was the backbone of transport between towns for the vast majority of Nicaraguans on business and vacation.

"Juanita, you said you're from this area. Are we going to pass your home?" I asked from across the aisle. We had been on the road for about thirty minutes.

"No, I lived in another direction from Jinotega."

"Does your family still live there?"

"No."

"Where are they?" Jamie asked.

"They moved away."

"What does your father do?" I asked.

"He's dead."

"I'm sorry to hear that."

"He was a simple man and worked a hard life. You do not need to be sorry. He died a couple of years ago."

"What about your mother?" Jamie asked.

"She also passed away, when I was young."

"Oh," Jamie said.

"I still have two younger brothers. They live in Managua and work in business. I visit them often."

"That must have been difficult without your mom," Jamie said.

"I do not think about it much. I was a little girl at the time. My brothers were even younger. My dad continued to work and I took care of the house like my mother did."

"How did you learn English?" I asked.

"I taught myself," she said. "I found books in the local store in Jinotega. The clerk would allow me to read them without buying them. I also tried to watch as much American television as I could. You can learn a lot from Sesame Street."

"That's commendable to improve yourself with a second language."

"When my mother died, I felt helpless. I watched as our local medicine man treated her with no improvement. We had no money to take her into the city for further treatment. My father just sat there. He understood as little as I did of what was wrong and why she was dying. I watched as the illness took over her body. I never wanted to feel that helpless again." She clenched her jaw as she paused looking to the front of the bus. "I taught my brothers English also."

"Well, thank you again for helping us," I said.

"I would not miss it."

We continued to drive further into the mountains. The forest became denser. The cloud cover grew closer. Occasionally, we took a turn over a precipitous cliff and my life flashed before my eyes. No one else was the slightest bit disturbed by our top-heavy Venus fly-trap careening around mountain ledges with half their life's worth strapped to the top. Within about an hour, we arrived safely in Jinotega. Although it was an experience, I was happy to exit the chicken bus.

"Where to now?" I asked.

"She said she would meet us at the bus stop," Juanita said.

It was midday so we found something to eat nearby and then waited. The day started to turn into afternoon, but the woman had not yet shown up. I began to think our trip was a mistake and I was foolish to travel here on a scavenger hunt. If she didn't show up, we would have to find a room for the night and then take the chicken bus back tomorrow. As the sun sneaked behind the mountains and darkness set in, we were about to leave when a 4WD truck pulled up and out popped our lady.

She apologized profusely and thanked us for coming while motioning to hop in the truck. She explained that the truck had stalled in a mud ditch and it took all day to wrench it out. Her brother would drive us to her hometown about thirty minutes away.

I began to have second thoughts. Would these people try to kidnap Jamie and me for ransom? Were they Contras luring us into a trap? The brother looked suspicious. He was younger than the woman. He looked straight ahead, not veering his gaze toward us. I glanced at the woman and she smiled. I took a deep breath and stepped into the vehicle.

We started up the northern road. The wife looked back and began to speak to me.

"She says that she is so happy that you are here. She knows that you will make her husband better. She says that he has been looking worse and he goes in and out of consciousness."

"I hope that I can help," I said.

Juanita continued. "They do not have a lot of money and cannot afford a doctor, but then she heard that American doctors were coming to Nicaragua and she knew that it was a blessing. After you healed her daughter, she felt you were the one to ask to help her husband."

"I'll do what I can." I became less confident as she continued to sing my praises. My medicine was magic to her and powerful enough to cure any illness. I didn't want to let her down, but how could I explain that my treatments were not supernatural, but cold, hard science. And I didn't have all the answers. If her husband was too far-gone, no amount of medicine would help him.

The ride was rough on the poorly paved, rutted road as we climbed further into the mountains. The sun had disappeared and the lights from Jinotega shrank behind us. Up ahead was just darkness. Our speed slowed with the night and after about forty minutes, we pulled onto an unpaved side road entering the woman's small town.

The main road continued through the middle of the town. A couple of side streets jutted off in either direction. Light radiated from the windows of a few of the small, indistinct houses. There didn't appear to be any large business or restaurants. A small, open market, currently closed, stood at the far end of the dirt road. The jungle encroached on all sides. We stopped beside one of the homes. It was about as small as a shed and made of aluminum siding.

"Come." She grasped my hand as I stepped out of the car. "*Sígame.*"

I ducked under the diminutive doorway and emerged in her home. A few candles illuminated the space. Sparsely furnishing the room was one simple wooden table and a couple of chairs. The floor was dirt and lined with rugs. The room smelled of earth and sickness. A small door in the back led to another room that looked like the kitchen. An old woman sat in a chair in the far corner of the room. She was silent and looked at me expressionless.

I saw my patient. He was lying in the corner on an old, sweat-stained, single mattress. Surrounding him were lit candles melted to the floor. His eyes were closed and his breathing was quiet and rapid. His dark, sweaty hair matted to his face. He appeared close to death. The wife pointed at the ill, near lifeless man in front of me.

I kneeled down beside him. "Juanita, help me. Ask them what he does and how this started."

"He is a farmer. This is his home. That old woman is his mother-in-law. The rest of his family has left in fear of getting ill. He came home a week ago from work and was not feeling well. He was very hot. He lied down on that mattress and has not wanted to move since."

"Did he have any other symptoms like a headache, vomiting or diarrhea?"

"Yes, he complains that his head hurts badly and he has vomited three times."

"Can he talk?"

"Yes, he can talk, but they say that sometimes he does not make sense."

"Juanita, I want you to ask him some questions."

"Does his head hurt?"

He made an almost inaudible "Si."

"Is his neck stiff?"

He tried to move his neck, but winced in pain. "Si," he said.

"Jamie, why don't you step outside for the moment? Juanita please step back, but unfortunately, I still need you in the room. I think he has meningitis and I don't want either of you to contract it."

I took the man's vital signs to include blood pressure, temperature and pulse. He had a fever and his pulse was fast, but his blood pressure was normal so he was not in septic shock yet. His fever could be the result of a number of illnesses such as meningitis, malaria, influenza, dengue, or others, but I didn't have the labs or the resources to confirm my diagnosis. If I were at the hospital, I would perform a slew of tests including a lumbar puncture to check for infection, but in the jungles of northern Nicaragua, that was not an option. I had fortunately brought a few vials of an antibiotic I used in the States to treat many different bacterial illnesses including meningitis. Typically, I would treat with two different antibiotics, but I didn't have that choice now.

"Juanita, tell him that he has an infection in the covering of his brain called meningitis and he needs antibiotics. I will need to give him a shot into his buttocks to deliver the medications and treat his illness."

I drew out the medication from the vial and injected it into meat of his left butt cheek.

"Now, Juanita, tell him that I will inject a second medication in the other butt cheek to help his pain and fever."

I pulled out another vial of a pain reliever similar to ibuprofen and stuck it in his buttocks. He groaned briefly, but then fell back into listlessness.

"Tell them to give him small amounts of water. He looks dehydrated. I will come back in a couple of hours to see how he is doing."

Juanita explained this to the wife and mother-in-law while I stepped out of the tent, washing my hands with extra hand sanitizer I always kept in my pocket. I gave some to Jamie and Juanita as well.

"I know you wanted to help, but meningitis can be infectious and I don't want you to come down with it. Your mom would kill me."

"I know, Dad, I figured as much. Maybe when I become a doctor, I'll be the one treating them," she smiled.

"Hopefully, you'll remember to bring a mask unlike me."

"Don't worry, you have a hardhead, remember. Nothing will penetrate it."

"Gee, thanks," I said. "We need to find somewhere to sleep tonight. I don't think the roads are safe to drive back to Jinotega in the dark. Let's talk with Juanita and see if she has any suggestions."

"I don't see any hotels around here."

"Neither do I," I said as we both looked down the small dirt road that was main street for this village community.

NINETEEN

HE WIFE FOUND the three of us temporary lodging in the house of a relative down the street. We commandeered a couple of mattresses set in what appeared to be the living room. Our host family cooked us a light dinner. As we scarfed down the food, the two young boys of the home watched us silently. Jamie and Juanita smiled and made faces at them. The mom stayed in the kitchen and kept to herself.

"Very good," I said to the woman after we were done. She smiled, but did not make eye contact.

Going to sleep was difficult. The silence in the home contrasted with the noisy jungle and amplified the insects, rustling leaves, and animal screeches. The air was humid and still, causing a thin sheen of sweat to cover my skin. Unable to sleep, I checked on my patient. He was resting comfortably, sleeping. His fever had broken. I woke him only to take his vital signs. He immediately fell back to sleep. The rest of the family slept except for the wife who was lying on the other side of the room. She looked at me as I tended to her husband. I smiled as I left and she smiled back.

When I awoke the next morning with the sunrise, I found my patient sitting up and talking. He was drinking water and nibbling on a tortilla. The wife rushed to me. She took my hand, rubbed it, kissed it, and put it up against her face. I took this to mean she was happy.

I smiled and then examined my patient. His temperature and pulse were within normal limits. He still had a mild headache, but his overall condition had drastically improved. I gave him the last dose of the injectable antibiotics.

Juanita staggered through the door still half-asleep from the early morning wake-up. The wife rushed to Juanita talking and gesturing.

"She says that she is very grateful and that you are a blessing." Juanita glanced at our patient. "He's better Dr. Handling. You cured him. I thought...he looked like he was too sick."

"The antibiotics worked. I also couldn't have done it without you," I said to Juanita. "But we aren't out of the woods just yet. He needs to take these oral antibiotics for another couple of weeks." I took them from my bag and gave them to the wife.

Juanita explained the plan and the wife seemed to understand.

I wanted to stay in town a few more hours to make sure he was on the mend. The plan was to leave late morning. As soon as we finished eating our spartan breakfast, the clouds descended from the mountain tops and it started to rain. And it continued throughout the morning.

We remained at our guesthouse. Jamie and Juanita talked while I watched the rain turn the dirt road into a mud pit.

"I bet the roads are bad," I said to Jamie.

"Do you think we'll have trouble getting back today?"

"I don't know, but some of those roads we drove in on weren't the best."

We ate our snacks for lunch. I felt bad taking food from these people who already had so little. Midday turned into afternoon.

"The roads are still too muddy," Juanita said, relaying the message from the wife.

"We won't be leaving today. Brenda won't be too happy," I said.

"She'll get over it," Jamie said.

By mid-afternoon, it had finally stopped raining, but as we antic-ipated the downpour had waterlogged the roads and they were unsafe for driving. My patient walked out of his hut for the first time in a week. His face radiated conquest with his wife in tow and their kids trailing behind. His clothes were baggy from his weeklong fast and he was still feeble from the illness as he shuffled along. He visited nearly every house on the small street. His neighbors congratulated him on his recovery. The wife would often point back in our direction where Jamie and I were sitting in front of our host house.

Most of the residents hadn't realized that two Americans were in camp much less treating the ill. A couple of locals meandered over and pointed to different body parts. I handed out a few Tylenol for their knee pain or back pain. Most walked by and stared at us.

When the town realized we were stuck for another night, the wife decided to put on a celebration in honor of my patient and me. It was a gracious gesture, but I tried to explain that it wasn't necessary. They should save their food.

"No, no, no." the wife said after Juanita explained my sentiments. "*Celebraremos.*"

"Does that mean the party is still on?" I asked Juanita.

"Yes."

"Well, I'm not going to argue with that."

"This should be fun, Dad."

"Yeah, you're right. This should be fun."

As afternoon turned into early evening, the women of the town gathered outside of my patient's house. Food streamed in. The air was cooler outside than in the houses so the lady folk set up the potluck on tables in the street. The modest village bustled with energy; workers returned from a hard day and kids emerged from the houses to play in the cool afternoon air. People poured into the street. A neighbor started a fire in a nearby pit. Villagers brought plates of fresh corn, large thick tortillas, cooked plantains and juicy papaya. The wife appeared with a large cauldron of food.

"Juanita, what's that? It looks good?" Jamie asked.

"It is *gallo pinto*."

"What's in it?"

"You have not eaten gallo pinto? How long have you been in Nicaragua?"

"I guess not long enough," Jamie said.

"Everyone eats gallo pinto. It is rice, onions, sweet peppers, and red beans boiled with garlic, mixed together and fried. It is very good."

"I can't wait," Jamie said. "I'm starving."

"I can tell. You're nearly drooling," I said.

My patient and I had seats of honor in fold out chairs near the food spread. We sat eating. Since he spoke little English and I only knew the requisite Spanish words to order a burrito and beer, not much was said between us, just smiles. His neighbors congratulated him on his recovery. He was beaming with pride after his miraculous turn around. He should have been grateful for his strong immune system to persevere long enough for the antibiotics to work. Most greeted me with smiles and thanks and the occasional stare as if I was an alien.

Juanita explained that the whole town was in attendance. No one was going to miss a feast. Everyone was enjoying the party except for one lone figure at the far end of the street, sitting on his porch. I couldn't make out a face as evening had arrived. I could only see the trace of a lit cigarette swaying back and forth on a rocking chair. He seemed to be looking in my direction. I left my foldout throne to ascertain his identity. Juanita asked the wife.

"Sukia," the wife said.

"He's their local medicine man."

"Why doesn't he partake of the festivities?" I asked.

"He does not want to be close to his rival," the wife said via Juanita.

"Who is that?" I asked.

"You are his rival. The sukia could not treat her husband. His medicine did not work unlike yours. So he stays away in shame," Juanita said.

"Is there anything I can do? I meant no disrespect."

"No, it would be better to say nothing."

I moved to sit next to Jamie. "Did you hear that? Another sukia. Apparently, he is angry at me."

"Makes sense. You invaded his territory and then treated his patient better than he did."

"True."

"He is probably afraid of losing the respect of his people, but you did the right thing, Dad. You had to treat that man."

"I agree. Juanita, can you ask the wife how long the sukia has lived here."

After some discussion, Juanita had the story. "He grew up in that house. He learned the way of the sukia from his father who learned it from his father. The family has been in this area for many generations. People have recently started to move away and he is losing his influence. He does not like the new ways. He is very traditional."

"Does he have any family?"

"His wife died a few years ago. He has a couple of daughters who live in the city. He also has a son, but he is not talked about around here. The sukia forbids it."

"Why not?"

"He was supposed to be the next sukia, but he did not finish his training. Now he works and lives in another village."

Time was passing the sukia and his way of life and he was powerless to stop it. His identity no longer carried as much significance as it once did. For anybody, this would be a difficult notion to swallow especially someone steeped in tradition. The sukia and his cigarette continued to sway with the chair until one of the locals cried out in laughter. As if on cue, the sukia snuffed out the cigarette and vanished into the shadows of his home.

Some of the villagers had gathered around the bonfire to eat and talk. Two men one with a small guitar and the other with a simple wooden flute began playing.

Juanita leaned over, "That is called a *guitarrilla* and that is a traditional Nicaraguan flute called a *zul*."

"What are they playing?" Jamie asked.

"They are playing a very old song. It tells the story of the first people to settle this land. They traveled from the north thousands of miles away. They came to make a new life for themselves because they could no longer farm their old lands. They started with nothing, but built many villages covering every mountainside. They prospered for hundreds of years."

Music filtered through the air. The onlookers were absorbed in the melody and the dancing flames of the fire.

"Dad, I'm glad we came to Nicaragua."

"I'm glad too."

"Do you think this was the path that we were supposed to follow?"

"It seems like it. We've done some good here and we're having a great experience."

"Yeah, we are."

For a few peaceful minutes, we listened to the music in front of the mesmerizing fire.

"Not to break up a good moment, but where's the toilet?" I asked.

"I saw people going around the back of the house earlier."

"I'll try and find one around the house as well."

Evening had set in and my eyes slowly adjusted from the glow of the fire. Thicker brush surrounded the back of the house and the edge of the jungle loomed just beyond the shadows. I started to urinate when I heard a rustle in the grass directly in front of me. I immediately withdrew, but not soon enough. I had stepped right on top of the animal. It attacked with lightning quickness and sunk its teeth into my left leg, hanging on momentarily before releasing its grasp. It slithered away in the brush only briefly exposing its long, smooth body. I let out a wail in pain.

"Dad, are you okay?" Jamie asked from around the corner.

"I've been bitten by a snake." I hobbled around the house. Two small streams of blood were dripping down my leg staining my white sock.

"Do you know if it was poisonous?"

"I have no idea. I know it hurts though."

"I'll go and get Juanita." Jamie returned with Juanita, the wife and my patient.

"They want to know what the snake looked like," Juanita said.

"I'm not really sure. The darkness and the glare from the fire made it difficult to see. It was big."

"Was there a color or did you hear any sounds?"

"No sounds. But if I had to guess I think it had yellow and red stripes."

Juanita interpreted this for the couple. They talked amongst themselves with looks that became more distressed. As their discussion lengthened, I also became concerned that I wasn't lucky enough to have stepped on a harmless garden snake.

Finally, I couldn't take it. "What's going on?" I asked.

"They think it is a poisonous snake," Juanita explained. "We call it *coral venenosa*. It has red, yellow and black stripes."

"The coral snake." Typical. A highly poisonous snake bites me while I'm urinating in a foreign country. At least he only bit my leg. "If I remember correctly, the coral snake has neurotoxin venom that can stop my breathing in a matter of hours. If the snake injected enough venom in me and I'm not treated, I could easily die. Vomiting and hallucinations often precede death."

"Dad, we have to get you treated," Jamie said with a frightened look on her face.

"They don't have treatment here, do they?" I asked Juanita.

"That is what they are discussing. They think there is treatment in Jinotega, but they do not know if you will make it in time especially with the poor road conditions."

"We have to try."

"There is another option, but I do not trust it," Juanita said.

"What is it?"

"The sukia."

"Oh," I said. I looked in the distance where the sukia and his swaying cigarette had been sitting.

"But, the wife thinks he will not treat you because of your rudeness and insolence for his treatments."

"Can't we explain that I meant no disrespect? I knew I should have said something to him earlier."

"The sukia is a very proud man. He may not listen."

"How do we know he can help?" I asked.

"The wife says he is a snake sukia and knows how to treat snake poisonings."

"Just like the girl we met," Jamie added.

"We should at least go and ask him," I said. "This seems to be his area of expertise. If he says no, then we'll have to come up with another plan."

"What if he says no, Dad?"

"We'll have no choice but to drive to Jinotega and hope the snake venom doesn't take effect before we get there."

Juanita and the wife walked the long road with Jamie and me to the snake sukia's house. The town followed behind us as they realized my predicament and were interested in the confrontation between the miracle worker with modern science and their medicine man with hundreds of years of tradition and natural remedies.

The sukia's house was bigger than the others. It had a small porch and two small windows looking out onto the road. Juanita knocked on the door. Leisurely, it opened and a man emerged from the darkness. He was medium height and thin. He wore a simple shirt and slacks with sandals. On his head was a thick, woven, snakeskin band that made it look like he carried an actual snake on his head. He held onto a simple wooden cane. The bonfire in the distance flickered off the wrinkles on his face making him look even more foreboding. He was surprised at first to see Jamie, me, and the rest of the town at his doorstep. Juanita explained my dilemma. He took a long look at me. I showed him the bite on my leg. He thought about it for a moment and then with a wave of his hand, he shooed us all away.

"Jinotega," he said with a deep miserly voice.

The crowd murmured in a low rumble, but their faces showed no dispute. They were resigned to my fate. Once this man spoke, there was no further discussion.

"No, wait," Jamie said. "This is my dad, you have to help him."

"No," the snake sukia said. "Jinotega."

The town started to walk away. I could see the remorse in the wife's eyes. Was this actually going to happen? Was I going to die from a snakebite in the jungles of Nicaragua?

"No, wait," Jamie repeated, but louder. Her voice rang through the town. The people hushed and turned to her. The forest rustled from the conviction in her tone.

"I have this." Jamie reached into her small travel pack and lifted up a gleaming figure. She held it straight into air for everybody to see. The firelight twinkled off its shinning, coiled body—the silver snake. The crowd gasped and a chorus of whispered words rose up like an oncoming wave. The silver stature possessed an indiscernible power over these people.

"Let me see that," the sukia said, thrusting out his hand.

He spoke English. There was more to this medicine man than he portrayed.

"Where did you get this?" He took the silver snake in his hand and examined it.

"It was a gift." Jamie reached for the statue unwilling to give it up.

"From who?"

"A girl in Matagalpa?"

The sukia's countenance changed. He seemed to grasp something that was beyond me or the crowd.

"Bring him in," he said. The wife and Jamie walked me through the door into an expansive but simple room. Along one wall was a large, thick wooden table with four chairs. Pushed against the other wall sat a sparsely shelved bookcase. A family picture dangled over the bookcase. Cushions covered the dark wooden floor on the other side of the room. A hallway led to the rear of the dwelling. In spite of the plain accommodations, it was surprisingly warm and inviting.

"Now leave us," the sukia said.

"I want to stay," Jamie said.

"No, you must go. Your time is done here. My people will take care of you. I will take care of your father."

"It's okay. Stay with Juanita," I said.

Jamie nodded.

"When the roads clear, go with Juanita to Jinotega and get the snake antivenom."

"Okay," she said behind the closing door.

"So, you still don't trust me? I take you in, but you still need treatment? Typical of you American doctors. You have no faith."

By this point, I was feeling woozy. The snakebite, my possible death, the sukia, and the long day of traveling had caught up with me. I was on the verge of passing out. I lied on a pillow. The sukia pulled out a long knife. Approaching quickly, he deftly opened up the bite wound with a slash. I let out a wale.

He continued to talk while he worked, ignoring my pain. He held up a small, round glass jar.

"Why do you think you came here? By chance? Do you think meeting that girl in Matagalpa was coincidence? I would never have seen you without that silver statue. That silver snake is an heirloom, passed down from sukia to sukia in my family. It is hundreds of years old. That silver was mined long before your European ancestors arrived."

"So that girl is your daughter?" I had little energy left. Only fear of what this man was going to do was keeping me from utter collapse.

He pulled from his clothing a long match, lit it and held it in the glass jar for a couple of seconds then quickly put the jar to my wound.

"No, granddaughter."

"Augh." The heat against the snakebite and incision was excruciating. The room closed in on me, my vision faltered, everything became silent and then blackness.

TWENTY

I OPENED MY eyes to the sound of voices. My vision was still blurry and my head spun. Strong hands grasped my armpits and hoisted me on my feet. The smell of sweat and tobacco smoke invaded my nasal passages. The pain in my leg cleared my sight. The sukia and a young man were dragging me out the back of his house. I couldn't help but rely on their supporting hands as I limped along. Blackness surrounded the sukia's backyard. Light from the house shone on a small two-wheeled wooden cart. I could barely keep up with their pace from my swimming head and the pain in my leg as they dragged me toward the simple cart. I hesitated, but they pushed on. The sukia said something in a language I didn't recognize. It wasn't Spanish or English. Before I could determine its origin, they flipped me onto the cart.

I was exhausted. I relaxed into the uneven wooden timbers that formed the large wooden plank supported by two central wheels. The cart lurched and I started to move as if floating along. After a few moments, the jungle blotted out the reach of the village lights and darkness enveloped me again. The forest was surprisingly quiet. The squeaking wheels of the cart had subdued all other living sounds. The hint of tobacco pervaded the air. I tried to turn around, but only saw shadows ahead of me pulling the cart. I closed my eyes hoping this would all disappear. I would wake up and find myself dreaming again.

The cart stopped after ten, twenty, thirty minutes. I wasn't sure. My skin was moist from sweat and the wet air of the warm jungle, but a chill had seeped into me. One end of the cart thudded against the forest floor jarring my painful leg. The sukia gave the muted boy a few directions in his native tongue. A hand grabbed my shoulder and with a grunt, eased me to my feet. The forest was pitch black, the moon and stars covered by thick dark clouds. The faint outline of the sukia stood in front of a small hut. Burning tobacco illuminated a long, slender pipe and his wrinkled face. He unfurled a thick, leather blanket attached to the hut, revealing an opening.

He shook his head to his assistant to put me in the hole. I resisted, but my strength had left me and my painful leg acted against me. As we passed the sukia, the light from his pipe revealed a familiar face. The assistant was the young man, who along with the wife, picked us up from Jinotega. His suspicious face was unmistakable. My fleeting anxiety of a guerrilla kidnapping me hopefully wasn't coming true. Before I could make a move, he pushed my head through the hole and I fell into the darkness.

It was cool and damp. It smelled of dirt and mold. Silence surrounded me. Time passed as I waited. My mind played tricks on me in the blackness as I saw flashes of light and shapes. My leg throbbed, but my anxiety about what was about to happen distracted me from the pain. A spark flashed in the middle of the hut and then a deeper light smoldered in the center. The door opened and moonlight flooded the area. Instead of the sukia, the Native American sweat lodge leader entered. He pointed to a scene outside the opening. My younger self was kneeling, helping the boy from the lodge. The doctor approached. He looked different this time, familiar. In fact, he looked like me. His stethoscope wrapped around his neck caught my interest. It shimmered. He examined the boy and held the stethoscope with a sense of purpose and pride. The boy and the doctor faded away.

Darkness overcame the hut and I could sense the walls shrinking in around me. The air turned hot and dry. Suddenly, out of the blackness stepped a gray bearded man. His elderly hand lunged for my neck, grasping a chain, and yanking me downward.

"You forgot the symbol," he said. "You forgot the symbol." His hand relaxed and a cartouche dangled from my neck.

He disappeared with another spark in the center of the hut that started a small fire, illuminating the young sukia helper. The assistant moved back and exited. The smoke meandered its way to a hole in the ceiling of the stone shelter. The sukia entered. He stood hunched over. He seemed enormous. He held in one hand his pipe and in the other his cane. He vigorously puffed on his pipe while incanting in his native tongue. Smoke filled the room unable to exit quickly enough. I became lightheaded and my vision blurred again. His recitations grew louder. The sukia then faced me and blew smoke directly in my face. Dizziness and nausea overcame me. He started undulating back and forth blowing more smoke at me, chanting louder and louder. He suddenly stopped and held up his cane. It was a nondescript cane, made of wood and ornamented with simple carvings. However, before my eyes it became a living creature with black, slippery scales and a writhing body. The light played off its reptilian skin as the hut spun around me. With one quick movement, the sukia thrusted the snake through the fire, its mouth agape and fangs displayed, stopping inches from my face. A final puff of smoke covered the snake and total blackness returned to the hut.

The nausea and dizziness left. I was quiet and warm. I opened my eyes. Instead of seeing the sukia's hut, I was in an empty white space. The room had no familiar markings. A pit knotted up in my gut. Had I died? Had the snake poison consumed me, blocked my respiratory drive and suffocated me? Dying without family in an old man's hut in Nicaragua was not part of the plan.

The white room changed and I was back in my bedroom holding the chalk portrait of myself. I could hear my patient with the crazy, blue eyes screaming, "Where is the painting?"

No sooner was I holding the painting than I was drawn inside the painting. I had become the two dimensional chalk head surrounded by rainbow colored bubbles. I was stuck, looking out into the world, but my mind was free to experience those self-censored ideas once again; ideas of spiritual medicine that I had forgotten and buried. To feel those thoughts without judgment was liberating.

I was abruptly pulled from the painting. The room changed again. I was at the hospital on call. I received a phone call that Gary had died. The freedom of thought dissipated with my dead best friend. The one person I had let down because of my alternative medical recommendations. I had to shut down to keep going, to finish my training. But now Gary stood in front of me. He was young—the age when we were the happiest before life got in the way. He had a goofy smile and held a baseball in his hand, flipping it up and catching it. He was happy. He told me I needed to let him go. I was not to blame for his death and was powerless to prevent it. Words I had held since his passing wanted to rush out, but I was speechless. He then flipped the ball up to me and before it hit my hand, he vanished.

My family lined up in front of me as if to wish me luck and say goodbye. Is this what it's like when you die? Instead of wishing farewell, each offered a bit of wisdom.

Tom shook my hand. "Don't forget your history. Symbols have been used throughout time."

My mom gave me a kiss on the cheek. "Remember that we are all destined to grow. Remember the symbols that we live by. They have the ability to change you."

My dad stepped forward and gave me a big hug. "Just follow your heart," he said, "and you will be okay."

Sara stepped forward, "I love you no matter what, but I need a partner and a friend as much as I need a bread winner." Sara was no longer sad or angry. She was resigned and the fight had left her. We felt so close and distant at the same time. She took my hand and placed it on her heart. She brought me into her space allowing me to experience her presence—no more games or defenses. I could sense her true self. More than resignation, she had a sadness for our marriage and family. The rush of her emotions almost brought me to my knees. I tried to talk to her, to tell her I loved her, but she slowly moved away and the connection ended.

Anna appeared behind Sara, smiling. She gave me a hug.

"Everything will be okay, Dad." I watched Sara and Anna leave hand in hand.

Finally, Judith stepped forward. She smiled knowingly. "Dreams are our subconscious guiding us, helping us to create connections. You have done well and followed your dreams. But one last thing," she looked directly into my eyes. "This is not a dream and you are not done."

My family disappeared. I found myself perched on a stone platform, encircled by blue sky. Supporting the platform was a gradual sloping mound of earth and rocks. A familiar face in a flowing colorful robe stood before me. He had grey hair and tanned skin. He wore a thick band of interwoven cotton on his head. His hands were old but strong. In his hand, he held an object that he thrusted toward me.

"This symbolizes you," he said.

I looked at him confused, unsure of what he wanted from me.

"Take it," he said.

I held out my hand. What appeared to be a ball of light suspended in his hand disappeared in mine.

"This symbolizes your family." He held out another sphere of light, which again disappeared in my hand. "And this is for your soul." The ball of light was blindingly bright, but disappeared as soon as he offered it to me. "Remember the power of symbols. Use them well. Now you have the answers to health and wisdom," he said.

"What answers?" I asked. He didn't respond, but continued to gaze at me as if looking through me. He started to turn away. "What answers?" I repeated louder. "What does all this mean?" I yelled. "This makes no sense!"

"Quiet!" he said. He took his old, bony finger and pressed it against my forehead making quick movements as if christening me. "Now go." His deep commanding voice vibrated to my core. I stumbled backward by the sheer force of his tone, but found no footing, only air. I was unable to stabilize my weight and began to fall. The platform rose before me as I plummeted to the ground, my head spinning. The old man stood on the platform smiling above me. Was he smiling at my impending death, my body crushed against the surface below?

Time then slowed. My only thought as I fell to Earth was how blue the sky appeared. I could see the stars gathering behind Earth's atmosphere. It was peaceful. Quiet surrounded me. Images of my wife and daughters passed before me, my parents, goals I achieved and failed, my regrets. Then the rush of the air snapped me back and bent my ears forward. I plummeted ever faster. My heart pounded and my breathing was incontrollable. I was falling to my death. I could feel the ground approaching, closer and closer.

My body came to a crashing thud, the air knocked out of me. I was paralyzed. In that brief second, I felt lifeless, but lighter than air. I couldn't breathe, but felt wonderfully oxygenated. A feeling of warmth and security enveloped me as if I floated in the gentle Hawaiian ocean.

I had a sudden urge to open my eyes. Instead of the sting of ocean water, a room formed around me. I took a deep breath and air filled my lungs as if for the first time. I knew this room. Again, an old man stood over me, grinning. Lit candles illuminated the space.

"Where am I?" I asked. The old man laughed.

"Nicaragua," the man said. "A better question is where have you been?" I was back in the home of the sukia medicine man, lying on a woven blanket on the floor. The bookcase was to my left and the table and chairs were on the other side of the room.

"I didn't die?"

"No, you didn't."

"How long have I been out?"

"Most of the night." I looked at my leg. A dark colored goop covered my bite wound.

"What is that?" I pointed to the wound.

"Sukia medicine," he said. It was some kind of herbal poultice he had plastered on my injury.

"The glass jar?"

"I used the quickly heated air in the jar to form a vacuum over your skin to draw out the poison."

"You took me to some place, another person was there, the smoke." It all seemed like a half-remembered dream.

"He is my assistant. I am an old man and you were dead weight."

I nodded. "The smoke. It made me feel…drugged."

"It was sukia medicine to prepare you."

"To prepare me for what?"

"Your healing."

I was still alive. I couldn't complain. "Thank you for helping me," I said.

"You should thank the animal that bit you. You needed a much more powerful healing than I could give."

I looked at him in disbelief.

"Yes, the venom was your healing," the sukia said.

"Are you suggesting the snake knew to bite me?"

"No. That is ridiculous. A snake does not think much less read your mind. A snake like all living things is a part of nature. It senses you."

"So it sensed what I needed?"

"No, you are not listening," the sukia said shaking his head. "It was not the snake. It was you."

"How can that be? I didn't want that snake to bite me."

"You came to Nicaragua. You drove to our small village. How could it not be you? Your mind may not have known you needed it, but somewhere inside of you did. And that is what the snake sensed."

The idea that I subconsciously led myself to this small village to have a deadly snake inject its venom into my blood stream was a bit

farfetched. But I didn't die, so I let it go. I didn't want to argue with
the man who had just saved my life. His views on illness and healing
were obviously much different from mine.

He noticed my internal dilemma.

"Don't worry American doctor. I won't tell anyone that sukia
medicine helped you last night instead of your own."

"And the snake? Was that a hallucination from the smoke or was
that real."

He smirked. "Do you mean my cane?"

I nodded.

He grabbed his cane that rested next to him. "A secret, but for
you, I will tell you. I think you would appreciate the power of suggestion as a practitioner of healing." He screwed off the handle of
his wooden staff and out popped a slithering snake. I lurched backward. "He is poisonous, but not as poisonous as your snake. I will
release him when we are done. He has served his purpose."

He reattached the handle enclosing the snake once again.

"Now I have one question for you. What does this mean?" the
sukia asked. He took his muddied cane and drew a faint marking on
the floor.

I leaned over and looked at the marking. "I don't know…Should
I know?"

"You made it," he said. "While you were fighting the poison, you
traced it over and over again on the dirt floor of the hut."

I looked more closely at the marking. It was two isosceles triangles one sitting on the angled end of another.

"You also kept repeating the word, 'symbols'."

Now it all started to come back to me. It was like a flood of
visions building in my mind.

"I had another dream. Actually, I had multiple dreams. My family
appeared and gave advice. I relived past dreams of past experiences
if that makes any sense. But this second time, I noticed things in the
dreams that I hadn't noticed before."

"The snake venom allowed you to see beyond yourself."

"My guilt was what I couldn't see beyond and what I've held onto for a long time. My family spoke of dreams and symbols. An old man presented me three gifts." The sukia shook his head in understanding. "He said the three gifts were for me, my family and my soul."

I paused and looked around the room. Evidence of my caretaker's activity shown throughout. A sleeping mat leaned against the opposite wall. A woven basket sat in the center between us. Everything was still so disconnected.

I studied the sukia's face.

"That man was you, wasn't he?" I asked.

"Only you can know who was in your dream."

"In the dream, I stood on a manmade structure, a huge mound of earth and stone that jutted into the sky."

"The stories of our ancestors trace back thousands of years even before the Mayans. Those stories describe a sect who tended to the faith of the people. They worked on monuments similar to what you describe."

"The old man was a priest. He initiated me after he gave me the gifts." The sukia nodded in agreement.

"What do those gifts mean to you?"

"Yes. Exactly. What do they mean to me? I understand now. It's beginning to make sense. He wasn't giving those gifts to me. He was returning them. They've always been mine. But they are more than gifts. They are symbols of who I am."

I felt around in my cargo pocket and pulled out my stethoscope.

"That is why this glowed in my dream. This has been my symbol all along. I'm a doctor. That's how I have defined myself ever since I was young. But my symbol, my stethoscope, lacked an important quality. I had denied myself an area of medicine that needed to be a part of my life and practice. I was incomplete without the aspects of health known as holistic medicine and spiritual medicine. Many years ago, I closed my mind to those ways of healing. I held a guilt that prevented me from using those treatments. It's time for that guilt to heal. I've held it long enough."

"There are many forms of health and healing."

"I'm going to be more open in my medical practice."

"It helped you last night." The sukia pointed to my leg.

I looked at a basket in the center of the room.

"Is that the snake? The one that got me."

"No. I suspect we will not find him. He completed his duty and left.

"What's in the basket then?"

The sukia smiled. He reached for the basket and pulled out a long black snake that coiled around his arm. "Even a sukia has friends."

"Your dream offered three gifts. What about the other two?" the sukia asked.

"You're right. The man in my dream said, 'For me, my family and my soul'. I must have two more symbols, but they weren't evident in the dream."

There was a knocking at the door. The sukia opened it.

"Where's my dad? Is he alright?" Jamie asked.

"I'm fine," I said from behind the sukia. The sukia opened the door further and Jamie burst in.

"I was so worried about you, Dad." She dropped to her knees and gave me a hug. "We tried to drive to Jinotega, but the roads were too bad. We came back a while ago, but I couldn't sleep. They said I shouldn't disturb you, but I needed to see how you were doing."

"Thank you for trying to help me. I'm doing much better now. The sukia cured me of the snake poison."

"Dad, I thought you might die. I didn't know what to do. I was so scared."

"I'm sorry to have put you through this, but you don't have to worry anymore. I'm fine."

"Please don't do that again. Go find a real toilet and don't pee in the woods."

"True wisdom that I will live by from now on," I said.

"Are you ready to go?" Jamie asked.

I looked at the sukia to see if he had anything further to say. He remained silent.

"Thank you," I said.

"Don't forget this." He pointed to the double triangle on the floor. "This was important to you."

"I won't." But why was it important?

I limped out the door. The sun had peaked over the horizon and most of the people were waiting for me to emerge from the sukia's house. A low rumble of praise rose up in the crowd. I saw a familiar face in the throng of people, the young sukia girl we had visited in the market. I met her gaze as we past.

"I told you, you would need this." She held up the silver snake.

"How did you know?" I asked.

"I know my grandfather. He does not like foreign doctors."

"No, I mean, how did you know I would need your grandfather?" She shrugged. "I just did."

"Good enough for me." We continued through the crowd and down the road to our guesthouse. The sukia medicine man had reestablished his standing in the community and I didn't die in Nicaragua. Everything was right with the world.

"I think it's time to get back to Matagalpa," I told Jamie.

Juanita, Jamie and I finally returned to Matagalpa and the medical mission. We had been gone nearly four days. Brenda was furious. She had even alerted the State department we were missing. However, she was relieved to have us back. We didn't give her the whole story. We said the town was remote and the weather delayed us. I did make note for her to add one more treated patient to the list, but she was not amused.

We settled back into seeing patients for the last couple of days. I continued to grapple with the idea of different symbols and their connection to the double triangle. I felt happy, happier than I had been in a long time. The weight of Gary's memory had lessened. This trip was complete, but a new professional path was before me. When we returned, I was going to explore how I could include complementary and alternative medicine into my practice. I wasn't going to give up the medical knowledge I had, but combine it. Integrative Medicine was the new term.

On the last day, we bade farewell to our guests. Jamie and Juanita had a tearful goodbye, as they had grown close in the short period of time we were together. We retraced our steps back to the capital, Managua, and stayed one night in the lavish hotel that had greeted our arrival, which seemed ages ago. How different things were now. I looked at my stethoscope. It wasn't glowing like in the dream. It was the same old stethoscope I had bought while in the Army almost fifteen years ago, but it possessed a different quality. It held more power and meaning now.

TWENTY-ONE

JAMIE AND I finally returned home after three flights and two long layovers. We left our medical mission colleagues in Miami. Brenda was more than happy to be relieved of us after all the trouble we caused her.

"You can never trust us crazy doctors," I told her.

"I never do," she said, expressionless.

Sara and Anna were waiting for us in our local terminal with all smiles.

"Hey, Dad, I missed you. Did you bring me any presents from Nicaragua?"

"Of course I did."

"Can I have them now?"

"No, they're in my luggage. But I promise, when we get home, gifts are the first order of business."

In the car, Jamie detailed our adventures to Sara and Anna; the hundreds of patients we treated, Juanita, our trip to the northern mountain village, my run-in with the snake and the sukia medicine man.

"I thought Dad was going to die," Jamie said. "He really didn't look very good right before he passed out."

"You passed out?" Sara asked. "You didn't tell me that."

"I didn't want to worry you. I'm fine now."

"And the sukia medicine man treated him," Jamie said.

"What is a sukia medicine man?" Anna asked.

"Yeah, who is this person who apparently saved your life?" Sara asked. Jamie explained the sukia, his granddaughter, and the market.

"Sounds like you two had quite a time," Sara said.

"We really did. It was great. Except for Dad almost dying. That wasn't so great, but he survived."

"Good thing for that," I said. "Not that I don't want to change the subject from my near death experience, but I'm starving. I can't wait for a home cooked dinner."

"I have something prepared. It shouldn't take long to get it ready."

Sara had cooked a delicious meal. We were still eating when Anna suspiciously disappeared.

"Dad, look what I found. Weren't you looking for this?" Anna returned from her bedroom with a multicolored painting in hand, which was the one I'd been looking for.

"Hey, where did you find that? That's mine," Jamie said.

"I found it in my closet."

"How did it get there?" I asked.

"Don't you remember, Dad? You gave it to me. I found it in the shed and you said I could have it. I liked the colors," Jamie said.

"How did it get in Anna's closet?"

"I must have left it there when we changed rooms. Anna wanted the room with the window and I wanted the bigger closet."

"Can I see the painting?" Anna handed it to me.

The painting was as I remembered it. The colors had faded a little and it showed some minor wear, but for the most part, it was the same. Why this painting was so important to engender a dream in Kim Travers still puzzled me. It had a familiar quality to it as if I had recently seen some aspect of it. The painting was my face with four bubbles floating above it. One was centrally located over my head and more luminescent than the others.

"It doesn't look like you at all, Dad," Anna said.

"It sort of looks like you, when you had a full head of blonde hair," Sara said.

"I still have a full head of hair, just not as blonde anymore."

"Nor as full," Sara said.

"This painting looks no different than what I remember of it. No streaks of grey in the hair or wrinkles under the eyes."

"Dad, you have more than a few streaks of grey hair," Anna said.

"Thank you, Anna, for reminding me."

"Even though the painting has retained its youth, we love the real thing much more," Jamie said.

"This person in the painting had many experiences still ahead of him," I said.

"And this person has many more also," Sara said, pointing at me.

Sara had been reserved, but pleasant toward me since our return. We had only talked briefly while I was in Nicaragua. Our discussions on the phone were short, pertaining to household chores. When we arrived, she gave me a quick, uninspired hug at the airport. Jamie then did most of the talking.

A distance still clung to our relationship. My time away hadn't bridged that gap. My Nicaraguan vision caused me even more worry that I was losing her and she was resigning to the eventual end of our relationship. Not only was her distance concerning, but also the sadness I felt in her. But things were different. I understood how she felt better now than I ever did. I could improve our relationship. The vision gave me that chance. I just hope I wasn't too late. I hope Sara was still willing to work with me.

"Dad, when's our next trip? How about somewhere like Thailand?" Jamie said.

"That sounds interesting, but why don't we wait a bit before planning the next one."

"As a consolation for Thailand, I was thinking tonight we could make our special cookies," Sara said.

"That sounds delicious," I said. All of us enjoyed making the special cookies. Sara's family had passed down the recipe through many generations. The cookies had chocolate, nuts and numerous spices

creating a burst of flavor that we all loved. We each had a job in making them. Mine was rolling out the tough, thick dough.

"Dad, are you going to help us tonight?" Anna asked.

"Of course. I've missed our cookie making too much recently."

"Yes, you have," Sara said.

"Dad, make sure you roll out the cookies real thin otherwise they won't taste right," Jamie said.

"I will, I will. Remember, I'm the rolling master."

"Sure you are," Jamie said.

"We should make these cookies more often. It's fun," I said.

"It's also fun to eat them." Anna was poised with her cookie-cutter waiting for me to finish.

"We do make them often. You just haven't been here to help us," Sara said.

"I'll be here more often from now on."

"I'll believe it when I see it," Sara said, but gave me a touch on the arm, the first sign of real affection since we had returned. Maybe I hadn't lost her completely.

"I will," I said.

"We know, Dad," Anna said. "Now roll that dough… please."

"One of these days, I'll have to officially hand over the recipe to both of you," Sara said to Jamie and Anna.

"So that when we have our own families we can bake them," Jamie said.

"Exactly," Sara said. "So when you have children you can bake them together."

"It's our own special family thing," Jamie said.

With all of my physical and mental faculties intently focused on rolling out the thick mound of dark goo, I almost missed what Jamie said. Nevertheless, her words cracked my concentration.

"Jamie, what did you say?"

"I said, this is our special family thing."

Jamie jogged something from my memory of the night I spent with the sukia and my snake poison induced vision.

"Our special family thing," I said. My mind churned for the missing connection.

"Yes Jeff, our family time. I know you haven't been here to make the cookies with us, but we used to do this all the time. Something you, the girls and I enjoyed doing together," Sara said.

"I love to eat them also," Anna said.

"Yes, exactly. This is our family thing. This is what we do as a family, how we spend time together and bond." I could see the sukia handing me the orb of light as it disappeared in my hand. He said that it represented my family. He was helping me discover my family symbol. "The sukia was right. It's been in front of me this whole time."

"What are you talking about, Jeff?"

"I hadn't said anything before because a lot of it still doesn't make sense, but when I was with the sukia, I had a vision of him giving me three gifts. Well, actually they were symbols and they weren't really gifts."

"You're not making any sense," Sara said.

"Yes, you're right, I know. But he gave me three symbols; one for myself, one for my family and one for my soul."

"That sounds cool," Anna said. "What are the symbols?"

"Well, I figured out that my stethoscope is the symbol of myself which is pretty self-explanatory, but I was unclear of what the symbol of my family was until now."

"It's the recipe isn't it?" Jamie said.

"Yes, it's one thing that ties us together. The recipe is our family symbol. It's a way we connect and express our love."

"And when mom gives us the recipe, the symbol is passed down," Jamie said.

"Yes, the symbol can also be used to pass on this loving connection to our children, grandchildren and so on."

"Makes sense. Some of my happiest memories as a child are making those cookies with my mom and my dad hanging out in the kitchen happily eating them. When I finally made my own batch, I was very proud," Sara said.

"Just like the silver snake that was passed down from sukia to sukia," Jamie said.

"Yes, just like the silver snake. The recipe is our family's symbol," I said.

"I like our family symbol," Anna said. "I can eat it."

"I think it's time to put the cookies in the oven," Sara said, "before Anna starts to eat the dough."

"That's the best part," Anna said. "I think we should change our symbol to cookie dough."

"Dad, what's the third symbol?" Jamie asked. "You said there are three symbols, the stethoscope and the recipe. What's the third symbol?"

"I don't know. I haven't figured it out yet. I wasn't given any clues except that it represents the soul." I paused as I watched Anna sneak another bite of cookie dough. "On second thought, the sukia also said that I made a marking on the floor in the form of two triangles. Maybe that has something to do with it."

"What did the marking look like?" Anna asked.

"I'm curious also. Show it to us?" Sara asked.

"I wish I had taken pictures."

"Draw it for us," Jamie said.

"You know I have no artistic ability, but the marking was of two isosceles triangles." I took out a piece of paper I had in my wallet and drew the symbol. One triangle was upright, the other upside down and they touched at their pointed end or vertex.

"Dad, let me see that," Jamie said. She took the paper, but instead of looking at the symbol I had drawn, she flipped it over. "Look," she said. On the front was an advertisement for the *Vitruvian Man* exhibit.

"I don't see anything," I said.

"Look at it in the sunlight,"

Jamie held it up to the light. "Remember the graffiti." Shining through the paper, I could make out my symbol etched onto the *Vitruvian Man* like the graffiti on the alley wall.

"You're absolutely right."

"I'm confused?" Sara said. "What are we talking about?"

"We went to a museum that had an exhibit of Leonardo da Vinci's *Vitruvian Man*. Da Vinci's drawing represents the perfect man and man's relationship to nature. There is also speculation that he used the golden ratio in his drawing."

"What is the golden ratio?" Sara asked.

"It is a number found in nature, architecture as well as the human body. This golden ratio can be represented in rectangles, pentagrams and even triangles," I said.

"Oh, I see. So you think these are golden triangles."

"Why not? It is a number that is innate in all of us and can even be found in our brain waves. This may not be what da Vinci had in mind, but my vision, which led me to draw this symbol, may have been trying to tell me something. Let me take a closer look at that drawing." Jamie handed me the paper. I outlined my triangles onto the front of the *Vitruvian Man*. "Look where the triangles converge."

"Right over the solar plexus," Sara said.

"Otherwise known as the seat of the soul," I said.

"Maybe that symbolizes the soul," Anna said. We all looked at Anna. She had been sitting quietly, nibbling on a piece of dough and listening intently to the conversation. We paused for a moment in thought.

"The soul symbol!" we all yelled minus Anna who was just smiling.

"Could these two triangles represent something more than the golden ratio? Could the triangles be linked to the three symbols?"

"Is there anything else that you can remember about the vision?" Jamie asked.

"Let me think. It's become more of a cloudy memory the longer time has passed, but I've had a good memory for dreams lately." I closed my eyes and tried to recreate the dream, but nothing happened. I opened my eyes, "Nothing."

"Dad, you didn't even try. Try it one more time. Was there anything that might have been said or done that you missed at the time?"

I closed my eyes again. This time I pictured myself in the sukia's house with the smells and candles. Pieces of the dream started to return—first the white room, then my family, then the priest with orbs of light, and finally my fall from the ledge. On second thought, the priest did utter something about the words *health* and *wisdom* as he gave me the spheres of light.

"The man in my vision said that I have the answers to health and wisdom."

"He stressed those two words?" Jamie asked.

"Yes, I'm certain of it."

"Let me see that drawing again?" Jamie asked.

We all looked at it more closely.

"I think I figured it out. If you put the soul symbol in the center as Anna said and then the rest at the edges, it fits. It doesn't make any sense, but it adds up. Look." Jamie began to write in words on the drawing matching each pointed end or vertex of the triangle with a word. *Soul* and *Family* aligned with the top two angles. *Health* and *Wisdom* aligned with the bottom two angles and *Soul* fit in the center where the two converging triangles met. When I placed the new symbol over the *Vitruvian Man*, the soul symbol lined up over the solar plexus.

"What is it?" Sara asked.

"I think you've found a fourth symbol," I said.

"What does it mean?" Sara asked.

"I don't know. Clearly, my vision was making connections of the perfect man and golden ratio to the three symbols. But I'm missing something. How does it all come together?"

I picked up the old painting again. Four orbs around my head and now a fourth symbol. Maybe this painting had a purpose after all. Ms. Travers would be pleased with herself. Why is this distant connection so important? I sat there perplexed by this new symbol. What did it mean—a fourth symbol? Neither the Sufi nor the sukia talked about a fourth symbol. The man in my dream had only given me three orbs. What were the connections between symbols, health, wisdom, soul, and family? Was I trying to make something out of nothing? When I created the markings on the floor of the sukia house, I was under the spell of a snake's poisonous neurotoxin. I could have been blabbering and doing all kinds of crazy things without any sense or reason.

But I had come so far. No matter how subtle, my path had taken me to this point. From one leap to the next, the dots had continued to connect in spite of myself. I wouldn't block my way again.

"The cookies are ready," Sara said.

"Yay!" Anna said.

"I'll get the plates," Jamie said.

"Jeff, can you help me get the cookies out of the oven?" Sara asked.

"Sure." I put the paper in my pocket to mull over on another day and extracted the cookies from the oven before the girls devoured my hands off. We sat and ate in a joyful satiated mood, happy to be back together again.

I wish I knew how Sara was feeling.

Later in the night, we had cleaned up dinner and were getting ready for bed. Sara was still distant. She moved around our bedroom putting things away as she normally did prior to sleep, but she was conspicuously quiet as if she was waiting for me to say something.

"So it sounds like you and Jamie had a good time on your trip."

"We had an excellent time, met a lot of interesting people and saw some fascinating sites."

"Something is different with you," she said.

"Yeah, how so?"

"I don't know. Different."

"Is that good or bad?"

"It's not bad."

"Well, I feel different. I feel better. I rediscovered some things about myself while on the trip."

"Like what?"

"Like I wasn't happy with work even though I was spending more and more time working. And I was searching for something."

"Did you find it in Nicaragua?"

"Yes and no. I found it within myself in Nicaragua. My identity is strongly tied to my career as a doctor. It's my life's work. When I became unhappy at work, it started to spill over into our relationship and the family. I shut you out and the girls. At the time, I didn't realize anything was wrong and much less how to deal with it. But I do now."

"What changed?"

"I wasn't allowing myself to be who I wanted to be. And I took it out on you. I'm sorry for that. It wasn't fair."

She was quiet for a moment. She still looked uncertain and conflicted. I wanted to be honest with her. Because of my vision, I felt much closer to her even though we had only said a few words since I had returned. I loved her now as much as I ever did. But she felt more distant than at any other time in our relationship. I couldn't recreate my experience for her, but I could be open. I could open my heart to her again.

"When I was in Nicaragua, I experienced something that made me sad, but also gave me hope."

"What was that?" Sara frowned, unsure of where I was leading her.

"In my vision, I also saw you. You were struggling with our relationship. You were resigned to its end. You allowed me in and I experienced your sadness. But when you let me in, I also felt an overwhelming love. Love that is still there between us, just buried underneath our everyday lives."

She nodded, but kept silent. I approached her, took her hand and placed it over my heart.

"I know it feels like our marriage is on empty and has run into a dead end. But I could feel and I know that we have a chance because love is still there. We can heal our relationship."

Sara remained quiet and still. She had a distant look. She pulled her hand from my chest. The pause, as I stood there, terrified me. I froze. I had no more to say. It felt like our marriage was on the brink. Then, as if a little fairy whispered in my ear, I remembered an experience we had early in our relationship. It wasn't a vision or a dream, just a memory. A month or two into dating, we had a bad fight. It was an argument that could have easily severed a new relationship. We were both about to walk out and give it up, when she turned around and gave me a hug and told me to never let her go. I in turn hugged her. I didn't want to leave her at the time, but my pride stood in the way. Thankfully, hers didn't.

"Remember when we had that big fight shortly after we met about something trivial and I almost walked out?"

She nodded.

"The important thing then was that you didn't let me go. And I won't let you go now," I said. "I'll do whatever it takes."

After a pause, she finally looked up. Tears were in her eyes and she was smiling.

"I know," she said. She took my hand in hers and pulled me closer. I tried to say something, but she stopped me.

We embraced for a long time. Hard work was still ahead, but we had passed a tremendous obstacle in our marriage. After a few minutes, she looked up smiling. "What was that fight about back then?"

"I think I called you a crazy Brazilian after you became angry for something stupid I did and you took offense to it."

"Yeah, that sounds about right," she said. "Nicaragua must be an amazing place."

"You're an amazing woman." I gave her a kiss; the first real kiss in a long time and I felt no reservation in her.

"This doesn't change anything," she said. "I still want to go to counseling and no more late night rendezvous with crazy patients. You scared me."

"That was the first and the last. And I agree with you. I think we should continue with the counseling." I paused. "But for how long are we talking about?"

"Don't push your luck. Now give me another kiss."

TWENTY-TWO

I HAD PROMISED Judith I'd call when we returned from the trip. I hadn't spoken to my dad since the night of our argument.

"Hi, Dad, just calling to let you know that Jamie and I made it back fine."

"How was your trip?"

"Good."

"Did you treat a lot of patients?"

"Yeah, we saw well over five hundred people and we even missed a couple of days."

"Why did you miss a couple of days?"

"Long story. Let's just say we wandered off-course in the jungles of Nicaragua only to be saved by a sukia medicine man."

"Sukia who?"

"A medicine man."

"It sounds like you have some good stories."

"The next time we come over, I'll bring the pictures."

I paused.

"Can I ask you something?" I said.

"Sure."

"If somebody was trying to find a symbol that represented their soul, what would you tell them?"

"That's a strange question coming from you."

"I've been thinking about things recently."

"This sounds like something I would be asking you."

"Yes, you're right. I guess you could say I've had a change of heart."

"I'm glad to hear it. Well, like I've said before, some people view the soul as our higher self and our connection with God. The first thing you need to do is figure out how you connect with God."

"How do I connect with God? I haven't been to church in ages."

"Many people commune with God in church, but it doesn't have to be there. Our connection with God is personal and intimate. Only you can know how you connect with God."

"Give me an example."

"I like to meditate and listen for God's guidance, others pray, some read the bible or sing hymns in church. Judith connects with God hiking on a nature trail while others find God surfing on a wave. There is no wrong answer."

"If the soul is our connection with God and our soul symbol represents our connection with God, what is my soul symbol?"

"I'm not following you."

"I'm just talking to myself. It's something I've been thinking about. My soul symbol. I've been trying to figure out my soul symbol."

"I'm not sure I fully understand what you mean by a soul symbol, but I'd ask yourself, what lights your path? What shows you the way?"

"Well, one thing is for sure. I've had so many dreams and visions that have scared the bejesus out of me I don't know which way is up or down. I've followed them and so far it's ended up well."

"Maybe you have your answer."

"What, dreams?"

"Yes, it sounds like your dreams are one way you have connected with God."

"I wonder if you're right. Somebody did tell me onetime that I have a talent for dreams. Could it be so obvious?"

"Sounds like it to me. It doesn't have to be complicated."

"And that same person, the Sufi mystic, told me not to forget symbols while grasping my cartouche. My cartouche!"—a symbol of royalty in ancient Egyptian times. Egyptian tradition considered the king the only true connection with the gods. "It must be it. That trinket is my soul symbol. Even the crazy Sufi mystic referred to it. I just didn't understand. I wonder what I did with it."

"It sounds like you have your answer."

"Thanks, Dad. Hey, uh, one more thing."

"Yes?"

"I'm sorry for yelling at you a while back. It was wrong of me whether I believed what you said or not."

"I understand. You have valid reasons for disagreeing with me. I know Gary's death was difficult for you."

"That's in the past now. I won't let it control my life anymore."

"You *have* had a change of heart?"

"I think you could say that. I'm going to start with a more holistic viewpoint in my practice and then go from there."

"I knew I would bring you around one of these days."

"It took a while, but here I am."

"I'm happy to hear it son."

Work quickly became busy. However, instead of being arduous, it was refreshing. My relationship with Sara continued to slowly heal. The tension was no longer there. And the trust was gradually returning. The girls acted as if nothing changed, but they were happier now that I was more available and involved. Jamie was doing well in school as usual and per Vice-Principle Buford's reports, she had relaxed some. Anna continued to be her free-spirited self.

"You know, my dreams are gone. All of them. It's like I've been given a break." Sara was preparing dinner while I was getting in the way picking at the food.

"No more dreams?" Sara asked. She swatted my hand away. I dodged her and gave her a peck on the cheek and then moved to clean some of the dirty dishes.

"Something continues to bug me about our trip," I said.

"What's that?" Sara asked.

"I still can't figure out what that fourth symbol means. I understand the first three symbols. My stethoscope symbolizes myself, the recipe symbolizes the family and the cartouche symbolizes my soul." I had found the cartouche in a box of my travel memorabilia in the attic.

"Why does it have to have a meaning?"

"Everything else has. There must have been a reason I scribbled it on the sukia's floor. On this long path toward self-discovery there has always been an underlying meaning no matter how subtle."

"Well, on your long path to self-discovery how did you discover things?"

"I was sort of forced to. I didn't ask for it at the time."

"How did it happen?"

"Mainly though dreams and visions."

"I'd start there."

"Where, my dreams? I can't force myself to dream."

"You can close your eyes. Maybe that'll be a start." I looked at her in disbelief. "I'm just offering suggestions here. You came to me."

"Dreaming can form creative connections as my psychiatrist said. Maybe it'll help make this connection. Recently, my dreams and visions have not only shown me the path, but also created one. You could be right."

"Once you accept that, this relationship will go much smoother," she said, smiling.

"I have three women in this house. I'm never right. The question is who I've wronged."

"Now you're learning." She patted my arm.

"Maybe all I need to do is set my intent on the fourth symbol. You're right, Honey. That's simple, but brilliant. I'll close my eyes, set my intentions and see what comes."

I wasn't able to find a quiet moment until the next weekend. I hid in my study at home. I closed my eyes and took in slow deep breaths. The room disappeared around me and everything became quiet. I sat and waited, but nothing. I didn't know how to activate this gift for visions. Until now, they had only spontaneously occurred. I felt silly as I wore the cartouche around my neck. What else was I sup-posed to do with it. Maybe it would empower me. I cleared all thoughts from my mind. I set my intent on the fourth symbol, the double triangle.

Suddenly, a circle popped into my head and then a circle within a circle. It looked like a single celled organism with the many different cellular components. The circle divided into two cells. Then the two cells divided further and further until it formed a creature vaguely similar to a fish. I followed the fish while it swam until it found a coastline. It rode the waves on to the beach, but instead of turning back, it slithered its way onto shore.

As if formed by the sand, the fish grew legs and walked onto land. Then the fish morphed into a four-legged creature. The four-legged animal sprinted over the land. Slowly, his legs straightened, his arms shortened, he reared up on two legs and walked upright. This animal gradually changed until he resembled a man.

He found others of similar characteristics. They made tools. They communicated via grunts and sounds. The man's features became finer and he walked upright. His tools became more complex and his communication formed a language.

Over time, his tools and communication grew as he evolved. He began to pray to the sun for blessings. The man continued to evolve using the written word and more complex tools that could reach around the world. The man then kneeled down to pray. He prayed inward, to an unseen God. His body filled with light and was lifted up as if floating just off the ground. The light faded and his body returned to earth.

A small boy joined him. The man gave the boy a miniature token of great significance. They walked off holding hands, the father's hand filling with light around the little boy's hand. They disappeared and the fourth symbol reflected in my mind.

The vision completed and I opened my eyes. I sat still for a moment. My study was quiet and peaceful. The vision was a simplified version of life's evolutionary progress on earth from a simple organism to the most complex being on the planet, humans. The praying man had reached a type of enlightenment and then passed a small gift onto his son. A symbolic gift no doubt, but of what?

Let me step back and review. I looked at my scribbled paper of the double triangle overlaid onto the *Vitruvian Man*. What did I know of symbols? They were representations of a person, place, idea, etc. to convey a certain meaning. We often empowered symbols, which when used could give us strength. Symbols could enable us to accomplish difficult tasks or to express difficult meanings. They allowed us to rise above ourselves.

Humans and our ancestors had used symbols throughout history as a tool for expression such as language. By using symbols as language, human thought processes became more complex activating our brain and increasing our neurosynaptic pathways. This led to a growth in our brain from one generation to the next. The human brain evolved as a result of symbols.

My visions and dreams had led me to believe that each individual possessed their own symbols. The first symbol was that of our self. It represented our identity, our personality and our psyche. It held our thoughts, goals, and fears. We could use the self-symbol to understand ourselves better as well as to enhance our purpose.

Our family symbol represented our family bond. It gave families a tool to share love, to work through family challenges, and to pass on learned experiences. Ideally, the family worked with the symbol as a group to nurture their relationship. If the group was unavailable,

an individual in the group could choose to work with the family symbol for growth. In a broader sense, the family symbol represented
our connection to all of humankind.

The third symbol was that of the soul, our connection with God.
We each had a unique way we communed with God. The soul symbol empowered this connection and brought us closer to God. We
used each of these symbols to improve our self, to strengthen our
relationship with our family and to enhance our link to God. The
symbols of self, family and soul formed the top triangle.

The double triangle linked these three symbols. But how were the
three symbols related to the bottom triangle? As before, I took in
slow deep breaths. A peaceful silence welled up within me. Again, I
had a vision of the praying man rising in the light.

The second half of the fourth symbol connected by the soul
symbol were the words *health* and *wisdom* as the man said in my vision.
Health was a broad term and included physical, mental, emotional
and spiritual health. Each aspect intertwined with the others. If one
part was ill, injured or out of balance, the others were affected.
Rarely did we think of our health except when it was lacking and
needed healing. Humans had used symbols for healing throughout
history. The snake and the medicine wheel were two examples. The
placebo effect was a modern day symbol used to heal. The placebo
effect empowered our own healing mechanisms.

Wisdom in its broadest sense was the ideal application of
knowledge and in this context most likely applied to wisdom of the
spirit or spiritual insight. Frequently, an old, experienced man with
many years of life behind him and declining years ahead personified
wisdom. However, that was a misrepresentation of wisdom. Wisdom was not feeble and lacking vigor. It was transformation of
knowledge beyond knowledge itself. Wisdom had an undertone of
action, energy, and growth. It implied doing and even evolving. Spiritual wisdom led to the growth of our soul.

Wisdom and health had gone hand in hand. When we heal from
difficult illness, we often grow spiritually. When we have spiritual

growth, we subsequently improve our wellbeing and health as has been shown in some limited medical studies.

Our health or health symbol and wisdom or wisdom symbol were influencing factors with the other three symbols. The double triangle embodied their connection. In essence, the fourth symbol, the double triangle, was a simple map for individual spiritual growth, health and healing when used with the self, family and soul symbols. Each built on the other.

From outside, someone slammed a door and shook my desk, which brought me back to the present. I was lightheaded, the vision still processing in my mind. Questions remained unanswered. The last part of the vision didn't add up. Why did the praying man give his son a gift and what was that gift? Did the gift have something to do with the fourth symbol?

"Hey, Dad, we're home. Where are you?" Anna yelled from the hallway.

I quickly wrote down my questions.

"I'm in the study." Anna opened the door. "Did you have a fun time shopping?"

"Yeah, we bought a lot of things."

"Don't tell him that," Sara said from the kitchen.

"I'm sure you did," I said, smiling.

Anna ran to me and jumped into my lap, her pig tails flipping behind her

"Look what we bought." She swung a shopping bag onto my desk. "Mom said to tell you that it's not as much as it looks."

"Is that all of it?"

"No, there is much more in the car."

"I bet I was not supposed to know that." Anna shrugged and so did I.

After a detailed story of Anna's shopping experience, I wrote down my vision underlining my questions. I was close and the answers were within reach, but I was still missing something. It would have to wait for another day.

TWENTY-THREE

MY LIFE HAD settled into a new rhythm. It had become lighter. I wasn't as weighed down by it. By opening my eyes and opening up, the many problems that were in front of me had disappeared.

A couple of weeks ago, as summer was fading and fall beginning, I went to a second baseball game for the season—the first time in close to twenty years. This time, I not only brought Anna, but Sara and Jamie also came along. Jamie was less interested than Anna, but I had promised cotton candy and funnel cake, which made it more appealing. Also, Anna wouldn't stop talking about the ball she had caught so Jamie wanted to give it a try. Sara came along for support.

We were four across, sitting behind home plate as Gary and I always did. Sara had scooched over closer to me and held onto my arm. Jamie and Anna were on either side of us. The stadium lights beamed bright and the night was cooler than the summer game previous. We all wore matching sweatshirts of the local team much to Jamie's chagrin, but she was a good daughter and played along. Anna was of course wearing her baseball cap, as was I, with her pigtails sticking out from either end. This time Anna brought her own mitt and was prepared for another foul ball.

"I'm not going to duck this time, Dad," she said.

I had given my mitt to Jamie who looked at it and said, "This thing is old and smells."

"It has aged well, just like its owner," I said, "except for the smelling part of course. Right, Honey?" I asked Sara.

"Of course," she said, giving Jamie a wink.

The full stadium buzzed with a fun, vibrant energy. This particular game was special, not only because it was the last of the season, but also because it was played in honor of Gary. The minors tended to be fan friendly. When I asked to dedicate the game to a friend, they complied and gave me the opportunity to throw out the first pitch. It also helped that the general manager of the team happened to be my patient.

With Gary's old pitcher's mitt, I walked to the mound with ball in hand. The audience clapped. I could hear Jamie and Anna yelling. I waived to them. After I ascended the pitcher's mound, I said a short prayer to the heavens, took my stance, looked down at the catcher's mitt and flung the ball straight down the plate. The throw was a little high, but had respectable velocity for an unpracticed veteran. I kept the ball, but left my self-reproach and grief on the mound. I had borne it long enough. It was time to let it go. Gary no longer symbolized a guilt-ridden memory, but instead many good memories, as a brother should. And I knew he was happy for it also. He would have given me hell for the weak pitch, but happy nonetheless.

The rest of the game went well. Neither Jamie nor Anna caught the elusive fly ball, but they weren't too disappointed. Jamie even thought she might join Anna and me next season.

The baseball game was a couple of weeks ago. Now, I sat in a lawn chair in my father's backyard and watched Anna and Jamie play with my father's dog—a Labrador/schnauzer mix. They were throwing a ball back and forth while the dog tried to intercept the passes. Sara and Judith talked while watching the girls. My dad had been sitting next to me, but had returned to his post to flip the burgers. Others milled about who had been part of the ceremony. The day had been perfect for the medicine wheel. Hunger pervaded the air as the smell of grilled beef and vegetarian patties floated about.

A few months had passed since my diagnosis of prostate cancer. I was in the process of treatment using a combination of modern medicine and alternative techniques. I came to the medicine wheel not for healing, but for acceptance and closure. I was looking back on a previous life and setting my sites on a new one.

The ceremony was peaceful. Sara and the girls surprised me with their participation. I had thought they were only coming for the get-together afterwards. I was glad they took part. It made the ceremony that much more special. A Native American shaman led the ritual. He was a friend of Judith's. He was an older man, tall and heavyset with long, grey hair. He smiled and laughed a lot with a booming voice. Along with my family, about ten people took part.

The shaman opened the circle. We prayed and drummed. The shaman sang in a deep confident voice. We prayed more. I prayed to the directions. I prayed for my prostate. I prayed for my family. I drummed with passion and felt the vibrations tickle my soul. Peace and reconciliation overcame me like a warm, gentle rain.

I had been in denial about the cancer. I wanted to ignore it, which was not the best way to deal with it. I would never counsel my patients to avoid their cancer. During the medicine wheel ceremony, I watched as my daughters danced, drummed, and enjoyed themselves. Their joy offered me a glimpse of where my intentions needed to be set. I realized the cancer wasn't a fight or a confrontation. It was a learning experience. It was as if the cancer was an unwanted partner motivating me to overcome certain challenges. This wasn't a revolutionary thought, but living life with passion was much more powerful than just knowing to do it.

Our physical illness can hold our emotions like fear or anger. Most people have experienced a stress headache. But did my guilt and fear cause my cancer? I didn't know. I did know that letting go of the guilt somehow made me feel that I would by fine in spite of the cancer.

I couldn't help but remember what Judith told me. "Form the question first and then the answer will come." I'd opened up. I followed an unlikely path to Nicaragua full of symbols and deadly snakes. I modified my medical practice to be more harmonious with who I was. I wasn't there yet, but getting there. And most importantly, I had become a better husband and father. Still, something was missing.

The wind picked up and rustled the trees. The dog paused from catching the ball for a quick sniff and then returned to playing with the girls. I felt a hint of lightheadedness or light-bodiedness. It was difficult to tell. Judith looked back at me quizzically, as is she was going to say something to me, but didn't. She stared for a brief second then continued talking to Sara.

Behind me, I began to hear faint drumming. I looked around, but found no one except my father at the grill and the girls playing further down the lawn. Sara and Judith had moved closer to them. The drumming grew louder and surrounded me. It was rhythmic and mesmerizing. The beat induced me into a slow meditation and I felt light as air. The fourth symbol of the double triangle flashed before my eyes. Then the man and his son from my previous vision walked before me again. The son held the gift his father had given him.

Why did the praying man give his son a gift and what was that gift? My chalk painting, sketched twenty-five years ago by my eccentric patient, glimmered in my memory with the central orb illuminated over my head. The scene shifted with the father now holding the glowing sphere in his hand. Did the gift have something to do with the fourth symbol? What else did I know of the fourth symbol? It was a link to the *Vitruvian Man* via the golden ratio. The fourth symbol was two golden triangles bound by the golden ratio. The *Vitruvian Man* represented the perfect man and man's relationship to nature through the golden ratio. As the golden triangle was intrinsic in nature, then the fourth symbol as two golden triangles must be fundamental in nature as well. With the *Vitruvian Man* representing man's relationship among nature, this would suggest that the fourth symbol was an inherent symbol in all humans.

The fourth symbol overlaid on the *Vitruvian Man* represented the fourth symbol's link to the self, family and soul symbols via the solar plexus. I recalled what the old mathematician at the museum said when he explained that the failed attempts to recreate the *Vitruvian Man* were a more authentic representation of man since we were all striving for personal growth and perfection.

Lastly and most telling, the *Vitruvian Man* as seen by Da Vinci was a microcosm representing a greater macrocosm. If the *Vitruvian Man* represented individual growth, then the greater macrocosm would be evolutionary change. Did the fourth symbol also have a dual symbolism, representing not only individual growth, reaching for perfection, but also evolutionary change? Did the old man in my vision when he said the word *wisdom* mean something beyond the conventional sense of the word. Nature and nature's laws directed evolution. Some might consider evolution to be nature's wisdom. Does evolution represent nature's transformation of knowledge that was greater than the sum of its parts? The praying man flashed before my eyes again. This time he departed with his son, hands clasped, light shining from both.

Symbols and evolution were historically linked. The symbols of language had helped our ancestor's brains to evolve to humans. Jamie made a good point when she asked if symbols continued to push evolution on a species level and not just individually. For evolution to occur, we must pass it down to our children. Our children inherited our physical characteristics via our DNA when they were born, but what about our spiritual growth, which DNA did not contain and which continued to develop after our children were born. Our children would have to inherit it through another method. That method could be the family symbol. That was it!

The family symbol acted as a thread that connected the generations. It was a subtle connection, almost imperceptible, that preserved and passed down our spiritual growth. That was what the vision was alluding to. The father imparted to his son his spiritual growth. He symbolically gave his son the fourth symbol.

In essence, the fourth symbol was not only a means for individual inner growth and healing when we used the different symbols, it was also a means to pass our spiritual growth to our children. It would seem that a higher spiritual growth and wellbeing would confer an evolutionary advantage. Those who did not use their symbols and subsequently did not pass down their spiritual growth would be at an evolutionary disadvantage. The fourth symbol was ultimately a symbol for a spiritual evolution.

I took a deep breath. The words echoed in my mind—a spiritual evolution. A different kind of evolution upheld through symbols. The fourth symbol not only advanced individual spirituality, but also ultimately, humanity's spirituality through successive generations. It was a way to build on each other's spiritual growth. The excitement and relief of finally putting answers to my questions swelled up in me and then slowly released as I exhaled.

My father's backyard gradually came into view again. My head still felt like it was in the clouds, but my body sank back into the lawn chair. Could this be true? Could the fourth symbol be a tool for spiritual evolution? It was somewhat farfetched, but it felt right. The only way to confirm this spiritual evolution would be to continue working with my symbols, connecting with my patients, my family, and with God.

My eyes were still glassy from the vision, but I noticed movement in the distance. Quickly, the movement morphed into a furry form. I had to blink my eyes to make sure I wasn't dreaming, but then Jamie yelled for me to throw the ball back that had rolled next to my chair. I picked it up and flung it over the dog's head. The dog looked at me, barked, and then chased after it.

The world still had a hazy look to it. The girls continued to play. Sara and Judith hadn't stopped talking. I felt a hand on my shoulder.

"Hey, let's eat," my dad said. "Burgers are ready."

Judith walked by. "You've been traveling," she said. "You'll have to tell me about it sometime."

"Yeah, you could say that," I said. "I think I need a burger. Nothing like tasty, saturated fat to bring me back to the present. I'm hungry."

Weeks and months passed. My practice continued along. My view of a holistic framework became clearer and my understanding of the healing process changed. Due to a new appreciation for the relationship between health, family, wisdom and symbolism, I had redirected my focus. The patient and their concerns were central to the visit as always, but I needed more. I needed a slightly different approach and intent.

I created a different clinic from which to practice. My clinic became a healing sanctuary. I treated each encounter as a healing ceremony. I wasn't doing the healing. I gave them the opportunity to heal. I meditated prior to the start of the day to focus myself for the healing process. If possible, I asked my patients to meditate, some giving me crazy looks. The waiting room was inviting and a peaceful place for meditation if desired.

Today, I waited for my first patient, Ms. Travers. Once again, her issue was a personal problem. My only hope was that she wasn't going to send my on another soul searching goose chase. I was still recovering from the previous one.

"Hello, Ms. Travers, how are you?"

"I'm well."

"You've changed your hair." She had dyed her platinum blonde to flaming red.

"Yeah, blonde wasn't my thing. A little too predictable."

"That is definitely not you."

She wrinkled her brow in confusion.

"Predictable."

She snorted

"I don't think the dogs liked it. But anyways, how was your trip?"

"It was enlightening."

"You're not dead I can see. That's good. I didn't think you'd make it."

"I almost didn't, but fate pulled me back from death's clutches along with the help of a local medicine man. I'm glad you are so concerned."

"I do what I can to help," she said.

"That you do."

"Did you see my jaguar?"

"No, never saw a jaguar. I did have a run in with a snake."

"Are you sure because I could have sworn it was going to be a jaguar."

"I have the bite marks to prove it."

"If you say so. By the way, I like what you did with the place. It soothes my frazzled nerves."

"Indirectly, you had a part to play in my redecoration of the clinic."

"Really, maybe I should get a discount."

"How about we see what your personal problem is and then we'll talk about it."

"Sounds fair."

"So tell me, what brought you in today? Are you going to detail another dream or another painting you envisioned of me?"

"No, why would I do that?" she said, shaking her red, frizzy hair as if I was crazy. "I need my blood pressure checked. These dogs are driving me crazy."

"Maybe you need a vacation. How about Nicaragua? It's cathartic."

"I need a new line of work."

"You still have painting to fall back on." She looked unamused. "Well, let's take a look at your blood pressure then."

After Ms. Travers, the day continued as usual, but overall my practice was different. It had evolved. Not only did I change the ambiance of the clinic, but I also better understood the importance of each segment of the clinic visit. The most sacred aspect of every encounter was the person's personal space. The introduction and handshake was the first step within the patient's personal space. From that contact, I sensed their openness and if the patient would allow further openness. While they explained their story, I resonated with their voice, expanding my energy around them and gaining a better sense of who they were. At the same time, I tried to tease out what their symbols might be, knowing that a person's symbols were a powerful indicator of each individual and a tool for healing.

After the patient finished their story, I performed the physical exam. It was the second time I entered into the patient's personal space. It was also another opportunity to expand my energy around the patient, mingling the physical exam with the spiritual exam. From my gut feeling and my intuition, I further utilized the power of my own symbols to help augment diagnosis and treatment if needed. As Judith asked, what did their illness smell like and what did that smell mean to me. Or what did it sound like or taste like. The fourth symbol represented the symbolic connection between my patients and me. Their intent for health and my facilitation of it was embodied by the fourth symbol. The wisdom of our spirit powered that connection. It was always the intention of the soul to reach for a higher self. It was the soul symbol.

With the exam completed, I reconnected with the patient via my voice for diagnosis, treatment plan, education and acceptance. I utilized the full spectrum of health treatments to include allopathic, naturopathic, osteopathic, and homeopathic. Evidence based medicine was always at the forefront of my treatments, but it could lose sight of the individual. Keeping focus on the individual and their unique needs was just as important. Although it worked for me, I never did recommend a snakebite—a little too dangerous. I was sure my sukia health provider would disagree.

Many times a patient already knew what they needed for healing. Their physical, emotional or spiritual self called out to them with the answer. They just didn't know how to say it or what it was called or how to put a word to what they were feeling. Part of my job was to help interpret those feelings into usable forms. Symbols could work in enigmatic ways.

Medical school and residency taught me many of these ideas, but my education never trained me in a spiritual context and I overlooked the spiritual connection. My upbringing opened my world to the possibilities of spirituality, health, and medicine. My medical training gave me the tools. Through the creative connections of life experiences, my path veered until a crazy trip to Nicaragua helped me connect the dots and reconnect with who I was. The discovery and use of my symbols rebalanced my life. I retouched with my higher self, allowing for positive healing and spiritual growth.

I felt as if I was starting over again. I was flush with anxiety and optimism about the new path ahead. I sat in my office after another typical day. I still had a stack of paper work to do, but I'd finish that later.

My phone rang. Jamie.

"Hey, Dad, Mom needs you to pick up bread at the store."

"Okay."

"Oh and also, can you get me some granola bars and Gatorade for my meet tomorrow."

"Anything else?"

"No. Oh, wait. Anna wanted something also."

I heard Jamie yelling to Anna for her request.

"She wants some ice cream, cookie dough."

"Cookie dough it is. Tell Mom I'll be home in a little while," I said. I hung up the phone and leaned back in my comfortable desk chair with my hands on my head.

My most important task was to keep focus on my family, to nurture our own spiritual light, and to pass on the few learned tidbits of enlightenment to my own daughters as we walked hand in hand.

I stood up and looked in the mirror. It was still too low, unadjusted after ten years. I flipped the mirror off the little nail affixing it to the wall, pried the nail out, and hammered it back in with my coffee mug, but this time twelve inches higher. I looked in the mirror again, unstooped—much more comfortable. My grey hair was in order. My tie was straight. I unwrapped my stethoscope from my neck. I was ready.

ABOUT THE AUTHOR

Jeremy B. Kent is a physician and military veteran. He has had a life-long interest in holistic health and the many different facets of spirituality. He has lived and traveled throughout the world and currently lives on the East Coast with his family.

Made in the USA
Charleston, SC
17 October 2016